PRAISE FOR JOSHUA CORIN

"*Assume Nothing* lives up to its title and will keep you enthralled from its opening chapter until its startling conclusion—leaving you longing for the company of Corin's memorable protagonist and sharply plotted page-turner."

—Alex Segura, bestselling author of *Secret Identity* and *Alter Ego*

"*Assume Nothing* is a wickedly entertaining novel that blurs the boundary between fiction and reality, perfect for fans of *The Good Girl's Guide to Murder*. Corin has devised the ultimate game of cat and mouse, where the stakes are as deadly as they are unpredictable."

—Michelle Gagnon, author of *Killing Me*

"Both a brilliant love letter to the mystery genre and a clever deconstruction of what makes it special. The voice will draw you in, and the ending will knock you out. The title says it all: *Assume Nothing*."

—Rob Hart, *USA Today* bestselling author of *Assassins Anonymous*

ASSUME NOTHING

OTHER TITLES BY JOSHUA CORIN

Xanadu Marx Series

Cost of Life

Forgive Me

American Lies

Esme Stuart Series

While Galileo Preys

Before Cain Strikes

Stand-Alone

Nuclear Winter Wonderland

Hollywood vs. the Author

Marvel Comics

Deadpool: World's Greatest Vol. 4 with Gerry Duggan, Ian Doescher, and Christopher Hastings

Deadpool Classic Vol. 21: DvX with Fabian Nicieza, Reilly Brown, Ben

Acker, Ben Blacker, Gerry Duggan, and Chynna Clugston Flores

Spider-Man/Deadpool Vol. 4: Serious Business with Elliott Kalan

Deadpool: World's Greatest Vol. 8: 'Til Death Do Us with Gerry Duggan and Christopher Hastings

Spider-Man/Deadpool Vol. 2: Side Pieces with Scott Aukerman, Gerry Duggan, Penn Jillette, Paul Scheer, and Nick Giovannetti

Deadpool: Too Soon?

ASSUME NOTHING

A THRILLER

JOSHUA CORIN

THOMAS & MERCER

This is a work of fiction. Names, characters, organizations, places, events, and incidents are either products of the author's imagination or are used fictitiously. Otherwise, any resemblance to actual persons, living or dead, is purely coincidental.

Published by Thomas & Mercer, Seattle

www.apub.com

ISBN-13: 9781662523533 (paperback)
ISBN-13: 9781662523540 (digital)

Cover design by Shasti O'Leary Soudant
Cover image: © Purple Moon, © GalapagosPhoto, © Street Boutique / Shutterstock

Printed in the United States of America

To my nephew Brayden,
for when he is older

1

"Want to see the novel I'm in?" I asked Dev, and he said yes, though I bet now he wishes he said no. I bet now he wishes he'd never met up with some girl from an AOL chat room, but he did. He didn't deserve what came after. But neither of us had any clue. Not when we first met in the chat room and not when we first met in person. How could we? I was sixteen and Dev was nineteen, just two book-obsessed dorks mingling online in a user-created room dedicated to mystery author Carissa Miller. Most of the other regulars were (much) older than us . . . at least, if they were the age they claimed to be . . . And if they were lying, well, lying online was for stupid people who enjoyed stupid games, and fans of Carissa Miller were supposed to be smart people who enjoyed smart games, and—

What, you were never young and naive? How nice for you.

Dev's username was WmbleyLnDet (as in Wembley Lane, the Central London street Dame Carissa's series detective, Adrian Lescher, lived on). I went by the much less creative KMcCann14 (because I was fourteen when my uncle first brought home our Packard Bell computer from a pawn shop and introduced me and my aunt to the wonders of the World Wide Web). At first, Dev was just one of the room's regulars, guaranteed to disrupt the flow with some new crackpot opinion, which he would then defend to the death. Like this one time, he suggested—without any supporting arguments *at all*—that Adrian Lescher's favorite composer was Richard Wagner.

Wagner?

Please.

Even a *casual* reader of the novels would know Adrian Lescher was a fanboy for Mozart. They were both, as Adrian himself stated in *The Devil in Ice*, "Austrian perfectionists in service to the world." And Wagner? One, maybe two references to him in the entire Adrian Lescher oeuvre.

That's right, ladies and gentlemen. Time to shame the troll.

KMcCann14: Do you smell burnt toast?

WmbleyLnDet: ?

KMcCann14: Answer my q. Do you smell burnt toast?

WmbleyLnDet: oh, i get it, burnt toast cause im having a stroke, u r so h1lar1ous

KMcCann14: It's not hilarious. It's serious. You might want to go to the ER. Or it could just be a concussion. It's definitely brain damage of some kind.

WmbleyLnDet: sooooooooo h1lar1ous

WmbleyLnDet: but srsly, heres 3 un1mpeach1ble reasons in ascend1ng order why adr1an actually preferred wagner

Dev's over-the-top online persona was (I guess?) his way of paying homage to Adrian Lescher (minus the wit and charm). He was never that way face-to-face, not once—not with me, at least. Especially not that first afternoon, when we sucked down an Orange Julius in the food court of the Chestnut Hill Mall and then approached our inevitable destination, Borders Bookstore, where I doomed him with my question—a question I knew he would say yes to because, I mean, come on, he was a book nerd, a Carissa Miller nerd, and maybe I asked him because I wanted to impress him, because I knew it would impress him, that it would make him absolutely lose his mind when he learned—

But I'm getting ahead of myself.

The chat room was the closest thing I had to a place where I could be myself. I didn't have to keep my mouth shut in the chat room. Not like in school, out of fear my classmates might think I was too dumb for my own good. And not like at home, out of fear my uncle might think I was too smart for my own good. The regulars in the chat room were my friends. We had running jokes. For example, whenever someone new showed up and tried to wow us with some iota of trivia about Carissa Miller, we all played along and pretended to be astonished.

She always traveled by train or boat because she was afraid of flying? Really? Gosh.

She based Adrian Lescher on a real person? Holy cow. That's amazing.

She disappeared on her seventy-fifth birthday? That's crazy. Tell us more.

It was all in good fun. Most newbies weren't there to impress anyone and were just looking to chat with like-minded weirdos. There were occasional pervs and trolls, but we all knew well enough to ignore them. Although there was that one time . . .

It went down like this: A user named AladdinZane became fixated on me, wouldn't really engage with anyone else but always replied whenever I said something. Then one day, he began IM'ing me. The usual crap—what did I look like, blah blah blah. By now, Dev and I had been chatting fairly regularly, so I let him know. Dev called out AladdinZane in the main room and told him to stop harassing me, and AladdinZane signed off . . .

. . . until the next night, when he showed up and posted Dev's name, address, and phone number.

Then he posted mine.

Marigoldeneyes, who was like the mother hen of the room, immediately contacted AOL customer support, and they assured us that everything was under control and we had nothing to worry about. And I guess they were right, because AladdinZane never showed up again.

On the other hand, that's how me and Dev found out we both lived in Boston.

The AladdinZane incident had creeped me out, though not enough to make me flee the chat room. It helped that everyone was doing their best to offer their support and understanding. They all really were good friends. Well, everyone offered their support and understanding except Dev . . . who said nothing. Eventually, I just had to send him a private message and poke him about his (uncharacteristic) silence:

KMcCann14: Is your keyboard broken?

After a minute more of silence—during which I wondered if maybe his keyboard *was* broken—he finally responded.

WmbleyLnDet: what are you doing on lescher day?

Lescher Day was July 7, in honor of Adrian's birthday, and July 7 was in five weeks. Did I have anything special planned? I was too concerned about

1. whether I would have to repeat algebra next year
2. whether my uncle would return early from his work trip
3. whether my aunt would keep her promise that I could spend every weekday this summer volunteering at the library
4. whether another AladdinZane was going to show up at my door with a butcher knife

KMcCann14: No, I don't have any plans for Lescher Day. Why?

WmbleyLnDet: because you shouldnt let one perv ru1n everyth1ng, bes1des hes in ja1l

KMcCann14: How can you be so sure he's in jail?

WmbleyLnDet: same way he got our personal 1nfo, i know how to use a computer

Oh. Good. Dev had stalked my stalker.

KMcCann14: I never asked you to do that.

WmbleyLnDet: you never have to ask me to help you

KMcCann14: Why did you ask about Lescher Day?

WmbleyLnDet: because i th1nk it would be cool if we hung out and like went to a bookstore or someth1ng, you know, s1nce we l1ve so close

My first response was no. Of course it was no. I'd just been some middle-aged carpet salesman's online prey.

But five weeks was a long time, and I didn't quit the chat room, and to his credit, Dev didn't keep asking me after I (kindly) rejected him, and my aunt didn't keep her word about allowing me to volunteer at the library every weekday, and my uncle did come home early, and it would just drive them both up a wall if they knew I met up with someone I knew only off the internet . . . and maybe my uncle *belonged* up a wall . . .

So on July 7, 1995, I put on my cleanest mauve shirt, gray pants, and boots (because, sure, it was ninety degrees of sunshine outside, but clothing was armor) and took the train to fancy-schmancy Chestnut Hill. We agreed to meet in the food court at noon. Dev would be wearing a purple T-shirt and jean shorts. How could I not find him?

Well, I didn't. Not at first. I did a circuit of the food court for a good fifteen minutes, checking out every guy whose T-shirt was even a little purple and whose shorts resembled jeans even a little bit. It occurred to me that I hadn't told Dev what *I* looked like. What if he spotted this short, strange redhead casing the food court and then changed his mind? What if this was all a prank and he never showed at all?

But he did show, finally, approaching me just as I passed Orange Julius for the umpteenth time. Purple T-shirt: check. Jean shorts: check. Dev wasn't much taller than me, but he was stocky and muscular and brown. Plus, there was a tiny stud in his right nostril and thick braces on his teeth. All the shinies. His purple T-shirt featured the Incredible Hulk raging his frustrations on an IBM PC.

The fact that he hadn't dressed up put me at ease. For a thin minute, I'd been worried he thought this was a date. We got Orange Julius and sat down, and aside from the first few minutes—which were awkward as heck—we soon fell into our rhythm as bickering amigos.

And then I had to go and ruin it all by asking him if he wanted to see the novel I was in.

We quickly made our way to the Mystery/Thriller section of Borders. As always, Dame Carissa's body of work occupied a shelf all on its own. These were the new color-coded ones her US publisher had printed a few years back, with scarlet spines for her Adrian novels, aquamarine spines for her historical mysteries involving Sister Mary Judith, and pale-white spines for her miscellaneous output. They bore a large Hulk-green number at the bottom to indicate order of publication. They didn't have all sixty-plus of her books in stock, but they did carry all the heavy hitters, and in no time, I snagged her most recent Adrian novel, *Double Frame*, from the shelf.

"Yeah, I didn't like it," he said. "The twist was f'ing implausible. And if there's a character named Kat McCann, I don't remember it."

"You know how every Adrian novel is loosely based on actual events?"

"So?"

I blinked. "Dev, are you sure you go to MIT and not ITT?"

He continued to be puzzled . . . and then, suddenly, he wasn't. Realization widened his eyes, and his face widened. He stared at me as if for the first time—which, in a way, it was.

2

"Tell me everything," he said.

"I don't have to tell you anything, Dev. You read it. You didn't like it."

"Are you pranking me? Is this a prank?"

I led Dev to the Art section, where we would be guaranteed more privacy. "It's not a prank. The little girl, Cora Brown, is me. Now, before I say anything else, I need you to promise me you're not going to tell anyone, especially the chat room."

"Why not? They find this out and they'll treat you like an f'ing celebrity. You *are* an f'ing celebrity! You're in one of Dame Carissa's novels!"

"Think it through, dummy. Would you want to be in one of her novels?"

He thought it through. This time, the realization made him shrink.

"Then that was your mom who was . . ."

I quietly nodded.

"And that means your dad . . ."

I glanced down at a dried stain in the carpet. "After he was found guilty, my aunt and uncle took me in and later adopted me."

"Jeez. I'm so sorry." He shuffled his feet. "This all happened to you? Really?"

"I was six when my father . . . did what he did. But if you were to ask me which are my memories from my life and which are my memories from the novel . . . I honestly don't know anymore."

"But still . . . you met Adrian Lescher . . . and he solved the case. He got justice for your mom."

"I never met Adrian Lescher," I said. "But I did meet Alik Lisser."

"That's so f'ing cool. What was he like? In real life, I mean."

"Very tall. But I was six; everyone was tall. We played Hearts. That's not in the novel, but it definitely happened. Alik Lisser had very large hands. Larger than the cards. And he smelled like cedar, probably from those thin panatela cigars he smokes in the books, though he never smoked around me. That's all I know about Alik Lisser. Everything else is Adrian Lescher."

"You really played cards with Adrian f'ing Lescher?"

"Funny thing about that was he cheated. Like, who cheats at Hearts? And who cheats at Hearts when they're playing against a child? I called him on it too. And he admitted it. He thought it was the funniest thing in the world."

"I can see why Dame Carissa didn't include that in the novel. But I guess she included everything else about your family. Didn't you feel exploited?"

"I was six. And in a way, Dame Carissa brought my mom back to life here. And people are going to be reading these novels forever."

"Which makes you immortal too."

I shrugged again. I didn't want to think about that.

"It's just too bad you're immortal in Carissa Miller's worst book."

He was smiling. All those metal braces and dimples like little crevices on display.

"You're such an ass," I said.

We hung out for another hour, and then we went our separate ways. I bought some socks at the Gap before taking the T home so I'd have something to prove to my uncle that I'd gone to the mall. Except my uncle didn't come home till the following afternoon, wearing the same clothes he'd worn the day before and reeking like he had taken a long bath in Listerine.

The rest of the summer trickled along. Sometimes I was allowed to bike to the library. Not as often as I wanted, but enough. Sometimes my aunt came up with chores for me to do around the house, like sorting the laundry or mopping the floors. Not that I was, like, Cinderella or whatever. My aunt spent her days disinfecting the countertops or re-papering the cupboards. Our apartment was on the second floor of a row house in Dorchester, where you can't tell the difference between the sidewalks and the sewers, but my aunt made certain none of that grime crossed the doorway. Every morning, I woke up to the smell of bleach and the roar of the vacuum cleaner.

She, I learned, was not the only obsessive in my life now. After that day at the mall, Dev dove headfirst down the rabbit hole that was Alik Lisser and used his considerable research skills to dig up anything and everything about the man, all of which he shared with me via email. By August, he had Alik Lisser's address and phone number in London, the names of seven Scotland Yard cases that Carissa Miller had not fictionalized but which Dev was certain Alik Lisser had assisted on, and the names of several prestigious universities throughout Europe and North America where Alik Lisser had taught criminology as a visiting professor.

This last tidbit tied nicely with the bombshell Dev dropped on September 3, 1995. I had already shifted my reading from its usual diet of mysteries to the books we were going to read that year in English (first stop: *Beowulf*) and was signing into the chat room per usual. Dev ambushed me maybe five seconds later with his news:

WmbleyLnDet: guess whos com1ng to boston next month, give up, its alik lisser

I knew why Dev was so hyped up. Ever since getting Lisser's address and phone number, he had been egging me on to call the man. Like, what was I supposed to say? *Thank you so much, Mr. Lisser, for figuring out who killed my mom even though it was my dad, and, oh, did you know my dad died in prison?* But Dev just couldn't wrap his head around any of that. And now . . .

WmbleyLnDet: hes g1v1ng a guest lecture @ harvard on oct 13 open to public

KMcCann14: You should go. I'm sure you'll tell me all about it.

However, the next day, as I shopped for school supplies with my aunt, I couldn't shake the wired current sizzling through my nerves. Alik Lisser was coming here. *Here.* Maybe he could tell me something about my parents, something only he knew. Maybe he had *disagreed* with the LAPD about my dad being guilty. Dame Carissa had invented new names to suit her novel; who was to say she hadn't invented new facts? All these years, I hadn't really thought about Dad's innocence. I mean, what was the point? I'd assumed the public narrative was *the* narrative.

But what if it wasn't?

3

To be honest, I haven't been completely honest.

What can I say? I learned from the best. A steady diet of Carissa Miller novels from age seven plus. Nobody did lies of omission like Dame Carissa, and a lie of omission is still a lie.

For example:

You've probably figured out by now that my uncle was a drunk. You might have even guessed that he was an *abusive* drunk. But let me clarify: it's not like he ever punched me or my aunt or anything. No knuckle-shaped bruises for the doctors in the ER to write up—nope, not for me or my aunt.

For me and my aunt, we got shoved.

Into walls, into doors. Into tables. One time he shoved my aunt against the stove when it was still hot, and she lost her balance and reached for the nearest object to keep from falling and got third-degree burns across her left palm from a simmering pan of tomato sauce. I soaked an ACE bandage with an entire bottle of aloe and wrapped it as slowly as I could around her hand while she gritted her teeth and stared out our second-story window at the falling snow. I was ten.

> *Q: But, Kat, why didn't you and your aunt just go to the cops?*
>
> A: Because my uncle was a cop. In Dorchester, all the men wore uniforms. Army fatigues, gang colors, factory coveralls, police blues. All the same.

Q: But, Kat, why didn't you and your aunt just run away?
A: With what money, fool? My aunt didn't work. I wasn't allowed to work. My trust fund was cleaned out to pay for my dad's legal bills. And where were we supposed to go? And what were we supposed to do when we got there?

Q: But, Kat, why didn't you or your aunt just defend yourselves?
A: Great idea. Let's switch places. You defend yourself against 220 pounds of crazy.

Q: But, Kat, what does this have to do with Alik Lisser coming to Harvard?

Now we're getting to it. Because when you're sixteen, you can't just hop on a train to go to a lecture on a college campus, especially not when your guardians are my uncle and aunt. It's not like they didn't let me get a job because they didn't want me to work; they didn't let me get a job because they didn't want me to leave the apartment. They were control freaks, both of them, in their own ways.

I already had one month of junior year done. It was a short month, what with starting after Labor Day and with a day off for the Jewish holiday, but it was still a month, and I'd survived. It wasn't the schoolwork that I minded—I probably would have loved school if it was just schoolwork. But then there were my classmates and my teachers and . . . no thank you. One of my (many) social workers diagnosed me with "social phobia," which meant that any situation in which I might be in a crowd of people sent me into a downward spiral. At best, it meant I was always, always shy. At worst, it meant heart palpitations and dry mouth and nausea.

I could handle the mall because it was all spread out. High ceilings. Plenty of open space. (Though the mall became a no-go zone between Thanksgiving and Christmas.) I was OK with the library because, let's face it, not many people went to the library. But school? Classrooms packed with thirty kids and then, between classes, hallways packed with hundreds of kids?

I took meds. Without them, I was throwing up on the bus every morning. Since my shrink had settled on my most recent regimen—two pink 150 mg pills with breakfast, every day, no exception—I'd been episode-free. I was still shy to the point of mute, but at least I wasn't passing out in my own vomit on the school bus.

Turns out, having your mom murdered by your dad and then having the trial become a total frenzy so strangers start snapping pictures of you whenever you leave your house, which is also a crime scene, does a number on your psyche. But this was why the chat room was so important to me. I could be around other people and not worry, even if every so often that meant dealing with some troll (although AladdinZane was the worst of them). The chat room was my safe hideaway.

A lecture hall at Harvard University would not be a safe hideaway. Who knew how many people would attend a guest lecture by the world's most famous criminologist, but if the number was more than twenty, I'd be in trouble. Even if there were only five other strangers there, I was going to sit in the back row. "Five other strangers" were still strangers.

Of course, I shared none of this with Dev.

Why bother? He seemed so ecstatic about the whole thing. Every night, he drew me into hypothesizing what Alik Lisser's lecture topic would be. We even came up with a sort of bingo game we could play during the lecture. Like, every time he spoke in his native German? Clap.

WmbleyLnDet: we better wear long pants or we m1ght bru1se ourselves from overclapping our knees

KMcCann14: It will be October. We better wear long pants or we might freeze ourselves.

Fortunately, the threat of a potential nervous breakdown during the lecture was overshadowed by the problem of how I was going to get around my curfew to attend the event. As always, the solution presented itself in the current book I was reading—but reading has always been like that for me. Whenever I've needed help, all I needed to do was lose myself in a book, and suddenly my brain would connect whatever dots in my life needed connecting. Dame Carissa's books were the most reliable for this, but other writers my brain meshed well with were Josephine Tey and Ngaio Marsh.

(Thank you to a very kind librarian named Miss Sharon for daring to lead a curious and shy little redheaded girl out of the children's section and introducing me to mystery fiction.)

I was rereading *The Daughter of Time* by Josephine Tey in homeroom on Monday, October 2, when I solved the problem of my curfew. I wasn't 100 percent absorbed in the book—in fact, I was well aware that Suzie MacIntosh and Fran Maguin were muttering behind me about whether Suzie should spit her gum into my hair—but I was absorbed enough by the words on the page and Inspector Grant's forceful arguments exonerating Richard III of the deaths of his imprisoned nephews that the magic took effect in my brain and the neurons connected the dots and I may have even said aloud, "Aha."

But before I could put my plan into action, I had to slog through six periods of blech:

Period 1. Trig. Fifty-five minutes of Mr. Roberts getting excited about sines, cosines, and tangents while the pit stains on his white button-down shirt grew bigger and bigger and bigger.

Period 2. English. Fifty-five minutes of Ms. Peorini reading to us about chivalric knights, which would have been fine except it was in Old English, meaning none of it made sense to anyone but her and it sounded as if she was trying to sing while gargling a quarter pound of Raisinets.

Period 3. Social studies. A video about how Harold II, the last Anglo-Saxon king, ended up with an arrow in his eye. Three and a half stars.

Lunch. Two limp hot dogs in stale, stonelike buns. At least I had the time to myself in my hidey-hole beneath the third-floor staircase.

Period 4. Gym. Basketball or Ping-Pong. I'm four-eleven, so not really a choice. I was made to face off against Fran Maguin. On match point, she spiked the ball so hard that it bonked me dead center of my forehead. She said it was an accident, but she was laughing when she said it, so . . . Zero stars.

Period 5. Chemistry. A test on covalent bonds. One star.

Period 6. Study hall. Fifty-five minutes, except it was the last period of the day, so it stretched on for eons, not helped by the fact that the clock on the wall of Mr. Benson's classroom was stuck forever at 12:02.

Finally, though, the bell rang, and I zoomed out the door so fast that I was the first person to board Bus #14. When I got home, my aunt was elbow deep in a deep clean of the oven. The Lysol in the air was so potent that I nearly gagged. Fortunately, I found my breath and was able to speak: "You know how my guidance counselor, Mr. Wintergreen, has been pushing me to take extracurriculars so I can get into a good college? Well, I joined the mock-trial team, and our first meet is October thirteenth, so I'm not going to be home till late."

She poked her head out from the mouth of the oven. "What's the mock-trial team?"

I actually knew this answer because I had a bunch of classes with, like, half the mock-trial team and they were always jabbering about it. Mock trial in the fall, school play in the spring. They didn't do school play in the fall because in the fall it was a musical, and they needed to do *something*. (*Did* they, though? *Did* they need to do something?)

"Oh, so, get this: in mock trial, we argue cases and stuff against other schools. It's like football. Except instead of, like, a quarterback, we've got a prosecutor. Or a bunch of prosecutors. Unless you're doing the defense side, in which case we're the defense lawyers. Except some of us are the witnesses—*pretend* to be the witnesses."

"So you would have to practice after school a lot?"

Oh, crap. I hadn't thought of that.

"I guess so," I said. "Especially since our first meet is on October thirteenth. But I won't need you to pick me up or anything. I can take the T."

She poked her head back into the oven, said something I couldn't hear, and went back to her spraying and wiping. She didn't say no, so that was a yes, but she was the easy part.

The hard part came home around 7:00 p.m., though 7:00 p.m. at least meant my uncle wasn't wandering in with a night's worth of booze sloshing through him. I was in my room, studying my chemistry textbook for the makeup test on covalent bonds my teacher Mr. Handy would (hopefully) allow me to take. I pressed stop on my stereo, interrupting Siouxsie Sioux right between "Dear" and "Prudence," and headed out to the kitchen.

My uncle was already hunched over a bowl of chili. Next to his bowl was a bottle of Sam Adams, already open, and two antacids for when he was done with his chili. Where my aunt had disappeared to was anyone's guess.

I sat down at the table.

"How was school?" he asked.

"It was fine. I watched a video in social studies class about William the Conqueror. I played Ping-Pong. Oh, and I joined the mock-trial team."

"Yeah. Your aunt told me you're going to have to stay after school a lot."

"Well, our first meet is on October thirteenth and—"

"I thought we had a deal." His eyes were brown and always a little wet. "You come home after school."

"I know, but my guidance counselor said—"

"Is your guidance counselor here? 'Cause I don't see him."

Ah, so my aunt hadn't stepped out. She had fled.

"We had a deal. You come home after school. You really need reminding how dangerous the world is?"

"It wasn't a deal," I muttered. "It was you saying so and me doing so or else. Same as everything around here."

He let his spoon clang into his bowl. His wet brown eyes fixed on me. "You want to say that again?"

This was the time for me to apologize. This was the time for me to take it all back and slink off to my bedroom. All would be OK. Not great, but OK.

Tolerable.

But how often was Alik Lisser going to be in Boston? In the novels, he was always the man with the answers, but this was real life—my life—and what if he had the answers for *me*, answers about what happened ten years ago between my mom and dad that no one else could give me? We're addicted to mysteries because they're puzzles to solve, but when the puzzle is your own life . . .

"Well?" asked my uncle, chili dribbling off the side of his mouth. "You want to say that again?"

Yes, I did.

4

When a bone is sprained, the bone itself is fine. It's the ligaments connecting the bones that get jacked up. In a severe sprain, the ligaments get so jacked up from pressure that they actually rip apart.

I learned all this the next morning as the school nurse wrapped my right wrist in a gauze splint. I told her that I fell getting off the bus. My ligaments had become so swollen that they bulged out from my wrist like a plump bracelet. She offered me some ibuprofen for the pain, but I passed. She must have thought I was being brave, because she offered me some again as I was leaving, but I wasn't being brave. I'd washed down a handful of ibuprofen about thirty minutes earlier in my kitchen with a glass of OJ, and I didn't want to overdose. Not that she needed to know that.

I know what you're thinking: Why did I have to go through the motions of making up an excuse for October 13 when I could have just told my uncle and aunt the truth? Wouldn't that have been easier?

Well, first of all, no, and second of all, *definitely* no.

If my uncle knew the real reason I needed to break curfew, he never would have allowed me to go and would have come home earlier that night and watched me like a hawk to make sure I *didn't* go. As far as he was concerned, I already knew everything I needed to know about what had happened ten years ago. This was all how he "protected me." So sure, I had to get shoved so hard against the stove that I sprained my right wrist, but that was just the price I had to pay in his "deal." And besides, I was left-handed. A few weeks without the use of my right wrist wasn't the end of the world.

When I came home late the next day, my aunt didn't say a word. If my uncle was going to do something more, he would have. After a week of crashing at the school library till five and then taking the nine o'clock bus home, I knew I was safe. My right wrist throbbed like it wanted to rip itself out of my arm, but nobody was going to stop me from going to "mock trial" on the thirteenth.

The thirteenth was a Friday. I considered dressing up—both to sell the lie that I was competing in a meet and to look presentable for Harvard University—but in the end went with a cheap vintage pastel-green dress that I liked because of the wide spotted belt that ran along the waistline (and because it fit). A pair of plain stud earrings, a pair of plain black boots. A bunch of ChapStick in my book bag to join my purse (which I found at a thrift store and was shaped like an itty-bitty frog), my can of Mace, endless Kleenex, and other necessities.

The morning was cold and windy, though October winds meant swirls of leaves the color of chocolate milk and lemonade. Autumn in New England. I don't really remember what I did at school. My mind was elsewhere. After school, I read some Nero Wolfe short stories and then, at 5:00 p.m., instead of taking the bus home, I strolled another six blocks against the breeze and the setting sun to catch the train. It was a straight shot on the red line, twenty minutes to travel from blue-collar Dorchester to crimson Cambridge and Harvard Square.

Dev had suggested we meet at a café called John's, which was on the side of Harvard Yard closest to Emerson Hall, where the lecture was set for 7:30 p.m. By now, the setting sun had set and gone, and I ended up walking all the way around Harvard Yard before finally finding John's.

Dev was fifteen minutes late, which I now suspected was his normal. What was not normal: Dev wore a long red necktie and a crisp light-blue button-down (both the button-down and, yes, the necktie were tucked into his dark-blue slacks).

"What's up with the outfit?"

I mean, sure, *I'd* considered dressing up, so I was being a little hypocritical, but I'd never thought Dev would dress up. I'd never even thought he owned a tie.

"Why? I think I look f'ing *sharp*."

"You look like you're in character for a play."

"I *am* in character. I'm playing the part of someone who's about to meet Adrian freaking Lescher."

"You may want to ease up on the caffeine there, dude. We're about to go to a lecture given by one Alik Lisser. Maybe, if we're lucky, we'll get to meet him. But we're never going to meet Adrian Lescher, because Adrian Lescher doesn't exist."

"Oh, don't tell me you're not excited, Kat. You're biting your lower lip so hard I'm f'ing surprised it isn't bleeding. Want a coffee? My treat. By the way, why's your wrist in a splint?"

I hadn't even realized I'd been biting my lower lip. Stupid unconscious habits.

Dev and I hung out for a while. We reviewed the phrases we'd chosen for our silly knee-clapping bingo game. Then it was time to head over to Emerson Hall.

I'd be lying if I said I wasn't nervous. The coffee didn't help. I popped in some spearmint gum to keep from biting my lip, but it did nothing to keep my mind from whirring . . .

Would we even get a chance to speak with Alik Lisser after the lecture?

What if he gave his speech and then went off to wherever it was lecturers went off to after they were through?

What if the thing they had was some sort of wine-and-cheese setup, and some grad student in a turtleneck asked to see my ID?

What if they asked to see our IDs at the door to Emerson Hall?

Dev had said the lecture was open to the public, but let's be honest, he was just a few years older than I was and had the wrong opinion about kindasorta everything, and I just knew some part of him was convinced we were on our way to meet his childhood hero, Adrian Lescher, and didn't that make him just a teensy bit of a flake?

We wiped the coffee residue from our mouths and returned our empty mugs to the counter and set out into the cold, dark evening. We crossed narrow Quincy Street and entered Harvardville: Fat redbrick buildings, sprawling green lawns. College kids, mostly white, walking briskly on their way to class, on their way from class, on their way to conquer the world.

Dev and I followed the crowd into Emerson Hall and then flowed along the corridor to Room 105. A trio of grad students sat at a table by the door, drinking Cokes and making everyone sign the guest book. Name, phone number, major.

I'd already told Dev that I wanted to sit in the back, but he must have forgotten, because he strolled down to the front of the hundred-seat lecture hall. Whatever. I took an aisle seat in the very last row and got as comfortable as I could. If things started getting hairy, I had the Nero Wolfe anthology in my bag.

The lecture hall filled up quickly. By 7:25, every seat was taken. Dev, sitting in the second row, looked back at me and mouthed, *I'm sorry.* Was he sorry because he'd forgotten my preference, or was he sorry because he'd remembered and chosen to ignore my preference? It didn't matter. I wasn't here for him.

The woman next to me had her gray hair in a tight bun and a pair of reading glasses dangling from a chain—so, probably not a student. Maybe a professor. Maybe a fellow townie. She offered me a piece of butterscotch hard candy, but I still had my gum, so.

I checked my watch—7:30 on the dot—and a man ambled to the podium. He was average height, a bit overweight, and had a long nose. In my memories, Alik Lisser was very, very tall and very, very thin. Either this wasn't him or my memories were as accurate as Dame Carissa's novels, and if I couldn't even rely on my memories of what had happened . . .

"Ladies and gentlemen," the man said. He mostly spoke through his long nose. "My name is Nathan Exley, and I am the assistant dean for the Harvard University Law School Graduate Program and International Legal Studies. It's my pleasure to welcome you to the Arthur Fielding Memorial Lecture Series. For seven years now, this series has invited luminaries in the field who share Professor Fielding's zealotry for criminal justice, and tonight's installment is no different.

"Our guest tonight joined the police force in Vienna, Austria, on the day his country officially severed itself from Nazi Germany—April 27, 1945. Over the next fifteen years, he garnered an inestimable reputation for closing cases, especially those involving violent crime, so much so that in 1959, Scotland Yard invited him to train its new crop of homicide detectives. While aiding on the infamous Reginald Baltry case, our esteemed guest became injured in the line of duty, and so began the second chapter in his storied career. He resigned from the active force, resettled in London, and over the past thirty-plus years, Alik Lisser has become one of the world's foremost consultants on criminal investigation. Were this not enough to garner his status as a legend in his field, we also have the hugely popular novels of Carissa Miller.

"It has been an open secret that tonight's speaker inspired Carissa Miller to create the immortal Adrian Lescher. Where Detective Lisser ends and Detective Lescher begins is a matter of debate, but what is not up for debate is Detective Lisser's unparalleled ability to obtain justice for countless mothers, fathers, and children; to punish the guilty and empower the innocent; and to demonstrate, time and again, in the words of Harvard alum Robert Kennedy, 'Each time a man stands up for an ideal, or acts to improve the lot of others, or strikes out against injustice, he sends forth a tiny ripple of hope, and crossing each other from a million different centers of energy and daring, those ripples build a current which can sweep down the mightiest walls of oppression and resistance.' Ladies and gentlemen, join me in welcoming Alik Lisser."

A door off to the side opened, and in he walked.

5

No, that's not quite right. Alik Lisser didn't walk. He *limped.*

Every step began with the tap of his bone-white cane against the floor—in this case, the soft carpet of the lecture hall. First the cane and *then* his feet shuffling behind, led by his left foot. He was as tall and thin as I'd remembered, but such a pronounced limp . . .

He'd been shot in 1960, so he must have had the cane and limp in 1985. But I had no memory of it—none at all. Was it because Dame Carissa had omitted it from Adrian Lescher's character? Again, the reliability of my memories from the time was being put to serious doubt. Children were supposed to be especially good at remembering details, except I'd blocked out the not-small detail of Alik Lisser's limp.

Why?

And what else had I blocked out?

Alik Lisser took his time reaching the podium, didn't seem in a hurry. Well, sure. We were here for him and he knew it. He grinned up at us with teeth as white as his cane, teeth so white they had to be fake. I mean, especially at his age, right? If he'd become a cop in 1945, well, how old did you have to be to do that? Eighteen? Twenty-one? Eighteen in 1945 meant he was now . . . ugh, I hate math . . . sixty-eight? Not ancient, but no spring chicken. His suit was a sunny blue, and his tie had happy sailboats sailing every which way. His hair was thick and black, but that had to be fakery too. Nobody that old still had thick black hair (except maybe Dracula). He was the great Alik Lisser, sure, but he was also this sad, vain old man. I wanted to give him a hug. I wanted him to take me out for ice cream. We could play Hearts. I'd even let him cheat.

Then Alik spoke: "Thank you so much, *danke*, thank you, all of you who have come out. I'm touched. I was fully prepared to speak to an empty house, but this is a much better alternative."

At least his voice matched my memory. Soft but precise, accent maybe 60 percent German, 40 percent London posh. Alik nodded to Dean Exley, who set a transparency on an overhead projector. The white screen behind the podium filled with the image of a painting: a naked man swinging from a tree in the center while groups of robed men and women cooked stews or signed parchments or examined the body of a half-dead, giant toad. In the background, a giant, skinless ostrich observed it all through eyeless sockets.

What. The. Huh?

"At the time Salvator Rosa painted this scene of a witches' sabbath, the mid-seventeenth century, fear of witchcraft still held its grip over much of the Christian imagination. To Rosa, and most of the Western world, this grotesquerie was accepted as probable. My ancestors in law enforcement, once they had a suspected witch in custody, employed a specific means for discerning his or her guilt called 'witch swimming.' Perhaps you've heard of it. They would push the suspected witch into a river or pond. The guilty floated and the innocent drowned."

When I was in fifth or sixth grade, a historian from nearby Salem had come to my class to talk about the witch trials, and she had mentioned witch swimming and shown us a clip from *Monty Python and the Holy Grail* that made fun of how ridiculous it all was. We'd all laughed—except the historian, who was not much taller than I was and also a redhead. Why had one of the world's foremost criminologists traveled across the Atlantic Ocean to lecture a hall full of Harvard students about witches?

"One theory," said Lisser, "held that witches, having been anti-baptized, could not be submerged under the water. Another theory suggested that the witches floated because their bones were hollow. This hollow-bone theory had the benefit of also explaining how the witches could fly. Lest we forget, these men—my ancestors in law enforcement—did not believe they were acting out of superstition. They believed they were doing what was right and just and that their methods were sound. But this was the 1600s. Skip ahead one hundred years, and let's examine the scientific methods used by my ancestors in law enforcement during the Age of Reason."

Lisser nodded again to Dean Exley, who replaced the projected image of the witches' sabbath with one of a human skull, in profile and sectioned off like a city map, only instead of the names of neighborhoods, the skull's sections were labeled with traits such as *constructiveness* and *concentrativeness*, which, excuse me, are not words.

"In my hometown of Vienna, a doctor named Franz Gall surmised that one could examine a person's head and determine from its contours and bumps and measurements what inclinations the person might have. This cross section is a diagram of Gall's conclusions as to where these inclinations could be found in the human brain and was used for decades by experts for concluding why certain people behaved the way they did and for, in some examples, predicting who might be predisposed toward crime based on the size and shape of their skull. We can laugh now at phrenology with all the superiority of the twentieth century and dismiss its theoretical truths as absurd as witch swimming. But let me direct you to an academic conference held in the twentieth century—in this very year—and to the conclusion of those in attendance, which will be published, I imagine, in the near future. Their conclusion? That some people possess a combination of genes which may make them—*ja*, you guessed it—predisposed to crime. They have an excess of what Dr. Gall might call *impulsiveness*, bound not in a chamber of their brain but in an allele in their DNA helix. If true, and if the scientists across the way at MIT and at fourteen other top laboratories reach their intended goal of identifying and sequencing the human genome by 2015, then that will be the day I am out of a job.

What use is a detective's mind in solving a crime when we have genetics to provide us a shortcut to the answer? *Nein*, a shortcut to the question! Round up everyone guilty of possessing this impulsiveness gene and call it a day! Let's just as soon round up everyone with a certain pattern of contours on the skull, or maybe let's just toss everyone in the river and see who drowns. Or perhaps let's take a step back from our shortcuts and consider the larger problem."

Another nod to Dean Exley. Another slide. A fingerprint, larger than life.

"This fingerprint belongs to a man named Bruce Basden. He was arrested in North Carolina in 1985 for the murder of Blanche and Remus Adams, and the primary evidence against him was a set of latent prints found at the Adamses' home. Basden sat in jail for over a year awaiting trial until, thanks to the efforts of his defense attorney, the fingerprint evidence was reexamined and found to be in error. Do I even need to tell you how common Mr. Basden's story is? In the past six years alone, fifteen convictions have been overturned in this country based on faulty evidence. Expand that to the UK and the number is doubled. Include Europe and the number is nearly tripled. Forty-four innocent men and women, tossed into the river. In the past six years. In the twentieth century."

Alik Lisser's words chilled me to my core. All I could think about was my father, dying in prison, abandoned by his friends, by his family. He and my mother had always been so happy. They had loved each other. I was sure of it. And I know what you're thinking: How can I be trusted to remember that when I couldn't even remember the limp of a man I'd maybe met once?

Love stays with you, and my memory of their love wasn't faulty because it wasn't a memory. It was as much a part of me as . . . well, as my DNA. And I was supposed to believe he'd stabbed her twenty-seven times with a steak knife, an act he never admitted to, not even after his conviction?

I didn't believe in fate, but for wrongful conviction to be the topic of this lecture . . .

And Alik Lisser wasn't finished.

"Am I an alarmist? *Ja*, I am an alarmist. I'm alarmed! Aren't you? Burden of proof as a concept dates back to Roman law, but what constitutes that proof is historically, horrifically slippery. I'm often asked the secret to my success as a detective, and it's really rather simple: assume nothing. The Cartesian maxim 'I think, therefore I am' is too often misunderstood to be an affirmation of identity, and it is not. It is an affirmation of *skepticism*. That all I know is that I think, and everything else is suspect. And yet in the West, we make a religion out of science and tithe all of our trust to it and leave nothing for ourselves. To appropriate a phrase from economics, we have forgotten the merits of diversification! We have made inductive reasoning a supplicant before the altar of technology when it should always, always be the other way around. Fingerprints, footprints, bite marks—all valuable, but none more valuable than critical thought. About this, surely we can agree, on the grounds of this college, on this place whose motto is *Veritas*. Truth. What nobler goal could there be? Thank you."

Everyone applauded. I must have as well, though I don't remember it. I was so caught up in what he had said. It was like I was outside myself. It was like I was six years old.

The guest book grad students set two tall chairs in front of the podium, and the lecture shifted to a Q and A between Dean Exley and Alik Lisser. Eventually, the questions were opened to the audience. Most of the questions were about the novels, because of course they were. On a normal night, I might have been on the edge of my seat to hear his answers, but these were not the answers I needed to know.

Dev raised his hand each time the dean asked for a question, but he was never chosen. At 9:00 p.m. on the dot, Dean Exley thanked everyone again for coming, reminded the attendees about next month's lecture, and dismissed us. I wanted to hustle down and speak with Alik

Lisser ASAP, but there was no way I'd be able to fight the anxiety (and pressed flesh) of traffic heading in the opposite direction.

Fortunately: Dev.

He grabbed his book bag and pushed his way against the grain toward the guest. The exiting crowd dwindled enough for me to dash down the lecture hall steps . . . in time to see Dev thrust five paperbacks and a ballpoint pen in front of Alik Lisser.

Ugh, seriously, Dev?

On the other hand, this bought me enough time to descend the rest of the way. Alik Lisser, to his credit, was patiently signing the books, though the dean looked appropriately annoyed. Once finished, Lisser handed the ballpoint pen back and then glanced at me, waiting (I assume) for my handful of books to sign.

"Thank you," said the dean, "but Detective Lisser actually is on a tight schedule. Have a good night."

My window was closing. I had to speak. Now was my time.

I opened my mouth.

Nothing came out.

The dean escorted Alik Lisser toward the nearest door. The old detective limped the whole way. I had at least a full minute. All I had to do was find the words.

Why was it so hard to find the words? Why?

Just open your mouth and speak. You do it every day, Kat.

Just open . . . your . . . mouth . . . and—

The door shut behind them. They were gone.

I still could have chased after them. I still could have stopped them on their way to wherever. I still could have asked Alik Lisser about my dad.

I didn't move a muscle.

What was this, cowardice? Maybe. Maybe I was too afraid that Lisser was going to tell me that my father, who used to scoop me up in his arms and carry me on his shoulders, was a monster. Or maybe it was my anxiety. Maybe I was just too weak willed.

Whatever the reason, my once-in-a-lifetime opportunity closed, and I was left alone in the lecture hall beside that fool Dev, who stood slack-jawed at his newly signed books as if he were a boy on Christmas morning with a new bike or something.

We headed out. He asked if I wanted him to walk me to the train station. I didn't. He asked me if something was wrong. I said nothing was wrong. Note that I had no problem talking to *him*, even if the words were lies.

I got home a half hour later. My uncle was out. Just as well. My aunt asked how mock trial went. I told her we won. The words came out without thinking. I just opened my mouth and spoke. Then I shuffled off to bed and cried myself to sleep.

I must not have set my alarm, because next thing I knew, my aunt was gently shaking me awake. I winced at the weekend sunlight. My eyes were sticky, so I wiped them and peered up blearily at her.

"What?" I muttered.

"There's someone on the phone for you."

Was it Dev checking up on me? Had I given him my number? Oh God. The last thing I needed was my uncle and aunt thinking I had a boyfriend—

"He said his name is Alik Lisser. Isn't that the amazing man who solved your mother's murder?"

6

"Hello . . . ?"

"There she is! Katie, Katie, Katie. At my age, surprises are few and far between, so let that context sink in when I tell you how surprised I was to see you last night. Surprised and delighted, *ja*!"

"So you . . . you recognized me?"

"Of course, my girl! Our past selves don't fade away. They remain within us and those that know us see us."

I fiddled with and tugged on the tuft of red hair that brushed against the top of my right ear.

He had seen me.

"But tell me, Katie, please: How have the past ten years treated you?"

The move to Boston. New home, new family. Loss. New kids at school. The news about my father's death in prison. So much lost.

I sobbed. I sobbed ten years' worth of tears in the span of a minute. Thick tears, soupy tears, dribbling down my cheeks to my chin to the floor. But sobs are more than tears. The whole body convulses, and the sounds that come out—like a cat's mewing.

Pain doesn't fade away. It remains within us, and those who know us see it.

Ten years and I'd had no one. For a while, I'd had a stuffed elephant named Harriet, which I must've gotten when I was tiny. Harriet was small and bright blue, and her trunk dangled from her face by a thread, and her bright-pink ears were misshapen from, I guess, my sucking on them as a toddler, and she had a permanent discoloration on her underside from some spit-up stain. I'd had her as long as I could remember, and I'd brought her with me from the West Coast, brought her with me on the *plane*, and then one day, two months into my stay at my uncle and aunt's, I came home from elementary school and Harriet was gone. I asked my aunt where she was, and she told me Harriet had come apart in the washing machine, so she had thrown her out and I was better off without such a filthy toy anyway.

How had the past ten years treated me?

When I arrived at my new school after my move, a bunch of my classmates knew who I was. The murder had been major tabloid news. Some of them stayed far away from me, maybe because they were afraid they'd catch murder cooties. Some of them did the opposite; they stuck to me like gnats to flypaper and peppered me with questions every moment of every day: What was it like having a killer for a daddy? Had I seen my mom's dead body? Did I think my killer daddy had killed anyone else? Had I heard the rumor that he killed my mom because she was seeing someone else?

I had just turned seven years old.

My dad used to send me letters from prison. He wrote with a black pen and signed them *XOXOXO*. He sent me twenty-nine letters. I found out about them the day after I learned he'd died. My uncle, in a rare moment of empathy, gave me the letters. He had been storing them in his underwear drawer in his dresser. Had kept them in their envelopes (their *opened* envelopes). He'd hidden the letters because, as a cop, he'd decided it was best that a child not keep in touch with a felon. The letters were mostly Dad turning the everyday horror show of his life into funny little fables to amuse his daughter. He turned the guards into rhinoceri, his fellow prisoners into pigs and ducks and horses. "Another Tale from the California Zoo."

Occasionally, Dad asked why I didn't write back.

How had the past ten years treated me?

The past ten years had torn me apart in the washing machine. They had thrown me away.

Did I tell all this to Alik Lisser? Did I unburden myself to this great man, who had recognized me after all this time and then reached out and actually phoned me?

No. Of course not.

Instead, after sobbing, after taking a deep breath to steady myself, I asked, "How did you get my phone number?"

"Ah! A puzzle! Not a difficult one. *Nein*, not to the girl who bested me ten years ago."

I considered the puzzle. How had he gotten my phone number? I went through it step-by-step:

Step #1: He recognizes me. He knows my name: Katherine McCann.

Step #2: He decides to call Katherine McCann.

~~Step #3: He looks up Katherine McCann in the phone book.~~ No, he would not look up a child in the phone book.

~~Step #3: He looks up McCann in the phone book and calls each McCann until he gets the right one.~~ No, again. My aunt and uncle's last name was Dundee. Plus, this was Boston. New Ireland. God knows how many McCanns were in the phone book. So how did he . . . ?

Oh, duh.

"The guest book at the lecture," I said.

"That's my girl!" he replied. "By the by, your penmanship has improved very much since last we saw each other, *ja*. Do you remember drawing my portrait? In the bottom-right corner, you wrote *By Katie McCann*."

"I don't remember that."

"You said when you grew up, you wanted to be an artist like your mom. Do you still want to be an artist?"

"Gosh, no."

"Why not? Humanity needs art! Who else is there to show us how silly and self-important we are?"

"Oh, I don't know if I agree with that," I said. I glanced over at the towers of books in my bedroom. All those mysteries. Did they remind me that life was silly? No. Life was strange and full of surprises. To call it *silly* was to say it wasn't serious, and that was just untrue. Life could be too serious. But Alik Lisser had led a very different life from mine. Maybe if I saw things through his eyes . . . as if I could ever see things through his eyes . . .

"Tell me, please, Katie . . . what did you think of my lecture?"

"You want to know what *I* think?"

"Of course I do! Do you think the sycophants at Harvard University gave me constructive criticism? They have been wooing me for years to be a visiting professor. If someone wants something from you, it is in their best interest *not* to give you an honest answer. Ah, but then again, you were going to ask me a question last night, weren't you? You were going to ask me a question last night and you didn't. Ask me your question, Katie. Just be forewarned: to you, because I respect you, because of our history, I *will* give an honest answer. Ask me whatever you want. Just be sure, *ja*, you *want* the truth."

This was it. This was the moment. Alik Lisser, the man with the answers, was going to tell me once and for all what I needed to know about my father and what had happened ten years earlier. My doubts about his guilt would either be confirmed . . . or destroyed.

All I had to do was ask.

I had to know. Even if the truth was awful, it was still the truth.

Better a hard truth than an easy lie, right? Right . . . ?

"Did my dad kill my mom?" I asked.

Alik paused. His silence lasted an eternity.

Then finally:

"Some truths can't be explained with words. Some truths need to be seen. What are you doing between Christmas and New Year's?"

"What do you mean?"

"I mean exactly what I said. I often do. What are your plans between December twenty-fifth and January first? Because if you haven't got any plans yet—any unavoidable plans—then I'd like to invite you and your family to my cottage here in Devonshire. All expenses paid, *ja, ja*. What do you say?"

7

Before my aunt could say yes (or no), she said she had to discuss it with my uncle, and that's when my hopes sank. She didn't really have to discuss it with him; we both knew what *his* answer was going to be.

Not that I expected my aunt to immediately jump on board. She was about as spontaneous as I was Martian. The tragedy of it all was that she *loved* British stuff. She sang Beatles tunes when she cleaned. She never missed *Masterpiece Theatre*. If we were at Stop & Shop and came across a magazine with Princess Diana on the cover, that magazine was an instant buy. As far as I knew, she had never left New England, not once in her life, and now she had an opportunity to go to Old England, *Real* England . . . and yet.

I was already up and in a sour mood, so I plopped down in front of the PC and dialed online. AOL announced, "You've got mail!" and I quickly skimmed and deleted whatever garbage spam had accumulated over the . . .

Oh. Hmm. I had an email from Dev.

Dev and I had mostly kept our online interactions to the chat room. But sure enough, in my inbox: one email from WmbleyLnDet. No subject line. I clicked on it.

Kat,

im really sorry i stole your time with adrian, i wasn't th1nk1ng, i w1ll 100% make it up to you

-Dev

What kind of lame apology was that? He had attended the lecture to get some books signed. I had attended the lecture to find out who killed my mother. How exactly did he expect to make it up to me?

I decided then and there that I wasn't going to tell Dev about the phone call. He didn't deserve to know. He may have exchanged pleasantries with the man, the legend, but I'd had an actual conversation with him. And sure, it would have been *delightful* to throw that in Dev's face, but no, ignorance would be his punishment.

Still, I had to tell *somebody*. I logged into the chat room.

It might surprise you to learn that our little rest stop on the information superhighway wasn't always hopping with activity. Case in point: that morning, only Kiwi_woolgatherer was online.

If Marigoldeneyes was the mother hen of our little fan circle (and Dev was the clueless contrarian), then Kiwi_woolgatherer was the peculiar old sage. He was a gay World War II vet from Christchurch, New Zealand. He worked on a sheep farm and, due to the fact that he lived literally halfway around the world, often showed up in the chat room at the oddest hours (although how or why a New Zealander was using an internet service called America Online was a mystery for another day). So while most of the western hemisphere was (reasonably) still asleep at 7:39 a.m. on a Saturday morning . . .

KMcCann14: Good morning! Or evening . . . ? What time is it in your neck of the woods? Have you even invented clocks yet in NZ?

It took Kiwi_woolgatherer a few minutes to reply. He was probably away from his keyboard. But when he finally did reply, it was with his typical mix of weirdness and wisdom.

Kiwi_woolgatherer: Time, much like the sky, is an illusion we've invented to help make sense of a vast and senseless universe.

KMcCann14: So that's a no on the clocks?

Kiwi_woolgatherer: I heard through the grapevine that you and WmbleyLnDet met a superhero last night.

KMcCann14: Do you even have grapes in NZ?

KMcCann14: I'm sorry, that was lame. It's before my awake-time. Time may be an illusion and all that, but it's got me tricked.

Kiwi_woolgatherer: Is this you not wanting to talk about meeting Alik Lisser?

KMcCann14: That depends. Are you sitting down?

And so I told him. I told him everything, which included:

- What happened with my parents and the media circus that followed
- Alik's role in the murder investigation
- The novel, *Double Frame*, Dame Carissa made out of it all
- My inability to speak last night
- Dev's inability not to speak
- Alik's phone call and invitation to visit him

I didn't say anything about my aunt and uncle. Why bother?

When I was through, I swore him to secrecy, especially from Dev. I was certain Kiwi_woolgatherer wouldn't tell. Well, I was *pretty* sure Kiwi_woolgatherer wouldn't tell. He didn't say much while I shared my story. Either way, it felt good to tell *someone*, someone who at least had read *Double Frame* and was aware of Alik Lisser.

When I was through, I waited to hear his thoughts, however weird and/or wise they were.

I waited five minutes. Had he stepped away from his keyboard again? At this moment? Was his woolly flock bleating for their shepherd?

Finally, his reply:

Kiwi_woolgatherer: When Alice passed through the looking-glass, she became a Pawn. Remember that.

Um, thank you?

I actually loved the Alice books. Girl suddenly finds herself in a world she doesn't understand and can't escape: relatable. *Alice's Adventures in Wonderland* was one of the books I clearly remembered my parents reading to me before bed. They tag-teamed it. My dad read the narrative and my mother did all the voices of the characters, even the male ones. And not just *Alice in Wonderland.* There was also *Charlotte's Web* (oh my God, I cried so much at the end) and *Anne of Green Gables* (my mother's favorite book as a child), though we never finished that one. Life interrupted. And by *life*, I mean *death*.

I still haven't finished it. I don't think I ever will.

Kiwi_woolgatherer offered up a few more pithy, inscrutable fortune cookie quotes, and then he had to go. It was late in Christchurch, and he had to be up at dawn to walk the sheep. By the time he left, the room had filled up with about a half dozen other regulars. I bantered a bit with them and then I, too, had to go. My aunt's vacuuming, combined with my early wake-up, had birthed a headache between my ears. I grabbed a banana from the counter, poured myself a tall glass of pulp-free OJ, and retreated to my bedroom, my door very much closed.

(By the way, if you ever wondered if dipping a banana in OJ might be a genius idea, it's *not*. I mean, unless, hey, a soggy banana and rot-flavored orange juice floats your boat.)

I cranked up my stereo for background noise (most of my music was either cassette rentals from the library or college-radio stuff I taped off 88.9 FM) and began to formulate an argument to convince my uncle to let me go abroad. This problem was a doozy. My uncle, Mr. Control Freak himself, who had shoved me into the stove when I mentioned I *might* have to stay after school for mock trial, was not going to roll over and let me fly across the Atlantic Ocean to spend a week with an old man, no matter the reason, no matter how famous the old man was.

Hmm. Putting it that way, it did sound sketchy. I needed to *not* put it that way. If I were a character in a Dame Carissa novel (a different character, that is), what would she have written for me to say to change a stubborn uncle's mind?

I must have fallen asleep at some point in my formulation, because suddenly my aunt was looming over me and shaking me awake (again). I snagged my headphones off my ears, rubbed my eyes, and asked her to repeat what she'd just said.

So she did:

"We're going to England!"

Was I still dreaming? I asked her to repeat what she'd said for a third time. Her face stretched into the biggest grin I'd ever seen her give, and she clutched me by my shoulders and repeated her news so loud that Her Majesty the queen of England could have heard her.

"But, I mean, how? You told me you needed to talk to—"

"I did. Your uncle called ten minutes ago. He wanted to know what we were having for dinner, and I told him that I'd tell him what we were having for dinner as soon as I told him about our big surprise! I figured it might be better to tell him over the phone than in person, and sometimes he's in a better mood when he's at work . . . Anyway, the point is, he said we could go! He can't go. He has to work. So it will be just us girls! Oh, we're going to need to buy luggage and get our passports and . . . I'll make a checklist!"

8

Alik Lisser had apparently given my aunt his travel agent's contact info, because after she hurried out of my bedroom, that was the first call she made. The next nine were to friends and relatives. She told them it was to cancel holiday plans, but come on, I heard the bouncy tone in her voice—she'd really called to brag.

I couldn't help but be happy for her.

For both of us. We were going to England! I still had trouble believing it. Most unbelievable of all: my uncle wasn't standing in our way, wasn't putting up a fight, nothing. At the time, I didn't question it. When you look a gift horse in the mouth, it bites your head off. Only later did I realize my aunt had been strategizing. She called all those people (including her priest) to brag so she could set up a fail-safe. What happened behind closed doors was one thing, but now these people were telling other people, and if my uncle turned around and said no to England, he'd be turning all these other people into liars.

So smart. So sneaky. So brave.

I'll bet my uncle probably thought he had beaten all the bravery out of my aunt. But he was wrong. However, while my aunt had all her people to call, I had nobody. But I did have a room full of chatters who were about to be jealous out of their *minds*.

I hopped out of bed and ran to the PC. It was nearly noon. I tried to log on but got a busy signal. Ugh. I had to wait until my aunt was done using the phone before I could use the line to dial into AOL. My stomach mumbled something fierce, so I made myself a PB&J (extra J) to shut it up while my aunt gabbed and gabbed and gabbed on the phone, wrapping and unwrapping the cord around her forearm. I was still happy for her, but I was also getting impatient.

When would I get *my* turn to brag?

Finally, after I finished my sandwich *and* some vanilla wafers *and* sat at the computer and basically glared at my aunt for, like, half an hour, she finished her last call and told me I could sign in online.

Seven people in the chat room, including Dev.

He IM'd me almost immediately:

WmbleyLnDet: did you get my ema1l

KMcCann14: Yes.

WmbleyLnDet: are you mad?

KMcCann14: No.

WmbleyLnDet: i have a surpr1se for you

KMcCann14: I have a surprise for you too.

WmbleyLnDet: really, what is it

KMcCann14: You go first.

WmbleyLnDet: one of the books i had adrian s1gn was double frame even tho you know i hate that book because it sucks but i got it s1gned for you

Well. That was both sweet and ridiculous. In other words, typical Dev.

WmbleyLnDet: whats your surpr1se

KMcCann14: Well, I don't know if it can compare with yours. Thank you, by the way.

WmbleyLnDet: its the least i could do

He wasn't wrong there.

KMcCann14: Alik Lisser called me this morning. He remembered me from ten years ago. We had a nice chat. To make a long story short, he's flying me and my aunt to stay with him from December 26-January 1.

WmbleyLnDet: haha, very funny, what's the real surpr1se

KMcCann14: That's it. That's the real surprise. I'm telling the truth.

Silence. Ten full, fat seconds. Then:

WmbleyLnDet: i dont bel1eve you

KMcCann14: Well, that's rude. Because it's true.

WmbleyLnDet: prove it

Oh.

He had a point. It *was* hard to believe. I had trouble believing it myself. How could I prove it? I couldn't, not yet. Had Kiwi_woolgatherer not believed me either? It was always impossible to tell with him.

KMcCann14: I'll take pictures in England with Alik Lisser.

WmbleyLnDet: ok

Well, hmm. So much for my support group supporting me. I logged off and tried not to let Dev get to me. I was going to England! I was finally going to get to sit down with *the* expert on what had happened ten years ago.

The "Adrian Lescher of it all" was nice, too, and over the next two months, as the temperatures dropped into the forties and my grades dropped into the seventies, I poured myself back into Dame Carissa's novels and short stories. I also made it a point to reread *Mrs. Mystery*, Dame Carissa's autobiography.

I didn't have a copy of my own, and so, one Saturday in November, I dressed for the New England Cold—chunky boots to keep from slipping on the ice, thick jeans to keep my legs warm (and to keep them from getting cut up when I inevitably slipped on the ice anyway), a wool sweater over a long-sleeve shirt, a wool coat (thank you, Salvation Army), and to top it all off, wool mittens and a wool scarf and a wool hat with wool earmuffs (thank you to all sheep, New Zealand and elsewhere)—and headed to my local library.

The two librarians at the desk, Shanice and Delilah, rushed out to give me a hug. I hadn't really seen them since volunteering that summer, and I guess they had missed me. Shanice got me to tell her all about my classes (and I may have exaggerated my enjoyment of them) while Delilah went in the back to make me some hot cocoa to warm me up.

The library was the same as it always was: Lighting a bit too yellow (making everyone look like they had jaundice). The wooden floorboards still creaked where the circulation area became the children's room. The floor of the children's room was a giant furry carpet designed to look like the United States of America. The part of the carpet sectioned off for Massachusetts was worn down the most. I had been too old for storytime here when I moved to the East Coast, but sometimes that past summer, when I needed a pick-me-up, I would take a break from shelving books and eavesdrop on the children's librarian, Miss Sharon, as she entertained a platoon of awestruck toddlers. If Miss Sharon hadn't retired, I totally would have shared my news with her, and she totally would have believed me. Without her nudging me, at seven years old, to indulge my curiosity and explore, I never would have found my love of mysteries, which led to my love for Dame Carissa in particular, which led to my joining the chat room, which led to Dev inviting me to the lecture, etc.

(And if you think it's bizarro to recommend murder mysteries to someone whose life has been stained by murder, if you think it's extra bizarro to *enjoy* murder mysteries if your life has been stained by murder, let me ask you this: When you're sad, when your heart's been ripped in two, why do you listen to sad music and watch sad movies? I rest my case, Your Honor.)

My project over the next month was to be as educated about Dame Carissa Miller and Detective Alik Lisser as I could be. As Adrian Lescher liked to say, "The difference between an amateur and a professional is that an amateur only does the work he enjoys, while a professional does all the work." I was going to do *all* the work. I could have leaned on Marigoldeneyes since she was the chat room expert in all things Dame Carissa (and had been writing a biography on her for years now), but I decided, for better or worse, this needed to be All Me.

I got a fresh spiral notebook (black cover) for this project and filled up the first page with a timeline (in black ink, coincidentally):

- September 1, 1920: Carissa Skint born in Sheffield, England; daughter of a typewriter salesman.
- 1937: Carissa Skint elopes with Winston Miller, a chemistry major at Oxford.
- 1940: Winston dies in France during the Battle of Dunkirk; to pay the bills, Carissa becomes a for-hire typist in London.
- 1947: Carissa writes her first novel, *Bridgeborn Manor*, a gothic romance in the style of *Wuthering Heights*; it sells well enough, but she doesn't quit her day job.
- 1948–1960: Carissa averages a book a year, mostly gothic romances with tawdry covers.

About those earlier novels, she had this to say in her autobiography:

"In autumn 1987, my agent brought to my attention the fact that Sotheby's was auctioning off a first edition of *Bridgeborn Manor* in mint condition. I had assumed all copies had been used for kindling during the winter months, a far better use of the three hundred pages than reading them, but to my astonishment, the dreadful book sold at auction for 32,500 pounds. I was suddenly curious what the buyer intended to do with his or her new acquisition, but the purchase had been made anonymously. I suspect that somewhere in England, there is a room full of artifacts to be found, such as the insurance policy for the *Hindenburg*, 'Wrong Way' Corrigan's compass, and a first edition of *Bridgeborn Manor* by Carissa Miller in mint condition."

- 1962: Carissa meets Alik Lisser at a party held by Princess Margaret at the 400 Club.
- 1963: *Turnabout,* the first Adrian Lescher novel, is published and is an instant smash.
- 1964–1988: Carissa averages two books a year, all mysteries and/or thrillers.
- September 1, 1990: Dame Carissa disappears, leaving behind only a brief handwritten plea that nobody try to find her.

This last bit wasn't in *Mrs. Mystery*, of course, first published in July 1990. What had made Dame Carissa, on the very day she turned seventy, decide to vanish? Where did she vanish to? Despite her plea, the police did search for her, both in England and abroad, but nothing had come of it. That part at least made sense. If I were as clever (and rich) as Dame Carissa and wanted to not be found, I would not be found.

What surprised (and disappointed) me about *Mrs. Mystery* was how little Alik Lisser was mentioned. Here he was, the inspiration of her wild success, and his name appeared on six pages in all (as per the index), and mostly with just incidental mentions. He was what we mystery nerds would call "conspicuously absent."

Adrian Lescher, on the other hand, was all over the second half of the autobiography and even had his own appendix, which cleverly presented itself as a mini-autobiography by the great man himself. How much of this was the story of Adrian Lescher, though, and how much was the story of Alik Lisser? I mapped out three key differences:

- Alik was real / Adrian was imaginary (duh)
- Alik, permanently injured from his gunshot wound, walked with a cane / Adrian, completely recovered from his gunshot

wound, sometimes strolled with a cane, but it was more of an affectation than a necessity
- Alik lived in a cottage in Devonshire / Adrian lived on Wembley Road in London

But what else? For the first ten novels, Adrian had a black cat named Macaroni. Did Alik have a cat at one time? Adrian enjoyed Mozart and pinot noir and cigars, and he always began the day, wherever he was, with a five-mile run.

Why borrow Alik Lisser's cases and emulate his genius and then change his character? Yet another mystery and puzzle. But I was soon going to be able to solve it, or at least have a one-in-a-million opportunity at trying. Though that was not the number one mystery on my mind . . .

Alik had told me that "some truths need to be seen." Would he make me fly ten hours during Christmas break only to show me what I already knew: that my father was guilty?

No, it *had* to be good news. It had to mean my father had been wrongly convicted. Unlike Adrian in the novel, who'd proved conclusively that my father had killed my mother, in the *real* world, Alik must have tried to convince the police otherwise, and for whatever reason, he'd failed. For whatever reason, Dame Carissa went ahead in characterizing my dad as a womanizer and a fiend and a murderer. She was an embellisher. Just look at how many liberties she had taken in creating Adrian.

The more I thought about it, the angrier I got. I wasn't a fool. I knew her novels were never intended to be taken as nonfiction. But didn't she have a responsibility to the dead? Didn't she have a responsibility to the living? How many other people had had their lives distorted for the sake of her book sales?

OK, OK. One step at a time.

Even though I continued to log on to the chat room every night, I didn't bring up my project or my upcoming trip. I felt guilty about this. These were my closest friends. I owed them for the many, many, many times they had given me support after a long and brutal day just by being there and being themselves. I never complained to them about my life. None of us really complained about anything serious. That was the point. The chat room was an escape from all that. Still, everything I was doing on the side involved Dame Carissa Miller, and this was *the* Dame Carissa Miller chat room, with the biggest Dame Carissa Miller fans on the planet. You see what I mean.

Meanwhile, Dev started pestering me about meeting up. He wanted to give me the signed book. He also implied that he'd gotten me something for Christmas, which stunned me. I hadn't gotten him anything. Was I supposed to? Sure, we were friends online, but we had hung out in person a total of two times. Did that make us Christmas buds? And if so, was I expected to know that?

I evaded him as best I could, but I could tell he was starting to get annoyed. He took longer and longer to reply to my direct messages, and when he did, it was with one- or two-word answers. All right, maybe *that* wasn't uncharacteristic of him, but it was the tone of it all. He was hurt. I had hurt him.

But he had hurt me, too, hadn't he? He had flat out accused me of being a liar. What did I owe him? And I was going to show him—all of them—the truth, anyway. I was going to take hundreds of pictures, and when I came back in January, I planned on sharing them in the room. Then they would all believe me, and Dev would be the one who would have to apologize.

For this to happen, though, I needed to gather evidence. Fortunately, the high school had a photography club, and the photography club had a Kodak DCS 200 digital camera. Unfortunately, the photography club kept their equipment under lock and key in the darkroom, which was adjacent to Room 214. Fortunately, I had chemistry in Room 214 with Mr. Handy, who ran the photography club (which was how I knew about the Kodak DCS 200, because he had shown it off to us), and the darkroom wasn't locked during school hours (so the club members could go in and use it during their free period or whatever). So on December 14, I tested the one advantage I got from being small and quiet: Right after my chemistry class got out and everyone was distracted, I zipped into the darkroom and stuffed the camera into my book bag. It took maybe thirty seconds. Nobody noticed.

Between the camera and my research, I was now ready for England.

9

My uncle's favorite spot in our cramped South Boston apartment (maybe in the world) was his recliner. It was perfectly angled so that he could watch the TV *and* enjoy whatever warmth he'd cobbled together in the apartment's small brick fireplace. The recliner was upholstered in plaid that had thinned over the years (like my uncle's hair) and was missing patches here and there (again, like my uncle's hair), and it chirped whenever he used the handle to shift out the footrest. But it was massive and soft, and even though it smelled like beer, I loved to curl up in it—especially if the sun was coming in just so or if the fireplace was in an orange mood—and read.

On the airplane we took to London, every seat was as massive and soft as my uncle's recliner. The seats weren't thin plaid fabric but a smooth blue leather. They didn't smell like beer; they smelled like adventure.

Or maybe I'm projecting. I do that.

My aunt, meanwhile, was a quivering mess. It was her first plane ride ever. Her eyes were shut, her lips mumbled the Lord's Prayer, and her hands gripped her armrests for dear life. I offered her some gum. She just shook her head. A flight attendant asked if she wanted a beverage. She just shook her head.

When we began to taxi toward our runway, I was sure she was going to weep.

When we accelerated to takeoff, I was certain she was going to scream.

When we finally left Planet Earth and flew into the wide blue yonder, I was positive she was going to faint. This time I was right. I pressed the call button for the flight attendant, but I had to wait another five minutes for the plane to steady before someone could come and check on us.

"Oh, poor thing," the flight attendant said.

"Is there anything you can do?"

He fiddled with the controls above my aunt's seat, and the oxygen mask tumbled down. Since I was closer, I put it over her mouth. Just like they'd said before the flight, the clear bag did not inflate, but oxygen was indeed flowing, because my aunt's eyelids fluttered to life and she made a soft moaning sound. Meanwhile, the flight attendant had magically produced a bottle of water. He offered it to my aunt, who took it with a grateful nod and slipped the oxygen mask off so she could take a sip.

Like I said: adventure.

"Think of a happy place," I told her. "That helps me sometimes."

The magical flight attendant returned with a pair of headphones and encouraged my aunt to plug them into her armrest and listen to the complimentary in-flight entertainment, which she did. She shut her eyes again, but I could tell from her fidgeting that she wasn't asleep. She didn't sleep at all during the six-plus-hour flight.

To keep myself busy for six-plus hours, I reread the first two Adrian novels: *Turnabout* and *A Dose of Murder*. Compared to the books that followed, *Turnabout* is a crazy read. For one, Adrian is still a member of the Austrian police, and is in London on a sort of foreign-exchange thing. There's a killer on the loose (isn't there always), and Adrian helps Scotland Yard catch him—but Adrian isn't quite Adrian yet. He's more of a, like, 1960s version of Sherlock Holmes. And I mean, sure, there is always some overlap, what with the self-confidence and the stubbornness and the encyclopedic mind, but Adrian is so much more empathetic than Sherlock Holmes ever was. Sherlock solves crimes not because he cares about the victims, but because he cares about the puzzle. Adrian Lescher always-always-always cares about the victims.

But *A Dose of Murder* is where all the familiar pieces fall into place. Here is Adrian Lescher, the human being. He's a genius with a weakness. He wears his heart on his sleeve, and it always leads him to danger. But through wit and intellect and guile, he survives the danger and solves an unsolvable crime and sets the scales of justice to their proper balance once again.

Or, you know, something like that.

The victim in *A Dose of Murder* is a beloved Anglican minister who has been killed by dehydration, as in not a drop of water whatsoever left in his body. Adrian, who has moved into a cottage on Wembley Lane, takes the case as a favor to his next-door neighbor, the minister's daughter, a dark-haired beauty named Penelope Sand. All the while, Adrian is learning how different England is from Austria and assisting Scotland Yard on another case involving a theft at the Royal Veterinary College. Naturally, the two cases converge in a way that . . . Well, I'm not going to spoil the surprise, but it's good stuff, and shows Adrian at the top of his game.

But how much of it was true? At one point in the novel, Adrian chases one of the suspects through Piccadilly Circus. It's an exciting sequence. But Alik and his limp weren't chasing anybody. Was that just Dame Carissa trying to liven up the story, or was she papering over something else? And what about Penelope Sand? Whom had she been based on?

More questions for my notebook. So many questions. So few answers.

We began our descent into Heathrow. The solution to all these puzzles was only a few miles away now, closing fast. I held my aunt's hand as we touched down on the runway, and she let out a breath she might have been holding for six-plus hours. As we gathered our stuff, I checked my shoulder bag to make sure the digital camera was still there.

I wasn't going to start taking pictures as soon as I stepped off the plane (that totally would have been something Dev would do), but I wanted to be prepared for anything.

My aunt and I strolled the walkway from the airplane to the airport. She was definitely not as anxious as she had been and in fact seemed to beam with more and more glee with every step. I was happy for her. I was happy for both of us.

Our flight from Boston had been packed full of passengers, and so the gate was packed full of passengers' sisters and brothers and fathers and mothers and children and friends, dozens and dozens of smiling faces calling out hellos in dozens and dozens of dialects of English. It was like every PBS show my aunt had ever watched all playing at once. She giggled with delight.

A few of the gate greeters also held signs with names on them. A tall, brown-suited man with short black hair and large black sunglasses held a sign listing mine and my aunt's names in pristine calligraphy.

"Herr Lisser can't be here in person," the man apologized. His German accent was thick, but there was something else about the way he spoke—a halting manner, as if the very act of forming words took effort. "I take you to him?"

OK, I'm *extremely* not a car person, but the vehicle he led us to was this chunky, swanky white five-seat sedan that looked like it was fresh from the factory—no scuffs, no key scrapes, no mud on the tires, nothing. Even its paint job glistened, which I didn't understand was possible on a day as overcast as it was. And the inside of the car was even more plush and luxurious than our seats on the flight.

It had been ten years since I'd even been near comfort like this.

The chauffeur—whose name I learned was Hermann—insisted we sit in the back. We stretched out our legs. Hermann popped in a cassette, and a melodramatic German soprano blew out the car with her big, big voice. I later learned that the song belonged to a musical called *The Threepenny Opera.*

Our scenery quickly melted from the cityscape of London (which reminded me a lot of Boston, actually, with both cities' main ingredients being red brick and gray iron) to the hilly countryside. Unlike Boston, there wasn't much snow on the ground, but the trees were just as winter-thin and the green fields just as yellow-white.

Almost two hours into the trip, just as a character called Pirate Jenny began to croon (in German) from the car stereo, we took an exit off the highway. I figured we were stopping to get some gas . . . err, excuse me, *petrol* . . . except I was very, very wrong because you know what is on the way from London to Devon? Oh, just a little circle of rocks called *STONEHENGE.*

(It took all my willpower not to use exclamation marks just now. You're welcome.)

What do you want me to say about Stonehenge? It's freakin' Stonehenge. Yes, it's as cool as it looks in pictures, even when the weather is crappy cold and it's begun to drizzle. I did expect the stones to be twenty feet tall for some reason, but they were not much taller than, like, a basketball net. However, I knew this was the perfect time to whip out the digital camera. I removed it from its case, figured out how to open the shutter over the lens, jogged a little bit away so I could get most of it in the picture, took aim, and . . .

Nothing.

I frowned. Maybe digital cameras didn't make a sound when you pressed the button. Or maybe I had to turn it on first? I searched the camera for a switch, found it, sighed at my foolish mistake, took aim, and . . .

Nothing.

Hmm.

I turned the camera over and over again. What was I missing?

"Need any help?" inquired an Irish lilt.

A pair of tourists (retirees, by the looks of it) ambled toward me. I showed them my camera, explained my problem. The wife (I assume) took the camera, slid open a tab, peered at a tiny meter, and said, "You got no battery."

Oh. I felt like an idiot. I needed to charge the camera. Right. Duh.

After fifteen minutes of taking Polaroids with their camera (thank you!), we returned to the car. Hermann was cleaning his sunglasses with the hem of his shirt, but he quickly put them back on before we could get a view of his bare face.

"You like the Stonehenges?" he asked.

"Yes," my aunt replied. "We loved it."

"It always made Carissa happy too," he said.

That news sent me over the moon, because of course he had known Dame Carissa too. He probably had so many stories he could tell.

"You remind me of her," he added. "You are both so tiny."

I could have died happy then and there. And my adventure in England was just beginning. A little over an hour later, we left the highway again, wove along a dirt road through a vast and fruitless orchard, and came to a stop at the foot of a white cottage about the size of a supermarket. Its front door and windows were ovals, its angled roof was tiled like a mosaic, and at the head of the pebbled driveway, leaning on his cane and carrying an umbrella in his other hand, stood our host and benefactor, Alik Lisser.

10

"I'd apologize for the weather," Alik said once we were indoors, "but I know Boston is just as dreary this time of year."

While Hermann delivered our luggage to our bedroom, our host gave us the grand tour. The cottage had only one story, but it was spread out so evenly that, by square footage alone, it may have been larger than our entire tenement building. We were first led through the foyer, and my aunt and I followed Alik's example by leaving our footwear by the door before stepping on the thick, colorful rug.

"Most people assume I acquired this rug at a bazaar in Turkey or Iran," Alik told us, "but the truth is, I found it in Taipei."

"Lescher in the Orient!" I couldn't help myself. "The killer used bamboo shoots."

"*Ja*, that's my girl," replied Alik.

"Bamboo shoots contain cyanide," I explained to my aunt.

"I did not know that . . ."

"Most don't," said Alik.

"And the chandelier?" my aunt asked, pointing up.

"That came with the cottage. As did the roof, the walls, the doors, and the ghosts."

"Ghosts?"

"One never knows." He winked at us. "Let's see the bedrooms."

There were three: two for guests on the east side of the cottage and one huge bedroom on the west side. Each bedroom had a different theme. The first bedroom—our bedroom—had two twin beds with feet painted on their, well, feet and heads painted on their heads, one head per bed. Only the bottoms of the feet were visible and were bare and pink. The equally pink heads had red splotches for cheeks and dimpled grins and closed eyes (for sleep, I guess). One was a blonde, one was a brunette; both had pigtails. A vanity occupied a corner of the room, although the mirror had a white lace veil over it, and our luggage sat atop the wooden dressers. The wallpaper was decorated with cartoonishly wet candy canes and elongated Christmas trees. The ceiling was low. Not too low for me or my aunt, but Alik Lisser was well over six feet tall, and there couldn't have been more than a foot between his scalp and the flat plaster.

"This property—the orchard, the garden, the pond, and this cottage—had been a holding of the Blanding family since the fall of the Celts, and by the early 1970s, it was under the ownership of Brian Blanding, who did quite well selling honey from his own apiary. It was through this business that he and I became acquainted."

"'A Bee in Her Bonnet.' From the collection *Little Deaths*, published 1974."

Alik nodded. "Just so. A tragedy befell his apiary—the tragedy essayed in the short story—and he moved from honey to pickled herrings. His gimmick was to dye the herrings red. Clever, but it never caught on, and in 1977, the poor fellow took his own life. Much to my surprise, he left all this to me."

"He must have been a good friend," my aunt said.

Alik nodded again, a sad look in his eyes, and led us through a shared bathroom to the second guest bedroom. Every inch of the single bed's frame was covered with bunnies, and the wallpaper depicted eggs in every variation imaginable: dyed, fried, scrambled, runny, hard-boiled, soft-boiled, and even some that were hatching baby chicks. And if that wasn't adorable enough, on the dresser was a small black-and-white photograph, framed, of a lamb chewing on a daffodil.

"And now, the great room," said Alik, and he led us through the doorway to the cavernous heart of the house. The chandelier here was indeed great, almost like a giant glass crown—a giant *glowing* glass crown, once our host flicked a switch. Except now I could see it wasn't just a great room. It was a *library*. Every wall was a series of bookcases, each one floor to ceiling, and every shelf on every bookcase was packed with books—not just any books but *old books*, so old that I could smell their purse-tight leather and fine paper, and in so many languages, thousands and thousands of books, and each one well read and well loved, I just knew it. I must have been gawking, because Alik was suddenly standing behind me, and he whispered, "Just return whatever you borrow to wherever you borrow it from."

Thousands and thousands and thousands of books . . . but not much fiction, and no Carissa Miller. Unless he had them in rare editions I didn't recognize (which was totally possible). Much like in the bedrooms, the ceiling here wasn't very high, maybe no higher than one of the monoliths at Stonehenge, and I suddenly remembered something I'd read once about how much shorter people used to be, and this cottage had been around since before Queen Elizabeth (by which I mean the first one, who loved plays and defeated the Spanish Armada; not the current one, who was most famous, I guess, for being Princess Di's mother-in-law).

The great room wasn't just bookcases, a fancy chandelier, and low ceilings, though. Over by the room's wide window, which peeked out on the grassy backyard garden, there was a fat oak desk and all the things you'd expect to find on a fat oak desk in an English mystery novel. Letter opener that can be used as a dagger: check. Fountain pen that can be used as a dagger: check. Stack of letters that may or may not contain blackmail: check. Half-full cup of tea that may or may not contain poison: check. The great room also contained several couches and chairs, all padded leather and all situated along the perimeter of a large rug done in the finely detailed Turkish style of the one in the foyer.

"This was the Blandings' summer cottage," said Alik. "Their main holdings are a few hundred kilometers north. As far as I know, and I've done the research, no monarch ever visited their keep in the north or this cottage here in the south, although William of Orange and his Dutch army landed nearby in 1688, so it's possible that some of his retinue quartered themselves here. I've set out a surprise for us in the dining room. Come."

We followed his lead, walked into the dining room, and that was when my aunt absolutely lost it.

On our flight here, especially during takeoff, she'd looked ready to scream bloody murder, but she hadn't. Whatever self-control and willpower she had now went out the window, though, because she just about *howled.* And it was instant too. One minute, we were entering the dining room; the next, my aunt was pointing at the wall and shrieking like she had seen, I don't know, the hanged ghost of Brian Blanding.

Except what was hanging on the wall was not a ghost but a painting. It did look familiar. The artist had used all these bright colors, a lot of oranges and greens, and created imperfect circles intersecting with squares (rounded squares with rounded corners), with the occasional appearance of parallel lines (slightly curved lines with slightly curved tips), and all these shapes and lines floated inside a black border, which itself was framed by, well, the painting's frame, which looked like white marble but probably was just wood done up to look like white marble . . .

And that's when two things occurred to me:

1. Even though my mom had been a very successful painter, my aunt did not have any of her sister's art hanging in her apartment.
2. This cool and weird painting had absolutely been painted by my mom.

Before I knew it, my aunt had left the dining room. She sat down on one of the couches in the great room and tried to catch her breath.

Hermann, black sunglasses ever present, appeared out of nowhere with a glass of water. Hands trembling, my aunt drank it down and then dragged the back of a trembling hand across her face to wipe away her tears.

"*Ja*, this is my fault," Alik said. He stood in the threshold between the two rooms. "Terribly short-sighted of me. The surprise was the Christmas pudding on the table, not the painting on the wall."

There had been something on the table? Sure enough, there was, right in the center, a round sort of fruit cake on a glass stand, with a small stack of plates beside it.

"I should add that I was a fan of hers—before, in fact, I became involved in the events surrounding her tragedy. Most people see the world the way most people see it, but the rarefied few see the world uniquely, and the rarest of them—and I do include Barbara Ackroyd in this company—are able to translate their unique vision into something shareable."

Hermann gestured for my aunt to lie down on the sofa.

"No, no," she said, "I'm all right. I just . . . It's like you said . . . I was surprised. And it's been a long day. Long flight. I should lie down. In the bedroom. If you don't mind."

"Want me to . . . ?"

"No, no, Kat, it's OK. I'll be fine. Thanks. Just leave me a slice of pudding."

She trotted off to the bedroom, taking her water with her.

Meanwhile, Hermann vanished back to wherever he'd come from, leaving me alone with Alik (unless you counted all those books and, well, the dessert in the dining room).

"So," he said, holding out a hand for me, "while we're on the subject, and since you've come all this way, let me show you what really happened to your mother."

11

I followed him into the small kitchen. Hermann was leaning against a cupboard and drinking from a mug. While Alik stopped by a door, presumably to the basement, and fished around in his pockets for a key, I thanked Hermann for helping my aunt. He nodded a silent *You're welcome*.

Alik swung the basement door wide open, flicked a switch beside it, and then motioned for me to go first. I didn't need to be asked twice. I bounded down the wooden steps. It was Answer Time, and I was ready.

"When I came into possession of this property," said Alik, descending the steps much, much slower, "this was all unfinished. Most cellars in this country are. I won't bore you with tales of the time and money spent transforming all this to suit my needs, but it's become my hearth, my sanctuary. Everyone needs a sanctuary. Wouldn't you agree, Katie?"

The basement/cellar really was extraordinary. The floor was polished white tile, and the space was divided roughly into three sections. To the right of the stairs was a row of filing cabinets (eight in all), a small desk (with a basketball-size TV set propped atop a bulky, wood-paneled VCR propped atop said small desk), and some framed documents fixed to the walls: news clippings in many languages and an old German/Austrian magazine with Alik's face on the cover, as to be expected, but there also was a pencil sketch of a cat and one sheet of paper covered only in squiggly lines.

To the left of the stairs was his laboratory, and this was what Alik, once he and his cane finally conquered the stairs, led me to explore first. The walls here didn't have framed documents but instead what looked like a spice rack . . . But then I took a closer look at some of the labels, and my obsessive reading of mystery novels came in handy for once, because I could translate the Latin names:

Conium maculatum. Hemlock.

Strychnos nux-vomica. Strychnine.

Atropa belladonna. Nightshade.

And others. Over a dozen.

On the perpendicular wall were his guns. Again, over a dozen of them, and all different kinds.

He then opened two drawers in the lab table and showed me a collection of his knives.

"Poisons, firearms, and knives. These are the three most common tools of murder. But each poison is different from the next, each firearm, each knife. An expert criminologist does his research. 'Data, data, data!' he cried impatiently. 'I can't make bricks without clay!'"

"What book is that from?"

"Not a book but a story. 'The Adventure of the Copper Beeches' by Arthur Conan Doyle."

"Sherlock Holmes," I said.

"The best man who never lived," Alik replied.

There was a third section to the basement, but a thick red curtain, like the kind on a stage in a theater, concealed it.

"What's behind that?"

"All the bodies of my ex-wives."

"Very funny."

"*Ja,* Bluebeard thought so. No, what's behind the curtain is a collection much more prosaic. I'll show you soon. But first: the reason you've come all this way."

We walked back to the file cabinets. They were unlabeled, but he seemed to know what was where, and after unlocking one in the middle and with some effort, he knelt down to open the bottom drawer. He removed a thick binder full of papers, set it on the desk, and said:

"My case notes for the murder of Barbara Ackroyd—if you're sure."

My stomach suddenly exploded with butterflies. Now that it was here, in front of me, I felt tentative. Why? Was I worried about what I might find? Was this a case of 'Be careful what you wish for' and all that nonsense?

Screw that. I was ready for the truth, whatever it turned out to be.

I opened the binder.

On top was a leather-bound notebook wrapped with a string. Alik took that for himself and began to read from it as I examined what lay underneath.

"30 September 1985. Invited by H. W. to consult on murder. RIP Barbara Ackroyd. Already a scandal, even in our papers. Flying to LA tomorrow."

I stared at a headshot of my mother, who was smiling all bashful at the camera, red hair dancing in the breeze. She was posing on . . . a hill, maybe . . . overlooking the city of . . . Los Angeles, I guess? No. Wait. I knew *exactly* where she was. She *was* on a hill. She was standing in Griffith Park by the observatory. I knew that view. We used to hike up that trail. Well, my parents hiked. I rode along on my dad's shoulders. Bounce, bounce, bounce . . . Look at the guy with the funny hat . . . Bounce, bounce, bounce . . . Ooh, a puppy! Bounce, bounce, bounce. Can we give the puppy some of our water? He looks thirsty. Bounce, bounce, bounce.

The headshot was paper-clipped to some articles about my mom from magazines and journals and stuff. Some of the articles featured pictures of her paintings. Some of them featured tiny versions of her headshot. Someone (Alik?) had highlighted the word *genius* every time it appeared.

It appeared so much.

Then I flipped to the next packet and nearly fainted.

Black-and-white copies of the crime scene photos. High-quality copies.

Every detail visible.

"2 October 1985. Tour crime scene with H. W. Glass shards, blood pools. Autopsy confirms c.o.d. repeated stab wounds to the stomach and intestines. Seventeen perforations, one inch in diameter, from a smooth, sharp weapon, no serrations. H. W. thinks burglary gone wrong. Why would burglar strike her seventeen times?"

I quickly flipped past the photos to the next packet. Here was the transcript of a police interview with my dad dated 29 September. The day after the murder. By then, I was staying with Uncle Mitch and Auntie Valeria (not real relatives but close friends of my parents'). They had a daughter my age named Michele who was really into arts and crafts. We built a whole neighborhood for her Barbie dolls out of Popsicle sticks and paste. God, I hadn't thought about Michele in ages.

"3 October 1985. Met B. A. husband, Bill McCann, in Santa Monica coffeehouse. His attitude: helpful, mournful. Regretful that B. A. will never see daughter (six) grow up. Begs me to find killer. Left eye bloodshot."

I looked up from the interview. "He had been crying."

"That's true," Alik replied. "And an overabundance of tears can make the blood vessels around your tear ducts eventually dilate from all the effort. And it's true that there are disorders which affect the tear ducts—Sjögren's syndrome, for example—so that one might, possibly, only shed tears out of one eye. It's also true, however, that when one shatters a pane of glass, especially with something like a wrench or a large flashlight, most of the shards will fall forward, but the physics of the impact will deflect some shards backward, perhaps into one's eye, perhaps irritating it for several days."

"That's . . . not in the novel . . ."

"At that point in the novel, she didn't want her readers to suspect that the character based on your father was the culprit. That would have been poor storytelling."

"And . . . and . . . one bloodshot eye isn't conclusive evidence."

"No. It's not. Even if, as I mentioned, there were an alternative theory for a bloodshot eye. High blood pressure, perhaps, which your father did have. But it encouraged me to scrutinize your father's alibi. Add to that the damning statistic that in eight out of ten homicides in America, if the victim is married, the spouse is the murderer, and you can follow the logic. Assume nothing but, to refer back to Mr. Holmes, never ignore the data."

"Are you saying . . . Are you telling me my dad . . . did it?"

"Oh, Katie," replied Alik, "what do you think?"

12

This was some bullshit.

"I don't believe you," I said.

"That's the beauty of truth, Katie. It doesn't need your belief to exist. But I'm not finished yet. I've taken the liberty of preloading a copy of the video evidence into my tape player. It's right there, ready for you to turn it on and press play—which, I might add, you are under no obligation to do."

Dame Carissa loved the video evidence in *Double Frame* so much that she'd made it her title (though her readers needed to make it to the climax to reach the reveal and get its meaning). The night my mom died, my dad was halfway across town editing his latest movie. He always edited his own movies in the same editing booth in the same suite of editing booths in the same building in Burbank where he'd first edited commercials back at the start of his career: 2240 East Magnolia.

2240 East Magnolia had security cameras monitoring each corridor, so if someone ever entered or exited an editing booth, they would be seen. That, combined with a guard desk manned twenty-four seven, made everything very safe. No footage had ever leaked out of 2240 East Magnolia.

(All this was according to the novel. Dame Carissa loved the finer details.)

My dad had entered his editing booth around 8:00 p.m. the night of the incident and didn't leave until the police showed up around 3:00

a.m. For some reason, he always edited at night. And I see what you're thinking, so don't you dare start to make a connection between him and my uncle.

The security-camera footage confirmed my dad's alibi. He left once, from 10:16 p.m.–10:21 p.m., which he confirmed was to use the bathroom, but otherwise, he was miles and miles from our home when someone broke in through the french doors in the back of the house, waited for my mother to come down to see what the noise was, and then killed her.

The videotape was everything. Or so it seemed.

I turned on the TV and pressed play. After a blast of static, the screen filled with the image of a brown corridor marked with two doors on either side and an elevator at the far end.

"Your father was the only person on that floor until 1:03 a.m. Notice the time and date code in the bottom left."

September 28, 1985. 8:00 p.m.

"The tapes can only hold six hours of footage. When one tape is full, the next one starts. It's a standard system, *ja*, although 2240 Magnolia saves all security footage for seven days. That bit especially impressed a certain author."

"She wrote about it in the novel," I said, staring at the screen.

Your father is in Bay C.

Present tense, as if he's still alive.

"You can fast-forward," Alik said. "The relevant part doesn't begin until ten forty-five."

Except I didn't want to fast-forward. I wanted to spend as much time as I could . . . here . . . with him. Look, I know it wasn't real. I know it was just a recording of something that had happened ten years earlier. I know it and I knew it, but Alik was wrong. Belief is a lot more powerful than he gave it credit for.

After about ten seconds, when I didn't reach for the fast-forward button, Alik leaned past me and pressed it himself. Horizontal lines of distortion appeared on the screen as the timecode zipped toward 8:30, then 9:00, then 9:30.

10:00. 10:15.

10:16.

Dad stepped out of Bay C and walked at double-speed up the corridor until he disappeared from view.

He looked tired. He looked like he needed a hug.

10:21. He returned from the bathroom, unlocked Bay C, and reentered it. His back was to the camera the entire time.

Bye, Dad.

10:30. 10:40. 10:43. 10:45.

Alik took his finger off the button.

September 28, 1985. 10:45 p.m. I was asleep in our Santa Monica home. My mom was probably watching TV in her bedroom. Maybe watching a movie on our own VCR. Dad was working on edits for his latest feature, a romantic comedy called *The Last First Date*. The studio never released it.

(In the novel, Dame Carissa had transformed my dad into a writer/director of horror films. His work in progress in that alternate reality was called *The Last Gasp*.)

The tape proceeded at normal speed. The corridor outside the editing bays remained empty.

I knew what was coming, but I had never seen it before, not with my own eyes, and that was the point. That was, I guess, Alik's whole deal.

Empirical evidence and all that.

10:47:32. A tiny ripple appeared on the screen, for maybe half a heartbeat. If I hadn't been looking for it, I wouldn't have seen it. That, too, was the point.

Alik rewound to that exact second and froze the screen, and there it was—there *he* was, my father, the image of him flickering in that ghostly way poorly frozen VHS images flicker, half in and out of life, and so, too, did the timecode flicker. Two frames superimposed, one recorded over the other but still the remnant of the first image, its ghost, visible for half a heartbeat.

A literal double frame.

"I must have watched this tape hundreds of times," said Alik. "Even when I had narrowed my suspicions, I had to contend with this perfect alibi. But there is no such thing as a perfect alibi. When the murderer came back from the crime scene—from the crime—he taped over the videotape evidence of him leaving and returning to make it appear as if he never left."

OK, fine, sure, but if the tape was still recording, he couldn't just sneak into the security booth and alter it. Dame Carissa sort of waved over this plot hole in her novel, except . . .

Except Alik must have read my mind:

"How he did it is irrelevant. Why he did it is irrelevant. I know there's cold comfort in that, but it's true. Your father never confessed to the crime, *nein*. But it's not our priority to solve for how or why, though they do often reveal themselves. It's simply our priority to solve for *who*, and then for a jury to acknowledge the truth and meaning of the empirical evidence."

My dad, there and not there.

It wasn't the only evidence, but it was damning evidence, and it had led Alik (and the police) to the *most* damning evidence: the blood on the sill of the bathroom window at 2240 East Magnolia—*my mom's blood*—from when he had climbed back in.

I knew all this. I knew all this before I'd hopped across the ocean. I knew all this from having read it in a novel when I was a preteen. But I also knew it had been fiction based on fact, maybe loosely, and that Dame Carissa had never visited my dad in prison (and had certainly never met my mom) and . . . and . . . and . . .

And nothing.

Because the ghost of my dad was flickering on the screen, guilty as can be.

"Would you like to keep going?" Alik asked, though that wasn't what he meant. What he meant was, Had I seen enough?

I pushed the off button on the TV. The ghost of my dad vanished into a bright dot in the center of the screen, and then that bright dot vanished, and then I got up. Alik had my answer.

We tromped up the wooden stairs to the main level. He locked the door behind us.

"I think," he said, "we both could use some Christmas cheer."

We adjourned to the dining room. Without thinking, I gravitated toward my mom's painting, leaning toward it till I could see the long brushstrokes. Had she held her brush in her right hand or her left hand? (My dad was left-handed; I remembered that.) I tried to picture her picking up a fork or one of my storybooks. Which hand did she use? Was it her left? (My dad had used his left hand to kill her. He probably held a knife as steadily as she'd held a paintbrush.) I hovered my left index finger over the long brushstrokes and traced them in the air. Had she listened to music when she painted? Was it the same music over and over again? Cassette or record? Had she played it loud or quiet?

Her studio wasn't in our house; it was downtown. I couldn't really recall what it looked like, but I know for a fact that it smelled awful. Like someone took a bottle of salad dressing and left it out in the sun way too long. It smelled so bad that I could taste the smell.

I sniffed the painting. I really did. But it had no scent.

"Her critics liked to compare her to Kandinsky," Alik said, "but that's like comparing a marsh frog to an Albanian water frog. Same genus, but vastly different species. That's the way critics are, though, when it comes to originality, *ja*. They need to tether it to a known quantity. Otherwise, they can't form the words, and as Carrie liked to say, 'A critic without words is like a monkey who's run out of shit to throw.'"

I turned around to face him. He had already carved two slices out of the Christmas pudding, taken a seat at the head of the table, and set my slice on a plate next to his spot. I took my seat.

"And yours, in a sense, *ja*, at least from her point of view. She regarded all of her fans as friends, and you've already proven yourself a fan."

Ah. Carrie. As in, short for Dame Carissa Miller. I quietly spoon-fed myself a little cake. On any other day, finding out that Alik Lisser's pet name for Dame Carissa was Carrie would have left me giddy, but right then and there, the only emotion I could find was . . . I don't even know what.

Is there a word that means grief *and* anger? If not, there *should* be.

"Carrie would have liked you," Alik added, "even if you weren't a fan. She always had a fondness for brave and clever girls. After all, she was one herself. I have a kettle on, if you want some tea."

"Maybe in a little bit," I replied between bites.

My aunt drank tea every afternoon, but I think that was more about her trying to be English than her actually enjoying it, because I'd never seen her smile after a sip. I'd really never seen her smile, *really* smile, until a few hours ago, when we'd gotten off the plane.

I excused myself to check on her. The poor thing. I mean, can you imagine? When I peeked into our bedroom, I found her on the blond-headed bed. She had kicked off her shoes, curled herself up tight, and fallen asleep. She looked peaceful. I left her alone.

Alik met me in the great room.

"I'm sorry," he said. "I know what you learned today, what you saw, wasn't what you wanted."

"Why do you think he did it?" My voice vibrated with grief-anger.

"It would be irresponsible to presume. Sigmund Freud, whose flat I actually grew up near in Vienna, proposed that all human emotion—and therefore, human action—stems from fear and/or desire. Despite all our pretenses, we really aren't much more complicated than that, so it's safe to say that your mother's murder, as tragic as it was, was the result of a man acting according to his programming."

"You make it sound like he had no choice."

"*Nein, nein,* we always have a choice. At least, the sane among us do. But you'd be surprised how many choices we make—what we eat for breakfast, what we wear, what we say, what we do—are entirely predictable. Yes, we have free will—but at a cost. But you have had a long day. Why don't you rest some, and I'll wake you up for dinner. I'm glad you're here, Katie. I hope to make our next few days together as enjoyable as possible. You and your aunt deserve some enjoyment, wouldn't you say?"

13

True to his word, Alik did his best to make the next few days as enjoyable as possible. That night, after a meal of goose in sweet orange sauce with caramelized brussels sprouts, Hermann drove us into town. The air was crisp and the sky was black, but the streets were aglow with Christmas lights and crowded with food stalls. We joined a queue for hot mulled wine. Nearby, a choir sang a carol I didn't recognize, something about a "bleak midwinter." Strangers bundled close together, and everyone, everyone, appeared to be happy.

Appeared to be.

Because I couldn't just forget what I'd learned, no matter how much cheer and joy surrounded me, no matter how sweet and delicious that mulled wine smelled. How could I? And although I'd gotten to spend five Christmases with my parents, I only had fuzzy memories of them, watching me sit on the lap of a mall Santa or unwrapping gifts at the foot of a fir tree . . . Or maybe those are just memories of children from commercials.

The facts were that my father had killed my mother, had murdered her in the middle of the night. Premeditated. Alik said the reasons were not important, but this was my *mom* and my *dad*. I needed to know why. But how? All I had to go on were my fuzzy memories.

By the time we reached the head of the line, the carolers had moved on to "O Tannenbaum." My aunt nixed the idea of buying some wine for me . . . but surprisingly did allow me to sip some of hers. It was yummy, kind of like hot apple cider mixed with spices. Alik then gave us a narrative history of the town, pointing out a church that was a thousand years old, a mill that had been converted into a pub, and, in the town square, a stone statue of Oliver Cromwell with his arms chopped off.

The next morning, I woke up in my peculiarly painted bed to the sound of raindrops on the roof. The view outside my window was a wet, gray gloom. My aunt was still asleep, so lost in Dreamland she wasn't even snoring. Well, she'd had a day. I probably should've been more tired due to, you know, jet lag or the time difference and all that, but I wasn't. I was a little hungry, though, so I shuffled out of the bedroom in search of breakfast. Did England even have bagels?

Alik was already awake (of course) and at work at his desk in the great room, jotting down notes from a book as if he were cramming for a test. He looked up, smiled at me, and said, "Good morning. Want something to eat?"

We moved to the dining room and the remains of the Christmas pudding. My mom's painting had been replaced by an arty black-and-white photograph of Paris (for my aunt's benefit, I figured). As soon as we sat down, Hermann appeared with a teapot and some teacups.

I really was living in a freakin' Carissa Miller novel.

After breakfast, I followed Alik back to the great room. He returned to his work, and I gaped at the thousands and thousands of books. Had he read them all? I bet he had. But it was the books he didn't have that got me talking.

"Why don't you have any Carissa Miller books?"

He glanced up from his notes. "I have all of her books. I keep a storage unit in Exeter. But I don't need them readily accessible, and so they aren't. Carrie used to kid that if I really didn't admire her writing, I should return my thirty percent."

"Your thirty percent of what?"

"My share of the profits. For my share of the contribution, *ja*. Only on the books based on my investigations, of course. But you see, I did admire her writing. Why else would I have agreed to the partnership? I'm not sure she ever got that."

He seemed lost for a moment in sadness. Because Carissa Miller wasn't just a name on a book to him. She had been his friend for more than thirty years. And now she was gone.

"What do you think happened to her?" I asked.

That broke him from his spell. "I could try to find out. I probably would succeed, but this is another example of Carrie's sense of humor. She knew that I detest questions without answers, and so, as a final ribbing, she gave me an attractive mystery and then forbade me from solving it. But that was our relationship. Every now and then, she liked to poke me and remind me of my foibles. Such as the whole Countess Oona du Perot joke."

"Countess Oona du Perot!" I perked up. "She's one of my favorite characters from the novels! Adrian Lescher's one true love, always just out of reach . . ."

"And that's the joke. I teased her once that if she was going to insert a version of me in her stories, she might as well insert a version of her. And she did. She took herself and some people's misperception of our relationship and stretched them all till they were nigh unrecognizable. But that's what the imagination does. It treats the real world like soft clay and then remolds it, *ja*?"

He was absolutely right. He always was.

"I need your help," I said. "I need a list of everybody you think might know why my dad did what he did."

"And if I created such a list, what would you do with it? Would you interview them one by one? That might supply you with a composite portrait of your father and a series of interpretations—but would it supply you with answers or just more questions?"

"Then what do you suggest?"

"You're not going to like it."

"I don't think I'm supposed to like any of this. But I need to know."

"Let it go."

"It's my parents."

"You know who one of my heroes was? Galileo Galilei. *'Eppur si muove.'* He understood that Saturn had echoes—he called them 'ears'—but it wasn't until two centuries later that the mystery of Saturn's rings was solved. Galileo was one of the best minds of his era. I am sure he came up with multiple valid theories based on the best data available. Could he have possibly known the rings were an array of particulate matter? No. That discovery belonged to the Victorian era. The lesson, Katie, is this: try as we might, some answers are beyond our ken."

I wiped at my cheeks. I hadn't even realized I'd been crying. "It's my parents. It's my dad. Who *was* he?"

"He was complicated and contradictory, and he did great things and he did awful things, and he ultimately is unknowable because he was human, same as you, same as me, same as Galileo. With all due respect to Herr Freud, there are no science kits for psychology. Some answers are beyond our grasp. But some, with the aid of reason and science, are within our reach, and those answers we should lean toward and grasp with all our might. Want a mystery you can solve?"

"Yes. Please."

"I might have one for you. *Ja*, a good one. Give me a few days. Is it a deal?"

He held out his hand. I shook it. It was a deal.

My aunt finally rolled out of bed around eleven-ish. She finished the Christmas pudding. I didn't ask her about Alik's thoughtful replacement of the painting, but I didn't really have to. Her good mood said it all.

Due to the weather being, well, gross, Alik suggested we skip a planned walking tour of the Cornish coast and instead drive to London.

"I've a flat in Chelsea," he said, "so why don't we relocate there? The rainy season lasts twelve months out of the year, and most of the city's landmarks can be enjoyed indoors. Let's make a list on the way."

Well, the idea of sightseeing in London sent my aunt into a fevered tizzy. She and Alik debated all the possibilities as Hermann drove us east, the melodramatic score from *The Threepenny Opera* accompanying us every wet, gray mile of the three-plus-hour drive. I mostly kept to myself, let my aunt have her fun. Occasionally, I jotted down random thoughts in my notebook.

It's not that I wasn't jazzed to explore London. Are you kidding me? I couldn't wait to climb the Tower of London or size up all the stolen artifacts in the British Museum. One thing about reading so many classic mysteries is you get an appreciation for culture. But this was my aunt's happy moment. I wasn't about to spoil that with my own selfishness.

Also . . .

You know that rush of anxiety you get because you're afraid you're going to get a rush of anxiety? Yeah, well, hello, darkness, my old friend. London was one of the busiest, most crowded cities on the planet, and as much as I wanted to climb an ancient tower or size up some ancient artifacts, the fact of the matter was that many, many, many people were going to want to do these things as well, and that meant crowds, and that meant heart palpitations, lightheadedness, and the apocalypse.

This pit in my stomach deepened as the cityscape, blurry though it was due to rain, came into view. Tall, majestic Big Ben? I clenched my teeth. The winding Thames and its thirty-plus bridges? I licked my lips with the saliva quickly drying up inside my mouth. The Gothic spires of Westminster Abbey? I swallowed down the nausea bubbling up my throat.

We left the highway and angled into Chelsea, which was apparently London's answer to Newbury Street (or vice versa, I guess). Block after block of fashion stores and jewelry stores with snobby names like Prada and Tiffany. Our destination was off the main road on a bumpy, cobblestoned side street called Mallowan Lane. We dipped down into an underground parking garage and drove up to a pair of valets standing in front of two gold-plated elevators. Fancy, fancy.

The inside of the elevator was gold-plated too. We rode up two flights. The doors didn't open to a hallway but to the apartment itself, and we stepped into what the old novels used to call an "antechamber," which featured red velvet walls and a large mirror framed by . . . a noose? Yep, definitely a noose, with the loop surrounding the glass and the knot dangling down below as if the mirror had a necktie.

While we stopped to take off our coats, Hermann gathered our luggage and vanished to the right. Alik led us to the left and into what he called "the reception room," but holy crap, the far wall was a massive window that overlooked a private harbor on the river, and I guess I'd never thought of the Thames River having private harbors, but of course it did, and of course the private harbor was docked with yachts, and I'd become so entranced by the million-dollar view that I didn't even notice until a good minute later that the wall to my right was nothing but bookshelves and that the bookshelves were stocked with at least one copy of every edition of Dame Carissa Miller's written work, including all the translations and special printings, all arranged chronologically and so overwhelming in beauty and perfection that I nearly fainted.

"I thought you said you kept your copies in Exeter," I muttered.

"Oh, these aren't mine," Alik replied, a twinkle in his eye. "This is Carrie's flat."

14

"She always let me stay here whenever I was in town," he added, or I think he did, because a persistent dull hum had suddenly joined the sound of the room, though I immediately knew the source of the persistent dull hum was just my brain breaking. That's what happens when someone casually tells you, *Oh, by the way, you're standing in your favorite author's freakin'* home. "It was here I found her final note. You would like to see it, *ja*?"

Her final note? I blinked. Wait, that meant something. She wrote a note.

She being Dame Carissa Miller. This being her home.

Why was her final note important again? Stupid broken brain.

Alik helped me out by pointing to the wall behind a grand piano, to a framed sheet of paper on the wall, and to the handwritten note scribbled in black ink just below a bloodred stationery embossment.

To All Who Read This:

I, Carissa Miller, of sound mind and wretched body, have decided to light out for the Territories. Don't come find me.*

It's been fun.

Love,

CM

***That includes you, Smart Alik.**

I'd read the note before. Every so often, we discussed it in the chat room. Some were convinced it was written in code and that a secret treasure awaited whoever could crack it. But to see the genuine article with my own eyes . . .

"Her office, where the note was actually found, is just down the hall. The door's locked, and will remain locked, I'm afraid, by request of her estate. For months and months, the note was held in a plastic bag by the Metropolitan Police, but once it became clear that they weren't going to find her, they returned it to her estate."

"Who runs her estate?" my aunt asked.

"A nephew with the Dickensian name of Willowby Swan. His main trade is banking. He and his family customarily celebrate their Christmas and New Year's on the island of Majorca."

The drive here had apparently jump-started my aunt's curiosity, because she then followed up her first question with: "And we have his permission to stay here?"

"I know I have Carrie's permission, and the law still considers her alive, so *ja*, I believe we do. More to the point, though, it looks like the rain has stopped, albeit temporarily. Have you decided which Londontown landmark you would like to visit first?"

"Buckingham Palace. Definitely. Will the queen be there?"

"I can't speak to Her Majesty's exact whereabouts," said Alik, "but the Royal Family does favor their home in Norfolk this time of year."

"Oh, that's all right. Me and Kat will still get to see the Beefeaters, right? Try to get them to smile?"

I bit down on my lip. Time for the inevitable. "Actually . . . I think I'm going to stay in . . ."

"Stay in? I mean, it's all nice and fancy, but we're in London, dear. London! Don't you want to ride on a double-decker bus around Piccadilly Circus?"

I looked down at the floor, and my aunt got the hint. Maybe she even realized why I was suddenly so reluctant. We had never actually spoken about my silly phobias, but she knew. I knew she knew.

"I don't know how I feel about leaving you alone. Detective, could your butler stay with her?"

"Now that you mention it, I was thinking Hermann accompany you and I remain here. I fear I would slow you down."

To accentuate his point, Alik tapped his cane on the hardwood floor. This also summoned Hermann, who gladly agreed to his new assignment and chivalrously held out an arm for my aunt. I rushed to our new bedroom, found the digital camera in our luggage, got Hermann to fetch us some AAA batteries (which were, thankfully, a thing that existed in Ye Olde England), and showed my aunt how to use it. Not long after, she and the camera and Hermann were gone.

Alik strolled into the kitchen, filled a kettle, and set it on the stove.

"Is it only crowds," he asked me, "or is it open spaces in general? If I'm not mistaken—and I'm not—you sat in the back row of the lecture hall while your friend sat near the front."

"Just crowds. Open spaces are actually a good thing."

"When I was younger, I had a crippling fear of the dark. My father was a miser and refused to leave a light on for me, but he did let me keep my curtains open. Full moons were the best. My bed was full with light, so much that I could read by it. New moons were something to dread, especially if there were large clouds obscuring all the stars. On those nights—on those quiet, dark nights—I was frozen in terror. I wet my bed on more than one occasion out of fear of getting up. *Ja,* it's true. That convinced my father not to let me turn on my light but instead to swallow raw cinnamon before I went to bed."

"That's awful."

"He meant well. Cinnamon dries out the bladder. As to my fear of the dark, eventually, I endeavored to find its cause. Fear of the dark is really fear of the unknown. Once I understood that, I dissected it, found its flaw, and eliminated it. In the meantime, though, there's always the comfort of a hot beverage."

He poured us each a cup of tea, his with milk, mine with sugar.

"I've been thinking about my assignment," he said. "A proper mystery for a bright and clever girl to solve. But I wonder if you're up to it."

"Only one way to find out."

He sipped his tea. "This is true. So. My good friend DI Cosmo Korban is retiring, and I agreed to host a small party here in his honor on New Year's Eve."

I perked up. Cosmo Korban had to be "Korba the Greek," Adrian Lescher's oldest friend at Scotland Yard and the character in the series with the most appearances (aside from Adrian himself). Would I get a chance to meet yet another real-life version of a favorite character? And what did this have to do with this "proper mystery" that I was definitely up for solving?

15

He hadn't elaborated, and as the day of the party arrived and the catering staff showed up to decorate the apartment and prepare an array of deliciousness, my phobia of crowds percolated anew. How small was this "small party" going to be? If I needed to retreat, I could slip out to the balcony, which had its own brick firepit, but what if the party then pushed outdoors? Where would I be able to retreat to then?

Alik must have noticed me biting my lip or shaking the nerves out of my hands, because at some point in the afternoon, when the catering staff had temporarily cleared out to change into their little butler/maid outfits, he asked me to help him move the recliner I had claimed as my reading chair to a new location beside the bay window. I wasn't sure why he wanted it there; it broke the circle of furniture. But then he said:

"This is your Spot. If anyone asks you to move, tell them *nein*. You have my permission to be as antisocial and misanthropic as you want to be. If the need arises, turn your back on them and stare out at the water. If it all becomes too oppressive, come find me and I'll devise you a new solution. How does that sound?"

If I were the hugging type, I would have wrapped my arms around his long, thin frame and squeezed so tight I might have never let go. *If* I were the hugging type. Which I wasn't. So instead, I just smiled and nodded and sat in my Spot like a dutiful child.

The party started around 8:00 p.m. Most of the guests were old men, the youngest maybe in his fifties. Some in shape, some not. All of them white. The guest of honor, retiring DI Cosmo Korban, seemed like the oldest of them all, at least from the looks of it. Vulturelike bald head covered with age spots. Vulturelike protruding nose. Yellowed teeth. Stooped posture. Like everyone else, he wore a plain suit, though the fit was loose around the shoulders and tight around the waist. As it happened, I had a copy of *Turnabout* in my lap. This was how Dame Carissa first described Korba the Greek:

> He met everyone in the room with a warm smile and glad hands. His fingers each bore a ring, some jeweled, and when he finally reached Adrian and noticed the Viennese detective's interest in his shiny accessories, he espoused, "My *mitéra* always used to tell me, she said, 'Korba, in this life, if you want to be treated good, you gotta look good.' But with a face like this, I can use all the help I can get, eh?"

Cosmo Korban's fingers were thin and gnarled, and there wasn't a ring among them, jeweled or otherwise. Had the whole ring thing been another fabrication of Dame Carissa's, or had time taken its toll with one precious item after another? I was tempted to ask him, but that meant standing up, and I wasn't about to relinquish my Spot.

My aunt seemed to be in her element. She drank and caroused with the guests, sometimes laughing, sometimes causing laughter. If it wasn't for her mint-green dress, which she also wore every Sunday to church, I might have thought she was an impostor.

My anxiety, meanwhile, remained under control, at least as long as I sat in my Spot. I didn't even have to turn away from the party. Occasionally, one of the adults would come over and try to start a conversation, but thankfully, they quickly ran out of things to say to an American teenage girl.

Where I sat gave me a fine view not only of the living room but also of the balcony, so I was perfectly placed to watch Alik lead the guest of honor across the room and onto the balcony itself. DI Korban needed to use both hands to keep his glass of wine steady. The door closed behind them, giving the two old friends complete privacy for whatever they needed to discuss.

I returned to *Turnabout*. Adrian was recuperating in the hospital after getting shot in the left ankle. By the next book, he would be up and running (literally), but Alik must have carried that injury, or one like it, for the rest of his life.

Maybe this was why he was so empathetic to my needs. He recognized a fellow broken human.

Or maybe some people were simply empathetic by nature. Just nobody who attended my high school, or junior high school, or wrote true crime pieces for tabloids, or took photographs of little girls at their mother's funeral, or—

"Help! I need help!"

Everyone looked to the balcony door, to Alik, who stood in the doorway, and beyond to Cosmo Korban, who was all but invisible behind the firepit. Along with everybody else, I rushed out to see what had happened, except the crowd prevented me from making much progress. Those who were quicker, though, those at the front, saw it all.

There were gasps. Cries. Questions.

Someone picked up the nearby telephone and dialed 999.

By the time I made it near the balcony, the New Year's fireworks had begun, making it hard to hear anything. The balcony lit up in explosions of color, which would have been perfect for me to see what had happened . . . but my aunt found me and forced me back to my chair.

"You shouldn't have to see that," she said.

What I didn't see (but soon learned just by listening) was this:

DI Cosmo Korban was dead. Several of the guests, many of them experts in the field, had checked for a pulse, etc. The EMTs arrived, and then the active-duty police. They secured the scene, interviewed everybody. The woman who interviewed me was kind and offered me a butterscotch as if I were a six-year-old, and I told her all I knew, which wasn't much.

Nearby, Alik was discussing the matter with who I assumed was the lead detective—a redhead like me, although much, much taller. She listened patiently while her handheld audio recorder took it all in.

"Everyone knew he was melancholic about retirement," said Alik, "but I never thought it would come to this. He came to see me a few weeks ago, a sort of private celebration of his career—*our* careers, if I'm being honest. He never got the respect he deserved. Maybe that was part of it. And then, tonight, out of the blue, he takes me to the balcony and thanks me for my friendship and tells me that when he was at my cottage a few weeks back, he nicked my vial of hemlock. By the time we were on the balcony, he'd already begun to lose his balance. I assumed it was the wine. In a way, it was. To think, I was the one who taught him about poisons . . ."

But this wasn't true. I knew it wasn't true. Alik had been the one who took Cosmo to the balcony, not the other way around. And Cosmo hadn't "nicked the hemlock" a few weeks ago. I had seen it a few days ago in the cottage's cellar.

Why was Alik lying?

16

Because the apartment was deemed a crime scene, we had no choice but to return to Devonshire. Hermann did so without complaint, even though it was well past 5:00 a.m. by the time we pulled into the driveway. This time there was no *Threepenny Opera* for our trip, no eager conversation about landmarks, no conversation at all. The suicide had dazed us into silence.

Well, I mean, no one was talking. But my brain was far from silent. A man was *dead*. Sure, people die all the time, blah, blah, blah, but he died maybe fifteen feet, at most, away from *me* . . . not that this was about *me* . . .

This was about Cosmo Korban.

And Alik Lisser.

What possible reason could have pushed him to lie to the police? What was he hiding?

Or maybe he wasn't lying. Maybe I was just *assuming* these were lies. Assume nothing, right? After all, what did I know *for certain*? Sure, I'd seen a full vial of hemlock in the basement. Alik had even pointed it out. But maybe he had noticed it was empty days after Cosmo Korban's visit and refilled it? It's not like he wouldn't have noticed something like that. He was Alik Lisser.

And maybe I had just *assumed* he'd led Cosmo Korban to the balcony. The man was frail. It could just as well have been the old, retired cop's idea to step outside and Alik was simply helping him make it from Point A to Point B. That seemed reasonable enough, didn't it?

Didn't it?

What was the alternative . . . ?

As I said, it was late when we returned to the cottage, very late, so my aunt went straight to bed. I didn't. I couldn't. Too many thoughts, too many unanswered questions.

I found Alik at his desk in the great room. All the lamps were off, but enough moonlight poured in through the window for me to see his shadow. He was holding a snow globe up to the moonlight, turning it slowly in his hand like a glass bulb.

"When I first arrived in this country, I was not welcomed with open arms. There was still plenty of anti-German sentiment because of the war, and even though I could speak English with an excellent level of fluency, I did so with a thick Viennese accent, and officers of the law can be cruelly xenophobic. Cosmo was born and raised on the same street as some of his compatriots at Scotland Yard, but because he was the son of immigrants, his patriotism and competence were constantly scrutinized. When I first arrived in this country with my thick Viennese accent, no one wanted anything to do with me—this, despite my undeniable credentials—and so Cosmo volunteered to be my partner, and I was no longer alone. And at the end of our first case together, he gave me this snow globe. Do you see it?"

I leaned toward the snow globe. It depicted a charming city center awash with white flakes of . . . well, whatever snow globes used for snow. The city center had a large church and medieval-looking buildings, and it could have been any city in Europe as far as I could tell, though I had a guess as to which one it was.

"Is that Vienna?" I asked.

He smiled. "Snow globes were invented there, *ja*, not that Cosmo knew that. What he did know was that I might like a reminder of home. We all do. How are you holding up? I'm sure tonight was traumatic. Why don't you lie down?"

"It was all so surreal, you know? One minute, a person's alive, walking across a room, having a glass of wine, and the next, he's . . . But I don't have to tell you. You were there. You were literally right there. On the balcony."

"Whenever someone tells me something they're well aware I already know, I get suspicious. Are you quite sure you wouldn't rather discuss this in the morning?"

That was the second time in a minute he had tried to get me to leave. If he was anyone else, I'd have thought he was trying to shoo me away. Maybe he *was* trying to shoo me away. He'd just gone on and on about how much Cosmo had meant to him. Even Alik Lisser needed alone time, right?

At that point, I should have left him alone with his snow globe and his memories. I really should have. Most people probably would have. I even turned to go . . . but my mouth didn't get the memo and my mind had a hunch:

"Why was Cosmo's retirement party at Dame Carissa's flat?"

Alik sighed, put down the snow globe, and stood. In the shadows of the moonlight, he towered over me. "Katie, are you sure you want to do this?"

"It's Kat, actually. It's been Kat for, like, five years. And all I want to do is make sense of something that doesn't make any sense. Surely you, of all people, can get that."

His shadowy head nodded.

I repeated my question.

He replied:

"She has a lovely home. He deserved a lovely send-off. Over thirty years of keeping the peace in the Old Smoke. Wouldn't you agree, *Kat*?"

"I would. Totally. Absolutely. So it was also your idea to have the party on New Year's Eve?"

"It fit the theme of the evening."

"Sure, sure. Again, totally agree. Except it limited your guest list, didn't it?"

Alik crossed his arms. "Did it?"

"Holidays are a crazy time for the police. Learned that in *Merry Christmas, Adrian Lescher*. The robbers broke into the Bank of England's main branch on Threadneedle Street at three a.m. on December twenty-fifth. Hard to forget a name like *Threadneedle Street.* But they got away with it . . . until he caught them."

"Until *I* caught them."

"Right. But holidays are a crazy time, right? Half of the police force take the day off, leaving everyone else having to cover their shifts. Who's left to attend a party except retirees? It would be the perfect time and place to get away with murder."

"Careful now."

"I am being careful. But so were you, when you spoke with the detectives. You said Cosmo must have taken the hemlock a few weeks ago. Except I saw you had a full vial of it a few days ago. I thought, sure, you just refilled it. But that meant you'd noticed he stole it and said nothing. But that begs another question: Why hemlock?"

Alik was staring at me, though I couldn't see his eyes. All the moonlight illuminated was his pale throat.

"I'm, like, a B student at best in social studies, but even I know hemlock is the poison that Socrates took . . . which is about all I know about Socrates. But he was Greek, right?"

"And all Greeks commit suicide by hemlock. Is that your point, *Kat*?"

"No, sir. But it's a strange way to commit suicide. Most cops use their guns. I learned that in a Ngaio Marsh story. She's great."

"What are you getting at?"

"Just this: either Cosmo stole the poison because he wanted to implicate you somehow, because everyone probably knows about your little collection downstairs, or he didn't steal the poison, which means someone else put it in his wine. And since it was a holiday, there was practically a guarantee that, in a flat full of policemen, none of them would probably be skilled enough or perceptive enough to spot a poison attempt . . . I mean, no one except you. That's means and opportunity."

"And motive?"

"You didn't need a motive to arrest my dad."

"*Nein*, I didn't arrest him. The LAPD arrested him. I was merely a consultant. Is that what this is all about? A child trying to obtain justice for her poor daddy?"

"No. It's too late for that. But there's still time to obtain justice for Cosmo Korban."

Alik went silent. He was judging me. I could *feel* it.

Then he dropped to one knee till we were eye to eye and held out his arms as if to accept me into an embrace, then said, warmly:

"That's my girl."

17

Huh?

His face was visible now, the moonlight slashing white across his lips, which were stretched into a wide grin because . . .

Damned if I knew.

Whatever adrenaline had fueled my interrogation only moments ago turned to ice in my veins. I felt suddenly unsure of myself, unsure of him, unsure of everything . . .

"Don't be so shy, now," he said with a chuckle. "Not after all that, my brave and clever girl."

"I don't understand. I just . . . I mean . . . I just pretty much accused you of . . . you know . . . murder."

"Oh, I know! And what a sight it was. Everything I'd hoped for and more. I realize it couldn't have been easy. All worthwhile accomplishments never are. But, *ja*, you did it!"

"I'm still confused."

"You solved the mystery! I did lay out the clues a bit thick. I couldn't help myself. But putting the pieces together was only half the test. The other half was summoning the courage to confront the 'great Adrian Lescher' with your solution, and you succeeded. Now, come here and give me an embrace."

I did. His hug was loving. But I still wasn't sure I understood everything. To be honest, I still wasn't sure I understood *anything*. After the hug, I asked:

"So Cosmo isn't dead?"

His smile shrank a few inches. "No, he's dead. Poison in the chalice, just like you surmised."

"Hold up." I took a step back. "You *did* kill him?"

"I did. And it wasn't easy. Actually, it was very easy, but we had been friends for so many years. That wasn't a lie. The irony of it all is that Cosmo was the most incurious man I'd ever met. Carrie captured his incompetence very well in the books—and he took her portrait as a compliment! That tells you everything you need to know about the man. Good heart, dim bulb. Salt of the earth. So when I tell you that shortly after he announced his intent to retire, he began asking questions about our past investigations, it came as quite a surprise to me. But I suppose retirement is an inflection point of sorts and makes one look back and weigh the events of one's life. Truth be told, he was more of a detective in the past six months of his life than he ever was in nearly a half century at Scotland Yard. So no, rest assured, I didn't dispatch him simply to give you a puzzle to solve."

The ice of terror in my veins must have caused me to tremble, because he asked me if I wanted a cup of tea. I just shook my head. He shrugged and ambled to the kitchen to brew some for himself.

"It was when I saw you at the lecture that the specifics fell into place," he said from the kitchen. "You have no idea how lonely I've been since Carrie went away. It turns out, I've more than a little in common with Harry Houdini. He was Austrian, too, you know. Well, Hungarian, but Hungary at the time was a part of our empire. Like all boys, I had so much admiration for Houdini. He was most famous for his escape tricks, and I studied those, of course, but he also was an expert at sleight of hand. I have several biographies of him on the shelves, if you're interested. The thing about Houdini, though, was that, as his fame grew, he became aware that each performance he gave was simultaneously for two different audiences. There was the majority audience, the everyday spectators who had paid their five quid or whatever to watch a magician slip out of his shackles and free himself from certain drowning in a glass tank—but importantly, there also was the minority audience, his peers, who watched an expert of his craft show off his skills. Carrie and I were that for each other, she with her writing and I with my particular activities. Any critic will tell you that her books reached heretofore untold heights once she began to write about me. I was her muse. And she was mine. Do you see?"

He popped his head back in. I must have been standing in the shadows now, because he took a few long steps into the room toward me.

"You . . ." I muttered, but my mouth was dry. "Your muse?"

"*Ja.* And I know what you're thinking. If she was my muse, why did I do away with her? Well, I didn't, and shame on you for concluding otherwise. Her disappearance came as a genuine shock. I still haven't gotten over it."

He vanished back into the kitchen.

On his desk, the snow globe still glowed in the moonlight. Beside it lay his letter opener, short and steely and sharp.

"I came to realize I needed a replacement if I were to continue to function. 'O for a muse of fire, that would ascend the brightest heaven of invention!' But it couldn't be just anyone. The person I required had to be clever enough to appreciate my machinations but also bold enough to point out when I wasn't doing my best. And then I saw you at Harvard. The gods had answered my prayers."

He returned with his teacup.

"You want to sit at my desk? Feel free. *Mi silla es su silla.* The seat cushion is filled with goose feathers for extra softness. Go ahead. *Nein?* All right."

"Why me?" I asked.

"Say again? You're speaking too softly, my dear."

"Why me?" I repeated, though if it was any louder, I had no idea. In that moment, he could have tapped me on the shoulder and I would have fallen into a bottomless void. I might already have been falling.

"Ah. Your characteristic modesty. Carrie sometimes was guilty of that too. I blame society. It encourages women to be humble and punishes those who dare take pride in their appearance or accomplishments. Are you surprised I've read Simone de Beauvoir? I met her once—in Morocco, of all places. She was on holiday with one of her lovers and I was . . . Well, that's getting off topic. Why you? We've already discussed much of it. When you were just a little thing, you bested me at cards, and I *had* been cheating. I admit, my sleight of hand skills are a mote compared to the majesty of Houdini, but I'm not sloppy. Maybe even as early as then, I was testing you, wanting you to be able to see through my legerdemain and be courageous enough to challenge me. Who knows? It wasn't the first time we'd met, after all."

What did he mean? But even as I asked the question, I could sense the answer shuffle itself awake in my mind after a ten-year-long slumber, a six-year-old girl waking up in her parents' bed, except where's Mommy . . . ?

"It was a remarkable thing," he continued, "showing you those photographs of your mother's murder. Another conscious test, *ja*, I admit it. Did any part of you feel déjà vu, seeing those images again after so many years?"

It's late and dark and I have to find Mommy. The bed is far off the floor, so I have to slide off and there's light from the hallway but a tunnel of darkness to get there, so I run-run-run. Bare feet on soft carpet. Same carpet in the hallway, same carpet at the top of the stairs, and something is happening downstairs. Is Daddy home? Oh no, is Mommy crying? I hold the banister and, bare feet on soft carpet, start to go down the stairs.

"I knew they had a child," said Alik from a thousand miles away, "but for whatever reason, I never anticipated she might make an appearance. Appallingly clumsy oversight. An expert is an expert because they prepare for all eventualities, and I suddenly had to make a choice in the moment."

Mommy is lying down on the soft carpet, and she's looking at me but she's not looking at me because Mommy isn't there anymore even though those are her eyes and they were crying but now they're not and there's glass on the soft carpet, too, and a man dressed in black is standing next to her and he has a wool mask over his head even though it's not cold, and his eyes are green and Daddy's eyes are brown so this isn't Daddy and the man is also wearing gloves and holding a knife, except the knife is not silver but red and wet, like Mommy's eyes were wet but aren't wet and—

"But you, my clever, brave girl, made the choice for me. You saw what you saw, you turned around, and you went back upstairs to bed. And when I questioned you a few days later, probing to learn what you remembered, I knew I was OK. Though I suppose we'll never know if your stubborn insistence that your father was not guilty stemmed consciously from family ties or unconsciously from having seen the real culprit at work. If only Herr Freud could get you on his couch, *ja*?"

I looked up at Alik through wet eyes. He was standing by the desk, absently toying with his letter opener.

"So," he said, "now to discuss where we go from here."

18

"You killed her."

"I did, *ja*. Please know, Kat—and this is important—it wasn't personal. It's never personal. But you want to know why. You always want to know why. The short answer is the same every time—I did it to show that I could. The longer answer varies every time, but in the case of Barbara Ackroyd, I did it because, while I was waiting in my dentist's office to have a crown replaced, I saw her home in an issue of *Architectural Digest*. Your home. Ernst Lubitsch's home, once upon a time. He was a director of romantic comedies. Have you ever seen any of them?"

"No."

"Pity. You grew up in his house."

"You killed my mother."

Alik took a sip of tea, then put his teacup down on the desk. He also put the letter opener down.

"Kat, I've learned that the best way to deal with bad news is to remember that we can travel through time only in one direction, and that direction isn't backward."

"'Bad news'? I didn't just find out I got a D on a test. I just found out you murdered my mother! Except it's not even that—I just found out I saw you do it! And I did nothing!"

"You were six years old. What were you supposed to do? Throw a stuffed animal at me? And now you're crying. Go ahead. Get it all out. You'll feel better once you do."

That's when I shoved him . . . and I don't think he was expecting it, because he teetered off-balance and had to use his cane to keep from falling. So I shoved him again, and this time I grabbed the cane out from under his hand.

He landed on the floor with a thud.

"I'm not six years old anymore," I said.

"This temper tantrum says otherwise."

"YOU MURDERED MY MOTHER!"

He nodded, let out a long sigh, and replied, "I've murdered many mothers; many fathers; many, many people, *ja*. And I've gotten away with it every single time. Just like I'll get away with tonight's murder, lest you're thinking about phoning the police and telling them what you know. Lest you're thinking they'll believe you over me. I've gotten away with it every single time because I'm smart. I've gotten away with it because I always make sure someone else is set up to take the blame."

"Like my dad."

"Yes. Which, again, was not personal."

"Maybe not to you," I replied, and grabbed the letter opener with my free hand.

He gazed at it, then at me, then beyond me to the doorway to the guest bedrooms.

"Hello, dear," he said. "I'm so sorry. Did we wake you?"

I turned around.

Nobody was there.

Alik snatched the cane and whacked it with considerable force against the side of my right knee. I crumpled like a marionette, the letter opener clattered to the floor, and just like that, Alik had it, the cane, and everything else.

Slowly, he rose. I clutched my throbbing knee. He calmly locked the letter opener in a desk drawer.

"So," he said, "this is how things are going to proceed. You can hear me down there on the floor, correct, *Katie*? Good. Are you sure you don't want some tea?"

"You'll probably just poison it."

"See, that disappoints me. It shows you haven't been paying attention. I *need* you, Katie. I need someone to, for lack of a better word, *perform* for."

"You mean *kill*. You're a monster."

"You need to stop being so closed-minded."

I couldn't believe what I was hearing, and that's saying something. "Seriously?"

"You use these words like 'kill' and 'monster' as if they're meant to be revelations. I know who I am. I accept who I am. I'm at peace with it. It didn't happen overnight. I struggled. But it did happen. If you want, I can help you come to peace with who you are too. All your anxieties will go away, *ja*, I promise."

"You can go to hell."

Alik sighed again and sipped some more of his tea. "Still such a stubborn child. So be it."

"All this time . . . the great detective is nothing but a sham . . ."

"Is that what bothers you the most? That your hero turned out to be human? Well, difficult as it might be to fathom, there is no sham. How many Adrian Lescher novels did Carrie write? Fifty? Not to mention all the short stories. I assure you that at least half of everything she wrote about me depicted real detective work. It takes months, sometimes years, to formulate a good trick. In the meantime, I solved many actual crimes. Rest assured that you will be an accomplice to greatness . . . one way or another. Now, if you'll excuse me, it is late even for a night owl such as myself. I'd recommend you get some sleep too. Tomorrow is your last day in Jolly Old England. You wouldn't want to waste it lying in bed."

He strolled into the kitchen, presumably to deposit his teacup in the sink, and then continued on, presumably to his bedroom. I heard his footsteps fade and then a door close.

Only then did I get up, leaning on the desk for balance. My knee had swollen to nearly twice its size. He must have hit a tendon or something. I sat at his desk, in his chair, and did my best not to absorb whatever crazy might have rubbed off.

So.

What were my options?

A: Find a weapon, wait until the Man Who Killed My Mom (and indirectly killed my dad) falls asleep, and then get revenge. Alik had a lot of heavy books. It would be fitting, wouldn't it? How many times would I have to hit him in the head with, say, *The Oxford English Dictionary*? How much blood would there be? What if the first blow woke him up and he started watching me as I killed him? Would I be able to do it? Would I even be able to do it with his eyes closed? He deserved to die; that wasn't the issue. But did I have it in me to *kill* him? And if I didn't, if he opened his eyes before that first blow, while I hesitated, what would stop him from killing me and then killing my aunt and then—

B: Be smart. Get revenge, but do it safe and do it right. I was in the house of an egomaniac. There *had* to be evidence here, somewhere, something that would incriminate him. All I had to do was find it. I didn't even have to take it. I had a digital camera. I just had to take pictures of it, wait until me and my aunt were safely back in Boston, and then email the pictures of the evidence to Scotland Yard . . . assuming they had an email address. And of course they'd believe pictures of evidence sent by an American teenage girl that proved one of the most respected men in the country was actually Jack the Ripper—

C: Do nothing. Let Alik use me as his sick muse or whatever. It wasn't as if I was innocent. It wasn't as if doing nothing wasn't something I already excelled at. I'd seen him take the life out of my mother. I was there. And doing nothing had been my instinctive response. Maybe this was my role in life, to just quietly observe how horrible life could be and then, eventually, mercifully, die—

Oh, screw that, Kat.

This is *not* the time for self-pity. This is the time for action. Do *something.*

I searched the desk for solutions and saw a stack of books, a fountain pen, some paper, some envelopes, a desk lamp, a mug full of rubber bands and paper clips. I grabbed the fountain pen—no matter what came next, it couldn't hurt to have something sharp—then turned my attention back to the mug.

To the paper clips.

Hmm.

I grabbed two paper clips and held them up in the pool of moonlight. What I was about to do was either brilliant or stupid. What else was new. Carefully, I unfolded each paper clip until it untwisted into a straight, long wire. Then I knelt beside the door (on my good knee), found the tiny lock on the desk drawer with my fingertips, and inserted one of the wires into the top of the lock and inserted the other wire into the bottom, and proceeded to do my best Simon Templar / A. J. Raffles / Arsène Lupin impression.

In other words, I tried to lockpick the crap out of it.

This technique worked in those stories. Something about the picks disengaging the tumblers inside the locks. You don't have to know how something works in order to use it, so I tried. I bit down on my lower lip, and I leaned my ear close to the lock to listen for those disengaging tumblers and I fiddled with my handmade lockpicks and I tried, even though the lock was so tiny, because if Alik was hiding anything, the best place to look would be in a place he kept locked . . .

Oooh.

Wait a sec.

I again used the desk to help me stand. Then I limped slowly toward the kitchen.

Into the kitchen.

To the door leading to the basement.

This lock was normal-size. And I didn't even have to kneel this time to pick it. I inserted both paper clips and fiddled for a minute or two. Everything I was doing was quiet, but I still nervously listened for footsteps, a creak in the floor, any sound that might indicate the approach of a certain tall, thin—

Click.

19

It worked?

I was as surprised as anyone. I turned the knob, peered into the darkness below. Then—duh—I limped back to the guest bedroom to retrieve the digital camera. It all took longer than I wanted, and by the time I'd returned to the basement door, the first pink rays of dawn had begun to poke through the kitchen window.

Scotland Yard might not believe whatever evidence I found, but someone might. There was a former Scotland Yard tech named Francis Fung, PhD, who was *certain* that Dame Carissa had been murdered and even maintained a website on GeoCities on which they compiled all their evidence. Some of the regulars in the chat room were avid followers of Dr. Fung. For all we knew, maybe Dr. Fung *was* one of the regulars in the chat room.

I used the digital camera's flash to guide my way down the stairs. My life may have recently become a horror thriller, but at least the steps didn't creak or moan. The basement was as neat and quiet as it had been a few days ago. I chose the office area first, snapping photographs of the cabinets, the cramped desk, and the weirdly framed newspaper clippings and animal sketches on the otherwise-bare gray walls.

The tape was probably still in the VCR. The tape that incriminated my father. The tape that Alik had to have doctored, right? I pressed the eject button. Nothing happened. I turned the TV on. White static filled the screen. I pressed play. Again, nothing. I slipped a hand inside the VCR slot.

The tape was gone.

Of course it was.

Still, maybe there was something in these clippings and sketches. Psycho killers kept trophies, didn't they? I'd need to get the German ones translated, but that's why God invented libraries and why libraries had English/German dictionaries.

I moved on to the basement's other workspace: the laboratory. The spice wall of poisons had seemed a wee bit eccentric, but now . . .

I took photos of everything. I wasn't sure how many the memory card could hold, and who knew how many pictures my aunt had taken during her adventures in London. I assumed the camera would let me know when it was close to full. But I had no idea what was important and what wasn't, so I wanted to document everything.

After the poisons: the guns. So many guns. I mean, come on. If most people strolled down those stairs and saw this many guns on the wall, they'd get suspicious. Alik had been lying in plain sight for decades. I then opened the knife drawers. Serrated steak knives, big fat cleavers, tiny paring knives, knives with wooden handles, knives in leather sheaths, even weirdly shaped knives that looked like props from a Bruce Lee movie. By now, there was enough light coming in through the basement's small rectangular windows that I probably didn't need my camera's flash . . . but I used it anyway. I wasn't about to lose any evidence in a shadow.

Then I saw the thick red curtain. How had I forgotten the thick red curtain? How had I forgotten that this lunatic had, for all I knew, *half of his frickin' basement* hidden behind a mysterious wall of fabric? No, nothing suspicious about that.

I set the camera next to a terrarium, grabbed one of the cleavers, and approached the curtain.

What would I find? Alik had joked the other day about the myth of Bluebeard and the chopped-up women he'd hidden behind his closed door. Not so funny now. My knee still felt as if it had an ice pick jabbed into it, so I limped the final few steps to the curtain, reached out, grabbed a handful of the thick red fabric, tugged with all my might . . .

. . . and revealed the world's largest collection of pickled herring.

Seriously, there must have been thousands and thousands of jars of dyed pickled herring, all stacked side by side and taller than me by at least a foot. Some of the jars glowed a devilish red in the meager dawn light. Most of it was still dark.

What a bizarre find. I'm not saying I would have preferred seeing a pile of chopped-up women, but it at least would have made more sense. Why had Alik kept his friend's unsold stock of gimmick fish? Surely by now, it was inedible.

Maybe there was something he was hiding behind the stacks? I turned around to grab the digital camera to take more pictures and instead came face-to-face with Hermann.

"It's time to feed plants," the sunglasses-wearing manservant said—or at least, I think that's what he said, because his sudden appearance had momentarily overloaded my brain.

Plus, he was holding my camera.

Crap.

How had I not heard him? Stupid non-creaking stairs. He had to know that I'd picked the lock, that I wasn't supposed to be down here, and now he had my camera, which was really the school's camera, and it had all the evidence I'd documented (and all the memories my aunt had documented) and he was going to confiscate it and tell his boss and . . .

. . . and he handed the camera back to me as if nothing was wrong.

"Thank you?" I replied.

He offered up a peculiar half grin and then returned to the terrarium and sprinkled what looked like coffee grounds onto the lamplit foliage. Maybe he assumed I'd been given permission to come down here and take pictures? That was quite a leap, but what other explanation was there?

I wasn't about to wait around and find out. I took my digital camera back to the bedroom, switched into my nightclothes, and just as the full blast of sunrise gray filled the room, I slid underneath the covers and shut my eyes and let my waning adrenaline lull me into a sort of waking sleep.

I woke up to snow. Snow fell outside. Snow seemed to be falling inside, too, or at least it was cold enough. I could see my breath. I took a quick, hot shower, changed into some clean clothes, put on my winter coat, and found my aunt in the dining room. She, too, was wearing a winter coat and was browsing through a chunky fashion magazine she must have picked up in London.

"Good morning, sleepyhead," she chirped.

Nice to see she was still in a good mood. No reason for this trip to suck for both of us.

I sat beside her. "Why is it so cold?"

"The furnace needs a new filter. Alik's butler went into town to get a replacement."

"And where's Alik?"

"Speak," said the man himself, entering with a tray of tea and biscuits, "and the devil shall appear."

He placed the tray in front of me.

"I'm not hungry."

"Suit yourself," my aunt said, and she grabbed a shortbread.

Alik sat across from us at the table. "It's our last day together. We can do whatever you want. Weather permitting, the entirety of this modest island country is yours to explore. Wherever our destination, be it the Midlands or the North, I will make a call and have your flight back to the Colonies depart from there."

My aunt suggested she might want to dip into Wales. She knew it wasn't too far from where we were, and she admitted to a childhood crush on actor Richard Burton, wondering aloud if every Welshman looked like him. Then there was Bath, home of Jane Austen, and was

Liverpool (hallowed home of John, Paul, George, and Ringo) too far away?

And so, after Alik had made a few phone calls, off to Liverpool we went. He advised us we wouldn't have time to come back, so Hermann helped us stuff our luggage into the back of the car and then mumbled his goodbyes. It would just be us and Alik for the rest of the trip.

Was it easy being stuck in a car with the man who'd murdered your mother? What do you think? It took most of my willpower not to reach forward and wrap my fingers around his neck and squeeze (putting aside the fact that if I tried to strangle him, he'd lose control of the car and we would all die), and whatever power I had left I used to keep from blurting the whole thing out to my aunt. But I wasn't about to endanger *her* too. I mean, she was whistling "Penny Lane" as we drove through a snow shower. Come on.

By the time we got to Liverpool, it was just about two, so Alik brought us to a small fish-and-chips place he liked. It overlooked the sea, which ate up snowflakes left and right as they set upon its currents, and my aunt swore she could see, in the far, far distance, the shores of Ireland. All I saw was fog. Maybe the shores of Ireland were made of fog. Maybe everything was fog and we just tricked ourselves into thinking otherwise.

My aunt excused herself to use the restroom, and that left Alik and me alone for the first time since our confrontation at his desk. I rubbed my aching knee and avoided his gaze. I could still hear him, though, breathing, tapping his fingers on the linoleum table.

"It doesn't have to be this way," he said. "What's going to happen is going to happen whether we're friendly or not, so wouldn't it be better to be friendly?"

I ran a finger up and down the length of my butter knife. "You really want to make things better?"

"*Ja*, always."

"Do you see the water out there? Go jump into it. How long do you think it'll take for hypothermia to set in?"

"Given the atmospheric temperature and the proximate temperature of the water, I'd say about twenty to thirty minutes. But if you're hoping I'd suffer, I have bad news. Within five minutes, I'd go into shock. I'd start to flail. I'd get confused. In all likelihood, by minute ten, I'd have drowned. But first, you'd have to get me in the water, and that is never, ever going to happen." Then he grabbed my chin and forced me to look at him. "What will happen is this: I will contact you. I will tell you that I killed someone and I will tell you how, and you will have to live with it. It really is best if you stop fighting. Give up. Give in. Let's at least be friendly about it."

Then a pair of cops walked in.

Sure, they wore bowler hats and black overcoats, but their badges were unmistakably "police" in any country. They were laughing about something while they nonchalantly bypassed the line of customers to place their order and, in doing so, were maybe seven feet from where Alik and I sat.

To get their attention, I wouldn't even have to raise my voice.

Alik probably *did* have Scotland Yard in his pocket . . . but Liverpool was the boonies. And if I did raise my voice, if I yelled . . . A teenage girl yelling about a creepy old man . . .

"Is that wee Harry Perkins?" asked Alik, standing.

The older of the two cops perked up. "Detective Lisser, as I live and breathe! Come here, you muppet!"

He then proceeded to slap Alik on the arm and introduce him to his partner while I simmered in silence. How naive of me to believe that Alik Lisser—Adrian freakin' Lescher—wouldn't have friends all over England (if not the world). And the way these two Liverpool cops smiled and laughed at everything he said, just Alik being Alik . . .

Eventually, my aunt returned. Eventually, she got to see the sights she wanted. Alik's eminence even got us a private tour of the Cavern Club. Here we were, standing backstage where her favorite band, The Beatles, had gotten their big break, and my aunt turned to Alik and said:

"You're really something."
In that moment, she was in awe of *him*.
I really, truly, deeply wanted to vomit.
"Isn't he something, Kat?"
"He really is," I replied.

20

Then: home. Back to normal.

Normal. Ha. *Normal* was not even normal by the abnormal standards of *my* normal, not with this monster looming over me like a giant swinging axe. When we came home, my uncle wasn't there. That was normal. My uncle wasn't there, but Alik's presence clung to everything. It had been there all along. Only now, I could see it. Now I could see the slime he had smeared across the past ten years of my life.

I sat on my bed and stared at my piles of Carissa Miller books and tried to implode.

There were a few dirty dishes in the sink, and the Kleenex box had been moved from the bathroom to the computer desk, but my uncle at least hadn't trashed the place. It was the middle of a Tuesday, so no one else was in the chat room. I would have been happy to spend the time with a random stranger. There were other chat rooms I could have gone to, but I wanted this one. If I couldn't have my comfort books, couldn't I at least have my comfort space?

Anxiety tingles started up and down in my arms and legs, so I logged out and shuffled back to my bed and cocooned myself inside the blanket and sheets. I went fetal. Maybe I cried. I don't even know.

At some point, my aunt woke me up for dinner. She was still humming, so I guessed my uncle hadn't come home yet. I barely touched my SpaghettiOs and maybe drank only half my glass of Diet Coke.

"Do you think you're coming down with something?" my aunt asked. "I notice you've been walking a little funny. Are you feeling dizzy?"

I shook my head.

She touched a palm to my brow.

"You're not warm," she said. "Want me to make some soup?"

I shook my head.

"How about this: When I go to the store tomorrow, I'll see if they have any English biscuits or tea. Then it can be like we're still there. How does that sound?"

How did it sound? It sounded like we were living in completely different realities. But I still wasn't about to spoil hers with mine. My mom had been her sister, and it was clear from the way she had reacted to the painting that she totally hadn't come to terms with her grief either. Plus, would she even believe me? I wouldn't believe me. And if I did tell her and if she *did* believe me, wouldn't that just put her in danger, and what kind of selfish freak would that make me?

So instead, I said thank you, and then I went to the computer. It was almost 8:00 p.m. By now, some of the regulars had to be online.

And there was one in particular that I absolutely *needed* to talk to.

Twenty-two people in the room! So many familiar names! Our mother hen, Marigoldeneyes, appeared to be moderating a discussion about the accuracy of Dame Carissa's depiction of Damascus in the Sister Mary Judith novel *Sayeth the Lord*. Specifically at issue was the color of the bricks at the Chapel of Saint Paul. A user named Professor. Tweed had "just returned from a Christmas pilgrimage to the Levant" and was insisting that the bricks were "of carbonate rock" and not sandstone, as Dame Carissa, via her narrator Sister Mary Judith, had noted.

Here's to the nitpickers and quibblers, arguing for hours over every detail in works of fiction, escaping into minutiae to avoid problems that really mattered.

My people. Now I was really home. The knots in my stomach untangled just a little bit.

And among the twenty-two people, my pal Dev.

I popped open a direct-message screen and typed away.

KMcCann14: Happy New Year, loser.

It took him less than ten seconds to reply.

WmbleyLnDet: welcome to the year o' the rat!!

The year of the rat? What the . . . ?

Oh. Those Chinese zodiac things, which I don't know are even real. But I wasn't about to say anything critical. I needed a Huge Favor. If anyone could tell me how to transfer the pictures from the digital camera, and maybe even enlarge them, it was Dev. I had to be nice. But I couldn't just ask.

KMcCann14: Make any fun New Years resolutions?
WmbleyLnDet: nope, already perfect.

Riiiiight.

KMcCann14: Nice to see some things never change.
WmbleyLnDet: x-actly

Then, as I was composing some more nonsensical small talk, still not sure how to segue into asking for the Huge Favor, this appeared:

WmbleyLnDet: i got you a chr1stmas g1ft

Say what?

WmbleyLnDet: its not a b1g deal but id love to g1ve it to you, when r u free

Hmm.

That might actually work. If I asked him in person, if I let him see the digital camera, maybe even asked him if he could transfer the pictures himself . . . after all, he had access to God-knows-what equipment at MIT. And there was no way I was going to take down Alik Lisser alone. I needed help. And Dev may have been a dumbass, but he wasn't *stupid*. And I could trust him.

Couldn't I?

So we set up a time: tomorrow, 1:00 p.m. Same place we first met, the food court at Chestnut Hill.

I hung around the chat room for another hour. It felt good to banter about nonsense, though I'd be lying if I said I didn't flinch whenever I saw the name *Adrian Lescher* pop up on the screen, which, in a chat room dedicated to Carissa Miller . . . well, talk about inevitabilities.

After I was through, I took some leftover SpaghettiOs out of the fridge. My aunt must have heard me, because she wandered in from her bedroom and offered to pop my food back into the oven for a few minutes, and I was about to say yes when we both heard the metallic click of a key in the lock of our front door.

Talk about inevitabilities.

However.

The man who came in wasn't my uncle. I mean, he *was*, but he didn't smell like booze and he seemed almost jovial. Somehow, within a week, he'd managed to grow a full beard, and the full grin he wore doubled the width of that beard till it nearly crowded the doorframe.

"My family's home!" he bellowed, and opened his arms to us like Santa Claus greeting his elves.

Um, what?

After what felt like a minute or so, when he realized we weren't going to rush into his embrace, he lowered his arms, shut the door behind him, and nonchalantly sat at the table beside me.

"So," he said, "tell me all about your trip, and don't spare any details."

OK. So my uncle had been replaced by an alien. Awesome.

My aunt and I took turns summarizing England. She showed him some of the outfits and knickknacks she'd bought, including a stuffed John Lennon walrus she got for me in Liverpool. Once we were through, my aunt asked him how his week was, but he just shrugged and said it was nothing special and that he'd missed us a lot, and then, with heartache in his eyes, he made us promise not to leave him alone ever again.

I almost felt bad for him—almost as much as I believed he had really changed.

Almost.

Because maybe my uncle really meant everything he said and maybe tonight would be all full grins and heartache, but all three of us knew this was just a commercial break and tomorrow, or maybe the next day, our regularly scheduled programming would be back.

Wasn't that the moral of the story?

21

The D train ran southwest on the green line from my neighborhood to Chestnut Hill. The whole trip took fifteen minutes. I'd taken it dozens of times.

The trip I took that Wednesday, on my way to meet Dev, was not like the other times.

It started ordinarily enough. I wore my winter outfit (boots, coat, scarf, mittens, wool hat). I sat with my backpack on my lap, with the straps looped around my wrists to keep anyone from stealing it. I'd grabbed my guardian angel of the day from my pile of Carissa Miller stand-alones (no Adrian Lescher for me, duh) and was already half-way through the first chapter when the doors hissed shut and the train lurched forward, and that's when everything went off the rails.

Let me explain.

When I first moved to my aunt and uncle's apartment, when I first settled in, I had trouble sleeping. It wasn't that I was scared of the night; I was scared of everything. Can you blame me? What finally helped me feel safe and go to sleep was this: I'd tuck myself underneath my blankets so that I was completely covered (even the top of my head, and *especially* the bottoms of my bare feet) and only then, only when I was fully covered in a force field of wool and cotton, was I able to relax.

The problem was, I couldn't take my blankets with me wherever I went, and as scared as I was in my bed, I was even more scared being out in the daylight, out in public. Crowds made it difficult to breathe.

I felt like I was being crushed inside a giant fist. Then Miss Sharon at the library introduced me to crime novels (her guilty pleasure), and I quickly found my way to Carissa Miller's novels (whose paperbacks alone took up a whole shelf!), and their pages became a force field I could take with me. They were how I made it through the day at school. They were how I survived every trip on the T. They were how I made it safely across the Atlantic Ocean while my aunt—who was unprotected—freaked out.

I was OK on the return trip because my sleep deprivation finally kicked in, and I slept most of the way. I hadn't thought to consider the fact that of all the things Alik Lisser had tainted and ruined, it included *this* too. Because believe me when I tell you that when the doors hissed shut, that book, in which Alik/Adrian did not appear at all, might as well have been written in Greek.

The train lurched out of the station, and I was unprotected.

And it wasn't as if the train was especially full. There were maybe more people than usual for a Wednesday at 11:30 a.m., but it wasn't *packed*. Most of the seats were filled, but only a few people were forced to (or chose to) stand. None of that mattered. I was locked in this metal tube with them. I had no real escape, and my only fake escape was now trembling in my hands—no, it was my hands that were trembling . . . trembling and tingling . . . and the tingling slowly worked its way up my forearms to my elbows, and then I couldn't swallow because my mouth had gone drier than a beach, drier than a mound of salt, and the world began to blur, so I shut my eyes *tight* and tried to think of something, anything, to distract myself from the fact that I was absolutely 100 percent having a nervous breakdown and it was Alik's fault, like everything else, Alik's fault, and I was going to make him pay.

But what punishment fit his crimes? Even if he was arrested, tried, convicted, and zapped on the electric chair, would that be enough? Would that balance out all the pints of blood he'd spilled like all those stacks of herring?

No, he had to suffer.

He deserved to suffer. Like I had suffered ever since that day. Like my father had suffered. Like my mother. Like so many mothers and fathers had suffered because of his insanity and ego . . . which Dame Carissa had supported. For decades. She was as good as an accomplice. She had literally profited off his murders. It didn't take a shrink to make me realize why her books had lost their magical powers of protection. She deserved to suffer too. Maybe she had. Alik said he hadn't killed her, but he was clearly a pathological liar.

How could I make him suffer? How could—

The train rocked to a stop. I glanced through the tinted window at the little green shed and its frost-covered signage, which read Chestnut Hill. I'd made it through without fainting or puking. That was something, at least.

The doors hissed open, and I darted outside. A cold breeze licked at my lips and cheeks, but my nerves were fine. No, they were more than fine; I felt renewed. I walked the thirty minutes to the shopping center, past a Star Market, past a bakery, past any number of stores and parked cars and snowdrifts, and I think I maybe even whistled a bit. It wasn't until I passed by the Borders Bookstore that I realized I'd left the paperback on the train.

I had a few minutes to kill. I wandered into the store. The Mystery section was exactly where it had been back in July, when I'd first shared my secret with Dev. I ran a finger over all the familiar titles, all arranged alphabetically but some so very different from the others. For example, the ones I'd gravitated toward for almost ten years now were the Golden Age mysteries and their later imitators, the so-called "cozies," where the puzzles were tantalizing but the good sleuth always solved them, often over a cup of tea.

But maybe it was time to shift to a different breed of mystery. I knew all these other authors' names well enough. Patricia Highsmith, Chester Himes, James M. Cain. I'd read a few pages here and there out of curiosity, but their stuff had been too dark for me—tales of femme fatales and men who were neither good nor bad but instead raw and vulnerable and capable of kindness one minute and cruelty the next . . .

Well, if I was going to set about revenge, I'd best do my research.

I made a mental list of some books to pick up the next time I was at the library and then strolled over to the food court. Dev arrived fifteen minutes later, as usual. He wore a puffy maroon coat and had gotten a crew cut since I'd last seen him in October.

"Happy New Year," he said.

I sat down. "Happy New Year to you."

"Did you do anything special?"

Oh, did I. But best to ease into it.

"This and that," I replied. "How about you?"

"Went to Nebraska. Competed in a college-wrestling invitational. Won second place. First time anyone from MIT won second place there."

"They had a wrestling competition during Christmas break?"

"No, the competition was December second. Why would they have a wrestling competition during f'ing Christmas break?"

"I don't know. I thought we were talking about—"

"Who would I wrestle? Santa Claus? He's not even in my f'ing weight class."

"Or real," I added, politely semi-sipping my Orange Julius, wondering who ordered ice-cold drinks in winter. But this was probably Dev just being polite too. I'd ordered an Orange Julius back in July. He probably thought I liked them year-round. Dev: polite dumbass.

The polite dumbass reached into his backpack and took out a small brown bag.

"I would've wrapped your Christmas gift," he said, "but I don't know how."

He handed me the bag.

I took it.

I peeked inside and then upended it over our plastic table. A smaller black box tumbled out. It took me a moment to figure out the picture on the box, the picture that indicated what was inside the box, because, well, I mean, it was not what I expected. I don't know *what* I expected, but certainly not . . .

"A pager," said Dev. "I have one too. I'll give you the number. So we can keep in touch."

The only people I knew who had pagers were drug dealers and doctors (who, I suppose, were *also* drug dealers). The fact that Dev wanted me to have one so *we could keep in touch* was such a weird shade of ick . . . except I couldn't let him see how weirded out I was. I needed him to help me with the camera. Speaking of, I reached into my bag.

"Oh, you got me something too?" he asked.

"In a way," I replied.

I showed him the digital camera.

He frowned. "You bought me a used Kodak DCS 200?"

"Well, yes and no. Yes, it's a . . . Hey, I am impressed you knew exactly what it was . . . not just that it's a Kodak DCS 200. And yes, it's used. By me. In London. Over Christmas break."

"I don't understand."

That was when I realized something important: he *wouldn't* understand, not if I told him everything then and there. He was Dev, the weird, polite dumbass. If I tried to tell him everything right then and there, we'd be stuck in that food court for the next five hours talking and talking and talking about every moment of my trip, especially every moment of my trip that I spent with Alik, and Dev would interrogate me over every single sentence that Alik had spoken, and I was very much *not* wanting to do *that*, so . . .

"I need a favor," I said, "but I need to be mysterious about it. You'll see why when you see what's on the camera. Which is what I need you to do: use all those fancy resources at MIT and see what's on the camera. Develop the film or the computer images or whatever you call it."

"But I already *got* you a Christmas present."

"Dev . . ."

"I'm kidding! It's fine."

"Thank you."

"Why were you *really* in London over Christmas break?"

"The sooner you develop the pictures, the sooner you'll find out."

He nodded, took the camera, and said with a grin, "And you'll find out when I find out, because I'll page you."

Awesome.

22

I felt guilty about using Dev like that. I mean, sure he was a tool, but that didn't mean I had to treat him like one. And sure, friends did favors for friends, but with the whole unprompted Christmas gift and all that, I was worried that might have been him wanting us to be more than friends—and if so, I definitely should have said something, right?

What I didn't feel guilty about, not in the least, was stealing the camera, not even when, on the following Monday morning, Mr. Handy began our class with a lecture on responsibility, building up to the revelation that someone had "pilfered the school's priceless digital camera," which he apparently had "obtained through a grant."

Why didn't I feel guilty about stealing the camera when I felt very guilty about using Dev? Both were a means to an end, after all. I think it came down to three things:

1. There is a difference between using a person and using a device.
2. I had every intention of returning the camera after Dev developed the pictures.
3. It wasn't like the photography club was going to need the camera anytime soon, or at least not the first week back from break. There was literally nothing new to photograph.

However, Mr. Handy was apparently not the only person in the school who disagreed with me, because when I went to my locker to switch out my science and English textbooks for my social studies and trig textbooks, a folded slip of yellow paper tumbled out of my locker and glided to my feet. I unfolded the yellow paper and read what someone had scrawled in barely legible black ink:

I KNOW YOU STOLE THE CAMERA.

MEET ME IN THE BAND ROOM AT 3PM OR ELSE.

Or else? Or else what?

Was it possible someone had seen me take the digital camera from the darkroom? I mean, I thought I had been careful, but who knows? And unless this mystery person had deposited an identical note in the locker of every other student in the school, they were targeting me for a reason.

And I suppose I should have been panicking, but I wasn't. Maybe I'd used up all my panic in England. I'd been threatened by Alik freakin' Lisser, and now I was being threatened by some overeager teenager over the theft of a camera? Please.

Or maybe—just maybe—I wasn't panicking because part of me had already realized what the rest of me took a minute to process:

Even if this fool had seen me take the camera, what was his proof? It was his word against mine, and it wasn't like I had a record of stealing school paraphernalia. I doubted Vice Principal Jeffers even knew my name. But let's say Vice Principal Jeffers believed the accusation and searched my bag or my locker or even my apartment. The camera wasn't there.

This joker, whoever he was (and that chicken scratch black-ink handwriting was 100 percent male), might have been able to intimidate the old Kat, 1995 Kat—but this was 1996 Kat, and 1996 Kat had seen some stuff and wasn't putting up with foolishness.

All of which is to say that, come 3:00 p.m., I went straight to the band room to confront and shame my accuser (though first I had to sit through a Mr. Roberts lecture in trig, its only entertainment value provided by the fact that his armpit sweat had pierced through the fabric of his brown button-down and occasionally released full, fat droplets to the floor). When the bell rang, we all gathered our things and bolted for the door. I can't speak for anyone else, but I made for the south stairwell and descended to the subbasement level, nicknamed "the dungeon," where the band and orchestra students (as well as the shop classes) conducted their day-to-day whatever. I'd been down there only once before, during the first week of my freshman year, when I was on the search for a quiet and secluded place to eat lunch. Secluded, yes, but quiet? Never. Despite the fluffy pink material the school used to soundproof the classrooms. Even now, at 2:58 p.m., the hum of buzz saws was so loud that it made my teeth shake.

I assumed the band room was the one labeled BAND ROOM. Its door, like all the doors down here, was closed, but the knob turned in my hand and I let myself in. The only other person in the room was a senior named Pedro Something or Other (we'd shared a gym class last year), who was playing some sort of fast, full-bodied jazz music on the upright piano—the kind of music requiring him to pump on the piano's pedals every few seconds to alter the tone. He had one of those bodies that was like stretched taffy—so long and thin that you could just about see the skeleton underneath. His skeletal head and skeletal shoulders bobbed with the quick rhythm of the music. His hair, shoulder length and streaked with green, bounced along with the beat like a roof-raising hand of snakes.

It wasn't my type of music (too all over the place), but it had a powerful energy and Pedro was clearly talented, so I let him finish. It seemed like the courteous thing to do. After all, it wasn't *guaranteed* that he was my accuser. He could have just been in here practicing and my accuser was running late, and I wasn't about to accuse a semi-stranger of accusing me of . . . Well, you get my point.

Then, suddenly, it was all over. If you had quizzed me, I wouldn't have been able to tell you what made the end *the end* other than it was the end. But Pedro swiveled around on his little stool and held out his hands and said:

"Well?"

"Hmm?"

"What did you think?"

He leaned forward, seemed to genuinely want to know the truth.

"I'm . . . not really a . . . you know . . . expert."

"Even better," he replied. "Experts are boring! Did you like it? Did you not like it?"

"It's . . . not my type of music . . ."

"Oh!" He deflated a bit. "What is your type of music, then? Wait! Let me guess."

He swiveled back toward the piano and started to pound out the melody to that overplayed Hootie & the Blowfish song. "Hold My Hand." Ugh. Gag my throat. Though it sounded a lot more funky coming from that upright piano.

"Well?" he asked.

"Not even close," I replied.

"'Not even close,' she says. All right. How about . . ."

He effortlessly segued from Hootie to Coolio, pop music to gospel hip-hop. "Gangsta's Paradise." Much less hokey, but still . . .

"Not really."

"You're killing me, Smalls."

"Excuse me?"

"It's a line from a movie that is clearly not your type of movie, just like none of these songs are your type of music." He swiveled around to face me again. "But that's OK! I will not be daunted."

"Well, I'd hate to daunt you."

He chuckled, his smirk punctuated by dimples for parentheses. "Good to know. But not helpful in narrowing down what you like."

"What does it matter what I like?"

He studied me for a moment, swiveled toward the piano again, paused, and began to play the first few bars of "It's Too Late" by Carole King, and my breath caught in my throat. I *loved* Carole King. Carole King and Joni Mitchell and all those amazing women from the early '70s who wrote their own songs and, with them, rewrote, like, the culture of America . . . or at least, that's what Miss Sharon said one day, years ago now, when I asked her what she was listening to on the record player in her office in the children's room, and I learned she was as enthusiastic about music as she was about books, and just as she'd opened my eyes to the novels of Dame Carissa Miller, she opened my ears to albums like *Anticipation* and *New York Tendaberry* and—

Pedro stopped playing mid-phrase.

"Well?" he asked.

He still had his back to me, but I could hear the smile on his lips.

"How . . . ?" I replied.

He spun around. "It's just a party trick, Kat McCann. Not that I go to a lot of parties."

"Me neither. Hold up. How did you know my name?"

"We had gym together. Last year. You were having trouble climbing the rope, and Mr. Ardebesian kept yelling, 'What kind of cat are you, huh?' What a fart-knocker."

"Ugh. Thanks, I'd forgotten all about that."

He shrugged. The room fell silent.

That pink fuzz on the walls really did absorb all sound. Or maybe it was just the palpable absence of the piano. Or maybe awkwardness was just that good at muting a room.

"I should probably get going," I said. "I was supposed to meet someone here, but I guess he's a no-show."

"Who were you supposed to meet?"

"This *dumbass* who left me a . . . It really doesn't matter . . ."

"Well, now you *have* to tell me. What did he leave you?"

I still had the note in my back pocket. I took it out and showed it to him. He studied the note the way he had studied me a few minutes earlier, as if every atom in his mind was tuned to this one focal point. It reminded me a little of . . . well, to be honest, it reminded me a little of Alik Lisser, and that encouraged my old friend Anxiety to flutter up my heartbeat and dry out my mouth.

"*Did* you steal the camera?" Pedro asked.

"He thinks I did. And he's probably going to try to blackmail me or whatever, which says all you need to know about him, right? But the joke's on him, because even if I did maybe do what he thinks I did, he doesn't know why I did it and he sure doesn't have any proof, so—"

Pedro then took something out of his back pocket. At first I thought it also was a note, but then he handed it to me and . . . nope, not a note.

It was a wallet-size black-and-white photograph.

Of me.

Scurrying out of the darkroom.

With the camera.

23

Welp.

Who's the dumbass now, huh?

"Sorry about the bad angle," he said, "but I took the picture in a hurry."

"You're sorry about the angle? Who gave you the right . . . the *permission* . . . to take my picture at all?"

OK, so maybe that was a little blame-shifting, but I wasn't wrong. And can you blame me, after being lured into a web by Alik and then forced to carry a pager by Dev and now *this* guy, stalking me, hiding in the shadows, and taking my photograph without even—

"You gave me permission," he replied.

I blinked. "Excuse me?"

"You signed the consent form. You signed it and your mom or dad signed it. For the yearbook. And, well, maybe I didn't, like, announce myself or anything, but that's the only way to get a candid shot."

"You plan on printing this in the yearbook?"

"No! I swear! The only people who've seen this picture are you and me. And Annie."

"Annie?"

"Well, sure."

I flipped through every Ann, Anne, Anna, Annabeth, and Annie I knew. It wasn't like it was a rare name. Neither was Katherine, Kathy, Kate, or Katie (which may have been one of the reasons I settled on

Kat). What made things harder, though, was that while I stood there trying to figure out which Annie was his Annie, which Annie knew I was a criminal, he had this look on his face like he was trying not to laugh, and the fact that this mischievous look on his face made his dimples plump up and look so stupidly pinchable . . .

"This is Annie," he said, and he took out his wallet and showed me a picture of a golden retriever peering up into the camera with unconditional love. "I tell her everything."

"I hate you."

"What? How could you hate Annie?"

"*You*. I hate *you*."

I punched him in the arm.

He shrugged, slipped his wallet back into his pocket.

"Why did you take my picture?" I asked. "And if you're really not going to show anyone"—I shifted gears—"why did you write that creepy note? Why did you want me to come here?"

"Did you sell the camera?" he asked.

"No. Wait. Why do you think I sold it? Do I look poor?"

He shrugged again.

"I didn't sell it. And I'm not poor. My uncle's a cop."

"I have an uncle who's a cop. Maybe we have the same uncle."

"I doubt it," I said.

Two boys reeking of pot wandered in, saw the room was occupied, and left. Their stench remained.

"I didn't sell it," I repeated. "I took it because I had a very good reason. I took it because I needed it. And I don't have to tell you anything because you said you weren't going to show anyone the photo. You can't blackmail a person without a threat. So maybe you'll never know why I took it. Maybe you don't deserve to know. 'Some answers are beyond our ken.'"

The words left my mouth before I even realized I'd said them, though I instantly realized who'd said them first, who'd said them to me. My cheeks pulsed with embarrassment, and my nerve endings sizzled with shame.

Why did I just say that?

Pedro clearly meant no harm—*probably* meant no harm. Sure, I wasn't ever going to tell him why I had swiped the digital camera, but I didn't have to be a jerk about it.

What was wrong with me? Alik Lisser had infected so much of my life. Had he now infected my soul too?

"I'm sorry," I said, sliding my backpack over my shoulder. "I shouldn't have come here. I'm the one who's the thief and here I am, trying to talk down to you, and all you did was—"

"—take a photograph of a pretty girl without her permission. Hey, facts are facts. You're a thief and I'm . . . What do you call someone who takes photographs of people without their permission? You know, like those losers who follow celebrities around."

"Paparazzi."

"Yes! Thank you! I'm a paparazzi. When really, all I ever wanted to do was show people a little bit of truth. With music, with pictures, whatever. So much of what we see is, like, painted over, you know? Everybody who thinks they know better, the first thing they do is crop out whatever it is they don't want us to see, and it pisses me off."

I didn't think I'd heard the phrase *crop out* before, but I had an idea of what he meant. I definitely knew I agreed with it . . . him . . . Pedro.

Who'd called me *pretty*.

Who'd called *me* pretty.

Me.

I was about to say something, maybe compliment him back or tell him how much of what he said made sense or who-knows-what, but we'll never know who-knows-what because my backpack suddenly turned into a beehive. I swear. One moment, it was a backpack, silent and still, and the next, it was buzzing and shaking with a life of its own. I shoved it off my shoulder, and it crashed to the band room floor and continued to buzz and shake and shake and buzz.

"Got an Energizer Bunny in there?" Pedro asked.

Not that I was aware of. What the heck did I . . . ?

Oh.

I reached into the backpack and fumbled around blindly until my fingers found what I was looking for: the pager. I took it out and pressed a button to quiet its tantrum.

"Are you on call?" Pedro asked.

My face flushed with embarrassment.

"I need to go," I said.

"Clearly," Pedro replied.

I slung my backpack over my shoulder. "You're really not going to tell anyone about the camera?"

"Are you going to return it?"

"Yes."

"I believe you."

And I *was* telling the truth, though for all he knew, I was full of it. He already had (correctly) clocked me as a thief. Was being a liar as well that much of a stretch? Maybe he was the liar. Maybe he didn't believe me and was just saying that.

Or maybe not everyone had the same trust issues I had.

"Before I go," I said, "I just need—"

"You want me to tell you the secret to my little party trick."

"Yes."

He nodded, sat back down on the piano stool. "Bring back the camera and I'll tell you all my secrets, Kat McCann."

He spun around and picked up exactly where he'd left off in "It's Too Late."

His playing was perfect.

I didn't want to leave. Maybe it was the comfort food of the song. Maybe it was . . . something else. But I had to go. I had to call Dev. I had to find out if he had printed the pictures. They were my best (and only) lead in catching the monster who had ruined my life.

Priorities.

Unfortunately: none of the pay phones at school actually worked. A few had gum jammed into their coin slots. A few were missing receivers. One of them was missing the numbers 1, 4, and 9. Was one lone idiot behind all this mischief? Was there a locker somewhere stuffed with Spearmint wrappers and phone receivers and, scattered at the bottom of the locker like metal teeth, the numbers 1, 4, and 9?

Fortunately: I only had to wait a few minutes to catch the bus home. While tucked away in a seat in the very rear of the vehicle, I dipped into one of my weekend grabs from the library, a slim paperback called *The Bride Wore Black*. It was just what I'd wanted. Something dark. A guilty conscience on every page. Heroes pushed to become villains in order to set the world right.

We came to my stop just before I was finished with a chapter. I tucked a mittened finger into the book to save my place and left through the side doors. January winds nipped at my face and nearly launched the novel out of my tenuous grip, so, with a sigh, I tucked *The Bride Wore Black* into my backpack and trudged the rest of the way home with my gaze set on my boring white boots as they splashed through puddles of muddy slush and then up the cracked wooden steps of my row house to the second floor and then down the paper-thin green-brown-carpeted hallway to the paper-thin once-yellow doormat in front of my apartment, where they stomped off whatever mud and slush was still stuck to their rubber soles before I inserted my key into the door's knob (always locked) and, eager to call Dev, quickly stepped into my home.

"There she is," said Alik from the kitchen table. "There's my girl."

24

He was sipping mint tea. I could smell it from twenty-five feet away. That was how close he was. Not an ocean between us, not thousands of miles. Only twenty-five feet.

Could he hear my heart beating from only twenty-five feet away? It was thumping so hard in my chest that I could feel it in my ears. Could he, famously perceptive, tell how on the brink I was to screaming?

My aunt sat beside him. She, too, was sipping tea, a look of carefree bliss in her eyes.

The kitchen table was covered by a large painting and the brown paper wrapping that must have once concealed it but was now torn into strips. Twenty-five feet away, I could see it was my mother's painting, the one that had been in Alik's dining room. All those colorful almost-squares and almost-circles.

"Look at her face!" my aunt said. "I bet I had that same look."

Alik put down his teacup. "I should have called first, *ja*. I do apologize for my rudeness. But there's nothing like popping in on friends—and I do consider us friends."

"Plus, you brought gifts! Kat, look at what he brought all the way from England."

"This painting belongs here more than it belongs there. I learned that. I was merely its caretaker."

My aunt's eyes welled up. "You're such a sweet man. Oh, Kat, don't just stand there! Take off your coat and have some tea. Or would you like a snack? I picked up some of those giant hard pretzels you like."

"She's just overwhelmed. Surprises can do that. Give her a moment."

Alik then raised his teacup in my direction, as if toasting my presence, and took another sip.

Was I overwhelmed? Uh, yes.

But I was also assessing the situation. My life literally depended on it.

1. Why was he here? If it was to kill me and/or my aunt, would he have just shown up in the middle of the day with a painting?
2. Why had he really brought the painting? Was he trying to use it to frame one of us (so to speak) for a murder he was about to commit (or had just committed)?
3. How long ago had he planned this "spontaneous" visit?

You're thinking, *Kat, he repeatedly swore he wasn't going to harm you or your aunt. What were you so worried about?* Oh, aside from the fact that Alik Lisser was a known liar (at least to me) and, oh yeah, *deranged*? There also was the small fact that he was Right There in My Kitchen! Sure, he'd said he was going to keep in touch, but that was last week, and now he was Right There in My Kitchen!

"Why don't we leave now?" Alik said, rising to his full height. "That way you don't have to take off that lovely winter coat."

Leave? With him?

"I told Alik you'd be happy to show him around Boston," my aunt said, "especially since he's going to be here for a while."

Especially since what, now?

"Oh no. It appears we have, in the parlance of journalists, buried the lede. You see, Kat, given the tragedy at home—Cosmo's suicide and all that—I just knew I had to travel. Then I recalled a standing offer made by the lovely gentlemen at Harvard University to guest-lecture in their law school's criminology program of study. That it gave me an opportunity to visit with new friends—well, sometimes the stars align."

He delivered all that while looking me straight in the eye. He delivered all that while the corners of his lips twitched a few seconds into grinning, letting his mask fall a few seconds at a time, just for me.

"What do you say, Kat?" asked my aunt. "Up for giving a tour? I'd join you, but Alik suggested I use this time to find a perfect spot to hang the painting, so . . ."

So that's how I ended up in the vast black leather back seat of Alik's rented Cadillac. He sat up front, of course, beside his driver, whom I was not at all surprised to recognize as Hermann (or to hear *The Threepenny Opera* racketing from the car's surround-sound speakers).

Would you have said no? Would you have come up with an excuse not to breathe the same air as Alik Lisser? The thought did cross my mind. However, another thought crossed out that thought:

This was an opportunity to learn why he was really here.

Not that I expected him to tell me. Or if he *did* tell me, not that I expected it to be the truth.

But I had to take any chance to gain an advantage.

"Where to?" Alik asked me.

"Does it matter?" I replied.

"It does to me. Come on, now. What is your favorite spot in all of New England? Name it and off we'll go. Provided you know how to get there."

"My favorite spot? Like the Spot you assigned me in Dame Carissa's flat?"

"*Nein*, Katie, that was by design. This is simply one friend offering to indulge another. Let's have a little fun together before we have our fun individually."

Yeah. I knew what his *individual fun* entailed. I dug my fingernails into my fancy black leather seat.

"My favorite spot? In all of New England?"

"Or at least within an hour's drive. I do want to get you home by a reasonable hour."

"I'll need a map."

"It's your favorite spot and you need a map to find it?"

"If we're driving there, yeah."

He took a map out of the glove compartment and handed it back to me. It took me a minute to orient myself, and then I told Hermann where to go. As we drove over the Charles River, snowflakes tumbled down on the city like salt from a heavenly shaker.

Alik opened his window, let the flakes land on his palm, and watched them melt. "I forgot how much winters in Boston remind me of winters in Vienna. You would like Vienna, I think, Katie. You see the beauty in the bygone. Vienna is a monument to the bygone. The Holy Roman Empire. Classical music. Oh, the museums! You would love the museums! Everybody loves our museums. The British, for all their virtues, clutter up their museums with pieces stolen from around the world, but Vienna's collections have always been hers. The Athens of the Pre-Modern Age. Someday I'll take you there."

With his window open, I was getting blasted by cold air. I had my coat on, sure, but we were going fast and the temperature couldn't have been more than twenty degrees. This was probably another one of his tests. Get me to ask him to shut the window. Demonstrate he was in control. So I went in a different direction:

"If Vienna was so wonderful, why did you stay in England?"

"There was an exchange between police departments. You know this. Carrie wrote about it in the books."

"I know why you left Vienna originally. But the exchange program was only for six months. Or at least, that's what she wrote in the books. You stayed for thirty years."

"I was injured. It took time to recuperate."

"If you don't want to answer . . . ," I said.

"There was, at the time, a politician in Vienna called Friedrich Peter. A member of the Freedom Party. In this, our Orwellian century, when a group calls itself 'the Freedom Party,' best be on your guard. One of my investigations ran afoul of Herr Peter. I should perhaps mention here that Herr Peter's job before joining the Freedom Party was to volunteer for Hitler's liquidation squad, wandering the countryside of Eastern Europe in search of Gypsies, Communists, and Jews to shoot in the head and bury in mass graves. I stayed in England out of fear for my life."

"Yeah, that's you—always on the right side of history," I replied, rolling my eyes. "What a load of bull."

He angled around in his seat to face me. "Listen to me when I tell you this: I'm not going to lie to you—not now, not ever. Our relationship will not work unless everything I tell you is true and that you believe everything I tell you is true. This is fundamental. So believe me, please, when I tell you this as well: it's going to happen soon. It took me some months to design, but I'm very pleased with the result."

"And by 'design,' you mean . . . ?"

"Ja."

"And by 'it,' you mean . . . ?"

"Do you really need me to say the words?"

"Well, it's just that I noticed we're not alone. We're not alone, are we, Hermann?"

"Alone?" our chauffeur replied. "I don't think, no."

"Oh, Hermann knows all about my extracurricular activities. Don't you, Hermann? See, he and I have known each other longer than some countries have been in existence. He knows all my secrets and I know his—although, to be fair, he has no secrets. So, yes, very soon from now, I am going to snuff the life out of a human being and someone else is going to take the fall. Is that explicit enough for you, child?"

Going by his reflection in the rearview mirror, Hermann's expression remained as stoic as always, though the top third of his face was hidden behind those chunky sunglasses. Nothing that Alik had just revealed shocked him at all.

"And it's going to happen here?" I asked. "In America?"

"Oh, *ja*. It's going to happen here in Boston. Well, *there*. It seems we've left the city limits. Might I ask our destination?"

"It's a surprise," I replied. "So I can see the look on your face."

He turned away, unsatisfied, which left me time to ponder the ramifications of what he had said. Because I was his "audience," he had let me know that he had chosen his next victim. He had also let me know that it had taken him months to design the murder.

This was what I was bumping up against.

If it had taken him months to design this murder, and I was to take him at his earlier word that he murdered only when he had a confidante he could brag to, then did that mean all this had begun back in October? And if that was the case, did that mean the victim was someone he had encountered during his visit?

Assume nothing, sure, but . . . maybe?

After thirty minutes, Alik again asked me to tell him our destination. The snow hadn't grown into a blizzard, but it had not stopped at all, and, he added, Hermann was not used to driving in "this level of weather." Plus, he wasn't a fan of the tolls on the Mass Pike. I took another look at the map and estimated that we were twenty miles from where we were headed, adding for a bit of light humor that "No one was a fan of the tolls."

I figured, when in a car with a madman, always good to add a bit of light humor.

Eventually, we left the highway and took a state road the rest of the way. Soon we were passing old signs for the army base that was nearby. I had learned all about the army base in my social studies class on Massachusetts history, how it had recently been named as one of the eighty most polluted sites in the country. Go, Massachusetts.

Finally, the signs for our destination began to appear.

"OK," said Alik to Hermann. "We can turn around now."

"But we're so close," I replied.

"Your favorite spot in New England is Fort Devens Federal Prison?"

"It will be," I told him. "Soon."

The drive back, none of us said a word.

25

As soon as I got home, I made a beeline straight for my bedroom and dialed the number on Dev's pager. It had been hours since he'd buzzed me. What were the odds that he was even still—

He picked up on the second ring.

"Where have you been?" he asked.

"First of all, hello. Hi. I'm fine. How are you, Dev?"

Not that I should have expected anything else. Dev was Dev.

"Sorry. Yeah. Sorry. It's just . . . do you know who's in these f'ing pictures?"

"Gosh, I have no idea," I replied. "I only took them."

"Kat . . ."

No, he was right. I couldn't imagine what was going through his head. He had just learned I'd been telling the truth and spent my Christmas break with his hero. He probably had a million questions. Join the club, pal.

"Are you sitting down?" I asked. "This might take a while."

"I'm always sitting down. What the heck?"

So I told him what the heck. I told him everything. If he was going to help me (and let's be real, I needed all the help I could get), he had to hear the whole story. My left ear ached from having it against the phone for so long. I switched to my right ear and waited for him to say something. Anything. After hearing all that, what did he think? Could he help me? Maybe there was a way he could help me that I could never have even conceived of. Compared to him, I was a tech newbie, and the internet knew everything.

Finally, he spoke:

"I don't believe you."

This wasn't a surprise. I mean, put yourself in his shoes. Would you have an easy time believing any of this? Would anyone? Convincing people was always going to be one of my biggest hurdles here.

"I know it's a lot. I couldn't believe it at first either. It's bonkers. It's like learning Santa Claus is actually Satan. It's very hard to accept."

"It's impossible to accept. And your analogy is totally f'ing wrong because eventually, sure, we learn Santa Claus isn't Santa Claus, but not that he's Satan. And neither is Adrian Lescher."

Oh, Dev. Why could nothing ever be simple with you?

I wrapped my phone cord around my hand like brass knuckles. "OK, sure, yeah, though he's not Adrian Lescher either. Adrian Lescher is as make believe as Santa Claus. And possibly Satan. Alik Lisser, though, is real, and he really did all the things I just said. All of it."

"You have no evidence."

"That's why . . . ugh . . . that's why I need your help!"

"To turn a legend, a *real* legend, into . . . what . . . into f'ing Ted Bundy? Are you crazy?"

"Have you even looked at the photographs?"

"Yes, Kat! I've looked at the photographs! And you know what I see? I see a . . . I see a great man opening his home to a . . . to an ungrateful brat! He chose *you*, and this is how you f'ing repay him? If he invited me to his home, you know what I would've done? I would've f'ing said thank you! Did you even say thank you?"

I shut my eyes. How could I convince him? How?

"I get that you had a bad childhood, Kat. And I'm sorry. And maybe this is . . . I don't know . . . transference or something? I'd have to check my notes from Intro to Psych. Which reminds me, you need to see a therapist. Someone who specializes in . . . delusions . . . or whatever."

"I'm not delusional," I said.

"Do you have any proof? That videotape you mentioned. Do you have the videotape?"

"He locked it up."

"How f'ing convenient."

"There has to be something in those pictures! You can blow them up, can't you? We'll examine them inch by inch and we'll find something. We have to find something. Because he's going to do it again. Soon, he said. He's been planning it since October, so it might be someone who was at the lecture. For all I know, it's you. He's going to do it again, and I don't know how else to stop him. Please, Dev. Help me stop him."

"I will help you," replied Dev.

"Really?" My eyes opened. Hope bloomed in my heart like a flower. "You promise?"

"Yes. I will. After we're done talking. I'm going to go straight to my psych professor, and we're going to find you a—"

I hung up.

Damn it, damn it, damn it.

I'd been a fool to expect anything else from Dev. I could see that now. It wasn't Dev's fault. OK, maybe it *was* Dev's fault, but it wasn't *only* Dev's fault. This was a heck of a favor to ask, and it involved a leap of faith so big that . . .

Well, I'd be lucky if I could find anyone to help me.

I was reminded again of *The Bride Wore Black* and all these noir stories I'd turned to since learning the truth about Alik Lisser. In the end, the hero was always alone.

In the end, aren't we all?

The apartment front door opened. Day #7 of my uncle skipping the bar and heading straight home, so not everything in my life sucked. I waited a minute for Dev to call back and apologize (as if) and then headed out to join my family for dinner.

My aunt had hung the painting in really the only place it could go: on the wall above the TV. She and my uncle were standing there now, staring at it.

"—and then Mr. Lisser left, and Kat gave him a little tour of the city. Oh, here she is."

"A tour of the city, huh?" my uncle asked. "You show him the harbor where we tossed all his fancy tea?"

My aunt piped up: "Actually, he's Austrian."

"I thought you said he was British."

There was an edge to my uncle's voice that all three of us recognized. Time to mediate before things got out of hand.

"He's both," I said. "Born in Vienna but moved to London."

My uncle nodded, clearly not caring. "I don't suppose Mr. European left you a padlock for the door, did he? 'Cause soon as word gets out we got this thing on display, every two-bit thief with a crowbar and a dream is gonna want to take it and sell it. Though none of that matters if you didn't go and blab about it up and down the street, but I already know you did, because what's-his-name already stopped me on my way home to congratulate me on my stroke of good luck! And I had to pretend I knew what he was talking about so I didn't look like an asshole who doesn't know what goes on in his own home."

"I only told Violet down in 1B. I tell Violet everything. You know that."

"And Violet tells the world! *You* know *that*!"

And it's my sister's painting . . . I wanted my aunt to say.

And I loved her and I miss her and I'm proud to have it on my wall . . . I longed for her to say.

But of course she said none of that. I could as much wish for her to be different as I could for my uncle, who, I guess, didn't need to be drunk to be a dick. I could as much wish for Dev to be different or Alik Lisser or me. I retreated to my bedroom, shut the door, and took out *The Bride Wore Black* to lose myself in, at least until the yelling stopped.

After I finished the book, I set it aside and reached for my to-be-read pile. By then, the yelling had stopped . . . though not before the other familiar sounds joined it: the clatter of dishes breaking and the smack of my uncle's hands on my aunt's flesh and the thump of my aunt hitting the carpet. Let Pedro play that tune. I knew it well. Eventually, the new book became too blurry to read, so I put it back on top of the pile and wiped my forearm across my wet eyes and willed myself to sleep.

26

The next morning was so bright I had to hide my head under my blankets and let my eyes adjust before peeking out again. A metric ton of snow had been dumped overnight on top of the city, like someone had emptied mashed potatoes eighteen inches deep over every sidewalk, streetlamp, and sewer grate. The cars parallel parked up and down the street weren't cars anymore but hills of mashed potatoes, and when you added the sunshine reflecting off all those miles . . . well, it's no wonder my poor eyeballs hurt just looking at it.

Maybe because I'd spent almost half my life in Southern California, but I've never, ever gotten used to snow. It's so weird. One moment, everything's the way you remember it, and a few hours later, your neighborhood's transformed into Pluto? How are we OK with that?

I was pretty sure school would be canceled, but I checked with my aunt to make sure. As always, on mornings like this, she was glued to Channel 5 on the TV to watch all the closings scroll across the bottom while Joan Lunden and Charlie Gibson did their gab thing with the author of a book I'd never heard of called *The Horse Whisperer*. The author was British, which reminded me of Alik Lisser, which turned off whatever appetite for breakfast might've been brewing in my belly.

My uncle was nowhere to be found, but I knew where he'd gone. On mornings like this, when ole Beantown became more snow than city, my uncle and, like, the entire police department and fire department and whatever all volunteered to clean up the mess. The way my uncle told it, the folks who showed up first got to man the snowplows, which was the prime gig because the snowplows were heated on the inside, and everyone else got stuck with salting or shoveling. Also, the cops were in a competition with the firemen to see who could clean the most streets and the winner . . . well, my uncle never was clear on what the winner got, which probably meant it involved strippers or something.

My uncle may have been gone, but his handiwork remained. The whole left side of my aunt's face had been sculpted into an overcooked eggplant. Her eyelid drooped, her cheek sagged, and her lower lip had a nasty vertical scab where she must have split it.

I just leaned in and hugged her.

She did her best to hug me back.

You have questions, I can tell. You want to know if that was the worst my uncle had ever laid out. Short answer: no. Longer answer: It's like my social studies teacher one day getting us to compare Hitler and Stalin to determine who was worse. At a certain point, does it really matter anymore? It *was* the worst my uncle had ever laid out that was *visible*. He normally was much more careful in his violence. Maybe her happiness post-vacation had pushed him past the brink. Maybe he simply couldn't tolerate the fact that she was smiling, so he corrected it.

But enough about that. You want to know why I let it happen.

OK.

First off, and I mean this with all due respect: fuck you.

Second off: What exactly was I supposed to do? I was five foot nothing. I was about eye level with his lungs. And if you couldn't tell from the way he tossed me and my aunt around, the man was strong. One time I did threaten him. I rushed at him with a fork. And that ended up with *me* knocked against a wall. I was seven.

So, yeah, sure, I did let it happen. I let him hurt my aunt. And me. For years.

Just like Boston let a metric ton of snowflakes stomp it down. As it had. For years.

What's your point?

"Oh, look, Kat. Good news. School's canceled."

Part of me wanted to ride that good news way back to my bed and catch a few more hours of sleep. But I didn't. I stayed on the little couch with my aunt. Joan and Charlie talked with a baseball expert about the (shocking!) announcement that there would be no new inductees that year into the Hall of Fame.

Tell me about it.

This segued into a segment on the blizzard, which had buried not just New England but whole swaths of the East Coast. Later, they learned from a marbled-mouthed Belgian chef how to make the perfect omelet.

After the show was over, my aunt shuffled into the kitchen to refill her coffee. She asked me if I wanted anything to eat. I said no, thanks and went online. I expected to encounter a bustling room due to the blizzard, but it was near empty. Then again, not everyone lived on the East Coast. Some of the semi-regulars were even international, and my favorite of them was one of the few names on the list of active users.

KMcCann14: Good morning from the cold and snowy US!
Kiwi_woolgatherer: Welcome to winter wonderland, Alice.

I smiled, remembering that the last time we chatted, he had also referenced *Alice's Adventures in Wonderland.* When your world is in upheaval, a little consistency is comforting.

KMcCann14: It's summer right now in NZ, isn't it?
Kiwi_woolgatherer: All day every day. December to March.
KMcCann14: That's so crazy.
Kiwi_woolgatherer: To think what's normal for one person is normal for every person, that's crazy.

He had a point . . . though, I mean, some things were universal. Everybody breathed. Everybody ate (even if the food was different). Everybody used the bathroom (even if the toilets were different). Everybody communicated (even if the language was different).

Everybody loved. Everybody hurt.

Everybody knew right from wrong.

Was my uncle feeling guilty about what he'd done? Would he show up at 2:00 a.m. blitzed out of his mind and slurring his words? I used to think his drinking made him violent, but he was stone sober last night. Now I wondered if he drank to shut up his conscience.

And then there was Alik Lisser, who had no conscience whatsoever, but he did have a compulsion, and he was going to act on that compulsion soon. And I still had time to stop him. Somehow.

So I said my goodbyes, logged off, and paged Dev.

I didn't expect him to get back to me right away. Heck, part of me didn't expect him to get back to me at all (probably the same childish part of me that wanted to ditch my aunt and nap). But a few minutes later, what do you know.

"Hey," he said. "Shouldn't you be in class?"

"Have you not looked outside?"

"I'm looking outside right now, actually. Watching my roommate use a cafeteria tray as a sled . . . and he just slid into a car. Uh-oh, it looks like . . . No, he's fine. He's laughing. Everyone's laughing."

"You don't sound like you're laughing, Dev."

"Yeah, well."

I heard a rumble outside and went to the window. Sure enough, a plow had turned down my street and begun to do its thing. Was that my uncle behind the wheel, sipping cheap coffee from his thermos as he shoved all this useless beauty into little hills?

"So what's up?" Dev asked.

"That depends. Have you changed your mind?"

"Maybe give me whatever you've been smoking, and we'll see. Otherwise, no."

I wasn't surprised. But I wasn't finished.

"Can I at least have the pictures from my camera?"

"Oh, I deleted the pictures from the camera."

I nearly dropped the receiver. "What?"

"Well, yeah. You had no right to take them in the first place. You invaded his privacy. You know that, don't you?"

"Are you kidding me right now?" I wanted to kill him. I wanted to wrap my hands around his thick neck and try to squeeze it. "Those pictures are the only evidence I've got!"

"Those pictures are evidence that my man has an f'ing awesome basement. And that your aunt is really into touristy crap."

"You really deleted the pictures from my camera . . . ?"

"I really deleted the pictures from the camera. Plus—and you didn't mention this part—it's not really your camera. It has an f'ing sticker on it and everything. *Property of Boston Public Schools*."

I wanted to club him on the head with a large book, like a dictionary or *Moby-Dick*. He didn't believe me. He'd deleted the pictures. And he was acting so *smug* about it, the jerk-off.

"Can I at least have the camera back?" I asked through gritted teeth.

Which was how we ended up meeting a few hours later. I wasn't about to let Dev see where I actually lived, and I figured with the weather and all that, our usual rendezvous spot would be closed, so our fallback choice was the fallback choice for every New Englander: Dunkin' Donuts. It so happened there was one a few blocks from my apartment, though there was a Dunkin' Donuts a few blocks from everyone's apartment.

He showed up wearing one of those ridiculous wool hats with the pouf on top, as if the pouf made it warmer or fashionable or I don't even know what. He also showed up with a Game Boy, a tattered paperback of Dame Carissa's novel *Pascal's Lost Wager*, and, at the bottom of his book bag, the digital camera.

"Thank you," I said.

He shrugged. "Sorry I couldn't help you."

"Listen . . . I know you think I'm delusional . . . and that's fine . . . I mean, no, it sucks, but anyway, just . . . watch your back. Especially if Alik Lisser, you know, shows up unannounced at your door."

"If Alik Lisser shows up at my door—"

"Dev, I'm serious. He's back in town. He's teaching at Harvard. But that's just an excuse for him to—"

"Right."

I wasn't going to convince him. I could see it in his eyes. The pity.

"Just promise me you'll be careful. Don't do anything stupid."

"He'll have to be careful of me," Dev replied. "Did I tell you I came in second in a college invitational in my weight class? I'm a wrestling beast."

"Yeah, you mentioned it."

"Kat . . . I think we should probably break up. You're clearly going through a lot, and I just got invited to pledge this secret society at MIT . . ."

I blinked.

Break up?

When were we together? I didn't know whether to laugh . . . or really, really laugh . . .

But I bit the inside of my cheek. No need to be cruel. Especially since, from the way he was starting to stammer, this wasn't exactly easy for him.

And *I* was supposed to be the deluded one? Oh, Dev.

"I still think you're great, Kat. And you'll find someone . . . closer to your own age . . ."

"Mm-hmm."

"I'd still like to be friends. Is that . . . something you'd want?"

I nodded.

We hugged. What else was there to say?

Then, on his way out, Dev stopped, reached into the outside pocket of his book bag, and took something out—something square and flat . . .

"I deleted the pics from the camera," he said, "but first, I burned them to a CD."

"Really?"

He shrugged, handed me the CD-ROM and said, "Don't do anything f'ing stupid."

I told him I wouldn't. And I meant it.

How naive I was. How naive we both were.

27

School was open the next day, and I took an early bus so I could sneak the camera back into the darkroom. I knew a bunch of the sports teams practiced before classes began, so I assumed the school doors would be open, and they were. The hallway lights were on, but the hallways themselves were eerily empty. Mr. Handy's classroom didn't even have its lights on, which made it eerier, especially with all those lab tables just sitting there in the darkness.

Or maybe I was still weirded out by spending most of yesterday afternoon and evening poring over every pixel of every picture either I or my aunt had taken at the cottage. Most of the pictures dated from before Big Ben rang in the New Year and the whole Alik-murdering-one-of-his-closest-friends-right-in-the-middle-of-his-party thing. I stared for hours at those pictures, at:

- The cottage's guest bedrooms.

And let's not forget my bed, with the human heads painted on the headboard and the human feet painted on the footboard? Like the bed was one of those medieval torture devices stretching a person apart? How had that not been a tip-off . . . ?

- The great room.

With its glass chandelier up above and its Turkish rug down below and everything else being walls and walls and walls of books. I had thought I'd discovered paradise. I tried to zoom in on the books for maybe a clue, but the image quality wasn't good enough or the books' spines were too faded with age—and besides, even if I *was* able to correlate a bunch of books to one of the murders, who was to say that he hadn't acquired the books *after* the murder to help him solve it rather than *before* the murder to help him commit it? The great room also had that fat oak desk, with its stacks of letters (zooming in on them just made them blurrier) and its locked drawers.

- The basement.

Below, in his lair . . . That was where I spent most of my time, well into the night. My aunt didn't say anything. She probably assumed I was in the chat room. She trusted me, which was nice, but she also trusted Alik, so.

And speaking of nice, it was nice that Dev had burned all the pictures to a CD, right? Yeah, he was still an arrogant tool, but he wasn't all bad, and he'd better take my advice and be careful. I actually wondered if Dev really was a possible target . . . I mean, if Alik Lisser really wanted to have this gross symbiotic relationship with me, he probably wouldn't start it off by killing someone he knew I cared about. Then again, maybe that's exactly what he wanted me to think, which was why he *was* going to target Dev . . .

Ugh.

All this fueled me well into the night as I pored over those digital pictures, but eventually, my eyes started to burn and my brain began to throb, and I had to take a nap before my eyes and brain liquefied. At the very least, I decided to check one item off my list.

Which was how I ended up at school shortly after the crack of dawn with the camera in my bag, braving the long shadows of Mr. Handy's lab tables so I could reach the door to the darkroom.

And if the door was locked? Well, then, I'd have to try again later in the day. Or after school.

I may not have been any closer to stopping Alik Lisser, but I was going to accomplish something, damn it.

Good news: the door was unlocked.

Less-than-good news:

"Hey, can't you read?" the dude inside the darkroom cried out. "There's someone in here!"

The last time I was in the darkroom, it was indeed dark, and I'd had to use a flashlight I'd borrowed from home to find the digital camera. This time, though, the darkroom was the set of a horror movie. Everything was bathed in a red glow and reeked so pungently that I actually winced. Maybe this was why I didn't recognize Pedro at first, even though he was standing, like, four feet in front of me, holding a glossy sheet of paper with a pair of tongs over a tray of—I'd have to guess from the smell—some foul combination of rye and battery acid.

"What the heck are you making in here? Moonshine?"

Pedro placed the glossy paper in a pan and replied, "That's right. You caught me. I'm a bootlegger. This is my speakeasy."

Now that I'd had a minute to process the scene, it all made more sense (darkroom, glossy paper, chemicals), and I felt foolish. Again. And Pedro was grinning at my foolishness. Again.

"What can I do for you, Kat?"

"Actually, I'm . . . Wait, why are you here so early?"

"It's the only time I know I'll be left alone. I like to moonshine in private."

"Ha ha. What are those photographs of? Other girls you like to stalk?"

"I don't stalk," said Pedro, offended. "I observe. If I see something interesting, I'll take a picture of it."

"You forgot the part about leaving mysterious notes in girls' lockers."

"One note in one locker. And isn't it just like a criminal to assume everyone else is up to no good?"

His angelic grin looked so goofy in that sinister red light, and it wasn't helped by the fact that he had his long hair bound back in a cute ponytail that I really, really wanted to tug on. But I'd show him. I opened my bag and took out the digital camera and placed it right on the table next to one of those shallow bins of chemicals.

"What do you have to say now, Your Honor?" I asked.

"Uh . . . thank you?"

"I'm not a criminal anymore. Plus, now you owe me a secret."

Pedro chuckled. "I've finally figured you out. You're a cookie-jar kid. My older brother was a cookie-jar kid, too, and he wasn't all bad, so it's OK. Me, I'm a frying-pan kid."

He then went silent, baiting me to ask me what a cookie-jar kid or what a frying-pan kid was.

Well, I wasn't going to fall for it. I wasn't going to give him the satisfaction.

Nope.

I was better than that.

I . . .

"What's the difference between a cookie-jar kid and a frying-pan kid?"

Apparently, he had soaked the glossy paper enough in its shallow bin, because he grabbed the tongs and airlifted the paper to another shallow bin, the last in a row of three. It reminded me of my aunt prepping chicken in egg, then flour, then basil, then breadcrumbs, before finally sliding it into the frying pan . . . Did Pedro's analogy have something to do with fried chicken?

"A frying-pan kid," he said, shifting the paper in the bin, "knows dinner is being cooked. Like, he can smell the pork, and he can hear the oil frying, and he's fine with that. He doesn't need to peek over the stove to see what's inside the frying pan and risk getting some oil splashing up into his eye. He'll help if his grandfather asks him to help, but other than that, he lets things take care of themselves."

"And a cookie-jar kid?"

"A cookie-jar kid, like you—like my older brother, Stevie—they're not thinking about the frying pan at all. They're thinking about the cookie jar. Because that's where the butter cookies are. And they know that because they stole two earlier in the day when no one was looking, but then they felt bad that they stole four and there's only so many cookies in the cookie jar, so they put one back. They don't put *all* of them back . . . but they're so proud of themselves anyway because they got away with stealing some dessert before dinner *and* because they're such a good person for not stealing even more dessert. Except then it's dinnertime, and they don't finish whatever their grandfather worked hard to make because they're not that hungry and, as punishment, their grandfather tells them they can't have any dessert, and that night they brag to their younger brother, because they share a room, that the joke's on the old man—except is it? Because later that night, Stevie can't sleep because he's hungry again, and I sleep like a baby because I got a belly full of pork and three butter cookies."

I wasn't quite sure what the point of all that was, but I had a feeling I was being judged, and I didn't like it, so I crossed my arms and asked him, "Is that supposed to be a lesson?"

"No. Just a story. You're always reading books. Can't you tell? Though how you can read all those books and not read a simple sign on a door that says *Knock Before You Enter*, but what can I expect? You're a cookie-jar kid. Why do you read all those books, anyway?"

"Why do I read books? What kind of dumb question is that? And don't think I haven't forgotten that you promised you'd tell me how you knew about that Carole King song!"

"And you haven't answered my question. Is it a hard question?"

"Are you kidding? It's the easiest question in the world! Why do I read? I read because books take me places I can't go myself. I read because books make me smarter. I learn about the world. I read because, yeah, I *want* to find out what's in the frying pan. I read because life is full of questions and books are full of answers, and which would you rather have, huh? I'm not saying the answers are always easy. That's why I like mysteries. Because you have to work. You have to think. But that just makes it all the better when you get it right."

I felt great. I felt vindicated. I didn't even mind that awful stench anymore.

Pedro seemed impressed, too, nodding in agreement. Then he fished the glossy paper out of its bin and hung it on a clothesline and pointed at the image. I had to stand beside him to take a closer look. Our shoulders were inches apart. The picture (which glowed red, like everything else) had been taken from the top of a stairwell during the break between classes, so it showed a crowd of teens rushing up, rushing down, rushing past each other, none looking up, most looking forward, some looking down.

"Every person in this photo is thinking something," he said, "and, I mean, we can guess what it is, right, but we'll never know. We can't ever know. Which means the answer can be whatever we want it to be."

"That's . . . not how anything works . . . at all."

"Kat, did I ever ask you why you stole the camera?"

Didn't he? He must have.

Except the more I thought about it . . .

"Here's a better question," he said softly. His face hovered near mine, so close I could trace the grooves in his lips. "Weren't you happier when you thought Santa Claus was real? Wasn't it cooler when you believed your dad really was making pennies come out of your ear?"

"I . . ."

Knock, knock, knock.

Damn it.

Pedro took a step back from me and said, "Come in."

Two boys he clearly knew strode in. One of them was toting one of those light-bulb-in-a-tin-hat things that the professionals used for our yearbook photos, and the other had a small camera dangling from his neck like a cross. They immediately engaged Pedro in some discussion about pictures for a swim meet, and the small room instantly became tiny, so I quickly, quietly slid away.

I didn't look back to see if Pedro watched me go. I'm not a complete loser.

Because, I mean, what was it with this guy? Was he real? He'd probably say that he wasn't real if I wanted to believe he wasn't real or some crap like that. And why was it that, after sidling out of the darkroom, I had some of my lovely anxiety symptoms (shortness of breath, tingling of extremities) but it didn't feel foreboding or bad . . .

Ah, well. At least I'd managed to accomplish something. Digital camera returned.

Least important item crossed off the list.

I had some time, so I tucked myself away in a corner of the library and dove into a book called *After Dark, My Sweet*. I mean, with a title like that! I liked the way it was written. Short, quick sentences. Very different from what I was used to. And even meaner than *The Bride Wore Black*, although I was beginning to get concerned that there wasn't really a mystery in this one. Just bad people doing bad things. As I made my way to homeroom, crowding down the stairwell, what I was thinking, Pedro, was whether to continue reading the book, because if I wanted to think about bad people doing bad things, well, real life had been more than generous there.

I took my seat in the back row and became invisible and listened to the morning announcements and zoned out a bit, so I didn't notice Miss Taggart, the nose-pierced, purple-haired lady who manned the front desk, standing in the doorway of the classroom, and I sure didn't hear her call my name, at least not the first time.

But everyone else did and had and were staring at me . . . and that, I *did* notice . . . and then I put two and two together when I noticed Miss Taggart and she called my name *again*, and I grabbed my stuff and joined her in the hall.

"What's going on?" I asked her.

"Oh, I'm so sorry, hon. It's bad news. There's been a death in the family. Your uncle Alik is here to take you home."

28

I walked to the front office.

I know I did, because a few minutes later, we were at the front office. I must have walked. I can't fly. I can't teleport. So I must have walked there.

I just have no memory of it.

I get that it's a coping mechanism. It's fight or flight, minus the fight. I just wish I had some control of it, you know? Like: skeevy dude on the train? Turn off the tape recorder. Uncle gets that angry look in his eyes? Fast-forward to the next scene, please.

Though then there's the problem of what if something important happens during my time-out? Like, it would have been nice to have remembered that it was *Alik friggin' Lisser* who had killed my mom. It would have saved me ten years of misdirected adoration *and* it would have saved my dad from prison and an early grave and—

OK.

Enough.

(I'm sorry. Like I said, I can't control it.)

I arrived at the front office. Alik was there. So very tall and thin. Leaning on his cane. Face all somber. If I'd had an axe, I'd have taken it to him then and there. I'd have chopped him down like the fairy-tale giant he was, and he would bleed half-melted ice and the police wouldn't be able to arrest me then, not when they saw what the monster had inside him.

"Hello, dear," he said, and outstretched his long, thin arms to embrace me.

We walked to his car. It was parked out front. Hermann held the doors open for us. I tucked myself into the back seat. Alik joined me there. Hermann shut the door on the empty passenger seat and walked around to his own. The engine was already running. The usual music was playing at its usual volume.

Alik asked Hermann to turn it off.

Hermann, sunglasses on as always, glanced at the rearview to make certain, then turned the dial until it clicked off and drove in silence from the high school's roundabout to the modest traffic on the main road.

Alik rested his left hand on top of my right hand, covering it completely.

"My clever girl," he said. "Indulge me, if you would, and tell me, please, did I choose the lady or the tiger? The housewife or the copper? Puzzle it out. I love to hear you think, *ja*."

That snapped me out of my stupor.

I recoiled my hand from beneath his and glared at him with the fury of a thousand suns. This was all just another game for him.

"Come on now," he said. "Guess right and you'll get a present."

I guess it was to my credit as, you know, an actual human being, that I could still be surprised by him, though if I had any chance of stopping him, he had to be the one who was surprised. I'd play his game, but just as he was taking notes on what I had to say, I'd do the same.

As to my grief . . . now that my state of shock had passed, I could feel it swelling inside me like a black balloon. Pressing against my organs. Filling me up to bursting. I had to push it down. I couldn't show weakness. Weakness was for later. Now was for the fight.

"You know my aunt better than my uncle," I said, "so it stands to reason you'd have a better idea of how to kill her than him."

"It's hard to argue with that logic. The more time you spend with a person, the more time you have to learn their vulnerabilities."

"And you were at the apartment just the other day to drop off the painting. Except dropping off the painting was the fake-out. You really were there to get a look at the place."

"Good," he said. "Go on."

If he'd killed my aunt . . . God, what a tragic life the woman had lived. My mother had died, sure, but I'd only known her for six years. She had been my aunt's younger sister for over twenty years. And then to have been shackled to my uncle for however long they were married. Every day on dismal repeat. The trip to England had been the best week she'd experienced in *decades*. And then the painting. And then the worst beating of her life. And then . . .

No. Stop. Keep your head in the game. Judging from the shops passing by, we were halfway home.

I continued:

"But none of that is *proof* you killed my aunt. It's just conjecture and assumptions, and we assume nothing. As far as I know, you've never even met my uncle. Just spoke with him on the phone. Maybe that was by design. What better way to remove yourself from the list of suspects if you've never actually met the victim? Like in Dame Carissa's short story 'A Hanging in Jerusalem.' The killer turned out to be a jilted lover that nobody even knew existed because they'd kept the affair so secret. Except, I guess, the killer was actually you."

"Nein," replied Alik, "that was one of the genuine cases. Some of them were actual crimes I solved, Katie. All habits aside, I really am an exceptional detective. And you're right. I have never been in the same room as your uncle. Did that change today? And if so, why today? And why him? You're running out of time if you want to earn your present."

"I thought 'why' was the least important question for a detective to answer."

"You don't know the 'who.' You can only guess based on conjecture and assumption. It would be nigh impossible for you to figure out the 'how' and 'where' without visiting the scene of the crime. 'Why' is the only question you have any chance of getting right. Why today, *ja*? Why him or why her? Work it out, clever girl. I have faith in you."

If it was my uncle who was dead . . . well, would that have been so bad? I mean, really? The man was a horror show. He brought nothing but pain into our home. My aunt would grieve, possibly, I suppose, but then a month would go by without having to get out the first aid kit, then three months, and then . . .

If one of them was dead, I hoped it was my uncle. Of course I did. I never would say those words out loud, but come on. And did that make me an awful person, feeling relieved that a relative of mine had been murdered? Hell, I apparently was already a cookie-jar kid. Why not add another demerit to my permanent record?

"You've given me next to nothing to go on," I told Alik.

"You're disappointing me, Katie. Why today? Why him or her?"

What was the date? January 10, 1996. Wednesday. Alik celebrated his birthday on July 7 and Dame Carissa celebrated hers on September 1, and neither my aunt nor my uncle celebrated their birthdays in January. What else happened on January 10? Ugh, thc ghosts of history quizzes had come to haunt me.

Did somebody famous die on this day? That was a likelier reason. Except, for as encyclopedic as my knowledge of the novels and stories was, it did not include specific dates. I mean, come on. Was it a holiday? Maybe a Viennese—

The car came to a stop.

"Sorry," said Alik. "We're here. Time's up."

We were double-parked beside a police cruiser . . . which was a bold choice. Hermann remained behind while Alik and I made our way to the front door. Once inside, we stopped at the foot of the stairs. We had two flights to climb and Alik had his limp, so I assumed that was why he had paused. I had paused because the black balloon had begun to expand again, and this time, I didn't think I could keep it in. This time, it was going to push out all my hot tears and howling anguish in the presence of Alik Lisser and allow him to bask in the satisfaction that he was the cause of it all.

"Did I ever tell you about my father?" Alik asked me. "I have, haven't I? *Ja.* His cinnamon cure for my fear of the dark. He also was fond of using his belt for lashing out discipline. Discipline was very important to him. He was, after all, a violinist, and a well-disciplined violinist could always find work in the City of Music. Mother died of polio in 1925. Her small photograph was fastened to the back side of our front door, so she was always the last thing one saw before leaving. Note that you'll find none of this in 'A Hanging in Jerusalem' or *Double Frame* or any of Carrie's stories. I forbade her use of my family biography."

We stopped halfway up the first run of steps. He let out a long breath. He seemed tired.

We in the Dame Carissa Fan Club were well aware of our author's evasiveness regarding Adrian Lescher's childhood. We all had theories as to what Young Adrian had been like. A few of us in the chat room had even had a contest to see who could create the best Young Adrian fan fiction, featuring the boy genius solving crimes at his grammar school.

Alik coughed in his fist. It seemed genuine. He sat on the step.

"Some hobbies take a toll," he said.

"Is that what this is? A hobby?"

"The only profit I gain from it is personal satisfaction. Is that not the very definition of a hobby? I can even tell you its origin. *Ja*, you'll like this. I was six years old. Quite an age for the two of us, isn't it? I, like you, was clever and curious. I endeavored to explore my little world and understand its design. I took apart the family radio and put it back together. I unscrewed a light bulb from a lamp, shattered the light bulb, and then spent the entirety of a day studying the filament, the contact wire, the insulator. I didn't explore blindly. My family had a full edition of the *Meyers Lexikon*—the preeminent German-language encyclopedia of its day—and I had an apprentice with whom I could discuss my findings. Even then, I needed an audience. In this case, at that age, my apprentice was my younger brother."

"You had a younger brother?"

"Don't look so surprised," Alik said. "Many people do."

I'd just never imagined Adrian Lescher (never mind Alik Lisser) having siblings. For one, Dame Carissa had never mentioned it (although now I understood why). But also, the idea of a monster having a younger brother seemed so . . . wrong.

Then again, I didn't have any brothers. Or sisters. Maybe one day I would have.

But Alik had put a stop to that, hadn't he?

"Why are you telling me about this?" I asked.

"By which you mean, what is my ulterior motive? Listen. And learn. I listened and learned, and soon my curiosity grew beyond the confines of my flat. I needed more answers. As fate would have it, it was about that time that my father brought home a parakeet, cage and all. It was a gift in lieu of payment, he said. He called the parakeet Wolfgang, and his warm affection for it was obvious—if only in contrast to the lack of affection he showed us—and he taught me and my younger brother how to feed it, refill its water basin, how to clean its cage. I assume you know where this is going now."

Yes. I did.

"Know this: when it came time to explore Wolfgang and understand its design, I did so alone. I did not include my apprentice."

"How nice of you."

"However—again, as fate would have it—my father came home before I'd had a chance to dispose of the detritus of my experiment, and I admit that in that moment, I acted a coward. I hid the remains in a shoebox and hid the shoebox underneath my younger brother's bed."

"Wow," I said, "your first frame job."

"It was an act in the spur of the moment. Had I a time machine, I would travel back to that day and that moment and force myself to make a different choice. It is the single regret of my life."

"What happened to your little brother?"

Alik shrugged. "My father asked us what had happened to Wolfgang. I said I didn't know. My brother, who had been in the den the whole time, listening to a Kurt Weill piece on the radio, said he didn't know. So my father searched the flat and found the shoebox and then went after my brother with a belt, all the while yelling, 'Why? Why?' and all the while my brother cried, 'I didn't do it, I didn't do it,' and on and on until eventually my brother stopped saying anything at all. You see, my father, in the carelessness of his fury, had struck my brother several times in the head with the metal buckle, caving in a small portion of his parietal bone. The damage to his brain was permanent. He was sent to stay in a well-respected sanitorium in Budapest. After I relocated to London, I sent for him to join me."

Oh. OH. Duh.

"And the sunglasses are because . . . ?"

"A sensitivity to light. Common, in cases of brain impairment. Any other questions?"

"Why did you tell me this story?"

"For the same reason I gave you a puzzle on the ride here that you couldn't solve. Our little sojourn the other day to the prison may have amused you, but to me, it demonstrated that you've still to come to grips with the Socratic paradox: you don't know what you don't know. Don't despair. It's a common flaw of youth. And meanwhile, in my benevolence, you'll receive your gift after all. It's waiting for you upstairs. Actually, come to think of it, it's no longer upstairs. By now, it's been transported, *ja*, to the morgue. Ah, well. Your uncle's blood is all over the fireplace bricks, so you've that to look forward to. Come."

29

The policemen's union sponsored my uncle's wake and, as per local tradition, held it at his favorite bar. My aunt and I sat in a corner booth. Every few minutes, another mourner came by to offer condolences. We heard maybe half of what was said because the jukebox was so loud, but we got the gist. Some of the mourners left envelopes of cash.

Several flyers in the bar advertised live fiddle music on Saturday nights, but here we were, Saturday night, and the stage was occupied by my uncle's coffin. Per local tradition, it should have been an open casket, but it's hard to do an open casket when the deceased no longer has a face.

Based on the evidence gathered by the police, this was the official approximate timeline of what had happened:

7:00 a.m.—Beer for breakfast. Evidence: half-empty bottle of Sam Adams on the kitchen table.

7:03 a.m.—Leans head and upper half of torso into fireplace to kindle or rekindle embers. Goes to stand and bumps head on top of fireplace. Grade 3 concussion leads to falling face-first into fire. Evidence: blood and hair on fireplace brick, trauma to the parietal bone consistent with impact, third-degree burns across face consistent with exposure to fire.

7:09 a.m.—Body discovered by wife. Call received at 911 dispatch.

7:18 a.m.—EMTs arrive. Code 10-55 received at main dispatch.

How long had my uncle lain there, face-planted in the fire, unconscious? Well, there would be an official update to the official timeline that would include the coroner's notes, should we be curious to know the specifics, but as to how accurate any of these events of the timeline were compared to what had *actually* happened, well . . .

I did ask Alik. He insisted this wasn't an instance of an impossible solution, like the test/lesson he'd given me in the car on the way home. He insisted I had enough clues to figure it out if I wanted to.

But that was the thing. I didn't want to. I didn't want to think about how Alik snuck into the apartment or how he manipulated my uncle in such a way that my uncle struck the back of his head on the brick fireplace or how Alik managed to do all that without waking my aunt. I didn't want to think about how Alik had come to the correct conclusion about my uncle's abusive nature. I hadn't said anything, and I was certain my aunt hadn't.

I didn't want to think about any of it.

Because when I did, I also began to think about how grateful I was.

And that made me want to vomit.

My uncle's death wasn't even Alik's coup de grâce. No, that came a few minutes after the police notified my aunt that she needed to relocate for a few days while the forensics team further analyzed the crime scene. They didn't suspect foul play, but due diligence was standard operating procedure, especially for a fallen police officer. Alik, having anticipated this (because of course he had), insisted on getting Harvard University to find us a place at the off-campus apartment complex where they were housing him. He added that Hermann would be able to drive me to and from school.

And in that moment, surrounded by my aunt's grief, I just didn't have the energy to fight him.

This was how Alik Lisser ended up at the wake, schmoozing with the attendees. Every so often, he returned to our booth to see how we were. Did we have enough food? Did we need our sodas refilled? Was there anything—anything at all—he could do for us?

My aunt, who recoiled a bit whenever my uncle's friends paid their respects (not forgetting, maybe, that they had treated her, at best, like their maid whenever they were at our place), visibly relaxed whenever it was Alik. She knew him. She trusted him. He made her feel better. And for that, I felt grateful too (even if, all the while, I reminded myself that he was the *reason* for her grief in the first place).

Also, of everyone I saw comforting her in those long days, only Alik had said anything about that continent of a bruise on the left side of her face, visible despite the borrowed sunglasses she wore to hide her dry, bloodshot eyes. Everyone else had offered their sympathies over losing my uncle, but none of them even acknowledged her physical injury, except with maybe a quick glance. Why? Because they knew who had given it to her. Or at least, they suspected. They'd probably known for years. And, as they had for years, they said nothing.

The next morning, while my aunt dressed for the funeral, Alik saw fit to remind me over the tea and scones he'd brought that my uncle's "dismissal from the planet" had been a freebie and that the "important one," the one he'd first set into motion back in October, was still scheduled for this week. He said all this with a twinkle and a smirk.

One week to prevent him from killing again, and most of that day was tied up with the funeral of his most recent victim. I read somewhere that all funerals remind you of the first funeral you attended. I'm sure I don't need to tell you whose funeral that was. Maybe that accounted for how painful this funeral felt, how hot the tears flowed from my eyes as Father Shannon, like all of us wearing a warm coat against the cold, quoted excerpts from Ecclesiastes and Proverbs, how much I sobbed when the three men in army uniforms lifted their rifles to the white sky and let off a three-volley salute in honor of my uncle's service during Vietnam, or how I nearly fell to my knees in agonized sorrow when a fourth army officer presented my aunt with a folded American flag as my uncle's coffin began its final descent into the dirt. At least the funeral was well attended. Neighbors, friends from the church. Sometimes I worried that my aunt's world was too tiny (and it was), but these people were here as much for her as they were for my uncle.

Alik had succeeded in getting us a two-bedroom apartment in the same building as his own (and on the weekend, no less), and since our apartment came fully furnished (including a PC), when we got home, my aunt napped on clean sheets and I logged on. Would Dev be online . . . ?

No. But many of my other friends were, and they, having not seen me in ever so long, swarmed me with virtual love (or at least it felt like it—so starved for virtual love was I). How was I doing? What had I been up to? Had I heard the latest theory from Francis Fung, PhD?

I navigated over to Dr. Fung's primitive GeoCities website and read his most recent post, which wasn't so much about Carissa Miller but about other recent instances "of injustice against prominent Englishwomen." His most notable example was also his most recent: how the authorities repeatedly failed to protect Princess Diana from the "ravenous vultures of the tabloid press."

I actually remembered her wedding (vaguely). It had to have been one of my earliest memories, sitting beside my mother, watching the processional on TV. My mother telling me in hushed tones that princes and princesses were real and here was proof. Diana's dress was long and white. He had all these shiny medals on his chest. Fairy tales were real.

(Though if princes and princesses were real, so were ogres and dragons.)

Reading Dr. Fung's website inspired me to an all-too-obvious revelation. Here was someone with experience in law enforcement, someone well respected, someone already invested (at least on the periphery) in what I was going through.

Why hadn't I reached out to him??

His email address was readily available on his website. I typed up a quick email. No need to lay it all on him and scare him away. I needed him to believe me.

Dear Dr. Fung,

Hi! My name is Kat McCann. I live in Boston. I have information about Carissa Miller. Please contact me.

Short, sweet, to the point, right? And no sooner had I clicked "Send" than I got a private message from Dev.

WmbleyLnDet: how u been?

I navigated back to the chat room.

Now that he was here, I wasn't sure what to say. So I did the best thing possible when at a loss for words. I told the truth.

KMcCann14: My uncle is dead. Nobody else in here knows. Please keep it that way.

WmbleyLnDet: oh, wow, that sux, im so sorry, was he s1ck?

Was he sick? What a question.

KMcCann14: He was killed.

WmbleyLnDet: jesus thats awful!! this city can be such a sewer <hug>

Moment of truth, once more. Don't let me down again, Dev. You're all I've got.

KMcCann14: He wasn't mugged or shot in the line of duty. He was murdered by Alik Lisser.

Silence. Of course.

But then:

WmbleyLnDet: you have proof?

That wasn't a complete dismissal, right?

KMcCann14: Sure. He even told me he did it. And he's going to kill again. Soon. I know how hard this is to believe, but I can't do this alone. PLEASE. I'll even talk to your psych professor if you want. But I don't have anyone else to turn to.

Except, as I typed those words, a part of me resisted the truth of it, and a brand-new idea for going forward bubbled up from the swampland of my brain—a dumb idea, a truly absurd idea, maybe even the worst idea I'd ever had . . . But when Dev responded with his inevitable *no* and again told me how sorry he was for my loss and that he (suddenly) had to go, well . . . I suddenly, dumbly, absurdly didn't feel alone and hopeless.

30

Just because Pedro was in the darkroom at the crack of dawn one morning didn't mean he was there at the crack of dawn *every* morning, but that artsy-fartsy frying-pan bozo struck me as a creature of habit, wouldn't you agree? Well, we would have both been wrong because Pedro wasn't there. Two kids I didn't recognize were in there, half-clothed, and I left before I could get any more details.

Instead, I did what I usually did. I idled in the library. I was striking out with the noir books, though. At first, it was empowering going on these proxy quests of vengeance, but the more stories I read, the more their cynicism began to rub me the wrong way. Like, I didn't need some spurned widow or woebegone orphan telling me that the world sucked. And even when they succeeded in their quests and punished the world for wronging them, it wasn't as if they lived happily ever after.

It reminded me of something someone (I forget who) had once said in the chat room about why Dame Carissa's books meant so much to them. Here she was, writing these Golden Age mysteries well past the expiration date of the Golden Age of Mystery, but she wasn't setting them in the '20s and '30s, when the Golden Age was the Golden Age, but today (relatively speaking). In other words, she was taking the tried-and-true form of the Golden Age—an eccentric and brilliant sleuth solving a crime in an exotic locale—and saying that it still held relevance. So while everyone else in the '60s and '70s had jumped on the spy-thriller craze, she wrote novel after novel of comfort food.

Was there maybe someone writing today who was writing Dame Carissa homages?

Normally, I'd just wander through the Fiction section, take out any titles that sounded like a mystery or any authors I knew who wrote in the genre, carry the stack to a cubicle, and go from there, but maybe because I had an hour before homeroom, or maybe because I was still a little icked by what I'd almost witnessed in the darkroom, I did something I had never done before. I went up to one of the two school librarians and asked for help. He was sitting crisscross applesauce by one of the tables, scraping gum off a chair leg with the sharp edge of a tape dispenser.

"Excuse me," I said. "Can you think of any new writers who write, like, classic mysteries?"

"If it's new, it isn't classic," he said without looking up. "That's how it goes, unless you're Coca-Cola."

"Yeah, sure, I guess, I mean . . . can you recommend someone who writes like Carissa Miller?"

"You mean cozies?"

"Carissa Miller didn't write cozies. Cozies are where old ladies solve murders over tea."

"Must be why they call them 'tea cozies,'" he said, again without looking up. "You want someone who writes like Carissa Miller that we got on the shelves?"

"Yes, please."

"Have you tried Carissa Miller? I think you'll find she writes like herself."

Whether he was being intentionally dickish or was just too focused on his job as gum remover to do his job as school librarian, I took the cue to walk away. I needed Miss Sharon. She would have been able to help me. Except she'd retired from the local library a few years earlier. For all I knew, she had moved to Florida.

I settled for a Dick Francis mystery I'd already read. At least his books always had horses. It kept me company until the first bell rang for homeroom. I returned the slim book to its place on the shelf and made my way through the halls. It remained very, very weird to have been at school for more than an hour already.

I settled into my seat in homeroom and doodled during morning announcements. The doodling was mainly to distract me from the sour ache in my stomach. The last time I'd been in homeroom was when Miss Taggart had shown up to bring me to the front office. As the principal rattled off yesterday's school-hockey scores and the victorious results of our basketball team, I found myself glancing again and again at the doorway, expecting her to make a reappearance.

I was nearly positive that my aunt was safe. I mean, for Alik to have her done in now, especially now that we were living a few doors away thanks to his intervention, would have just made him a likely suspect, which would then cause the police to take a closer look at my uncle's death, etc., etc.

No. My aunt was safe. I was safe.

But, Dev, you good-hearted twit, you'd better be taking precautions.

Homeroom passed and the Grim Reaper never showed. My classes passed and the Grim Reaper never showed. Some of my teachers took me aside (which was out of character) and offered their condolences for the loss of my uncle. They must have read about it in the newspaper or heard about it through school gossip.

None of my classmates said a thing. I was grateful for the normalcy.

After the final bell, I went down to the subbasement for my second attempt at catching Pedro in his routine. I knew I'd succeeded even before I stepped in the music room, knew he had to be in there once I heard those oddball jazz rhythms doing the Charleston up and down the dungeon's lockerless hallways.

"Well, look who it is," said Pedro, glancing in my direction. "If you're here to steal the piano, can you wait till I finish this song?"

"Ha ha. I'm not here to steal the piano."

"Then what are you here to steal, Kat? There's been a lower joint of an oboe sitting in that corner since I was a freshman. It's all yours if you want it."

"I'm good, thanks. Hey, could you stop playing for a minute? There's something serious I want to talk about."

He stopped playing and spun around in his seat. "Serious, huh?"

"Have you ever heard of Carissa Miller?"

Pedro grabbed a half-eaten apple from the top of the piano and took a bite and thought about his answer. The fact that he had to think about it at all, well . . . sometimes we fans forget that not everyone has our obsessions.

"She writes mysteries," I added.

"Oh yeah, sure, yeah, OK. I read most of a book she wrote. Took place in Paris. There were these jewel thieves."

"That's *The Left Bank Robberies*," I replied. "It's one of her later novels. Why didn't you like it?"

"I did like it. I wouldn't have read any of it if I didn't like it."

"But you said you didn't finish it. Or, I mean, you *implied* that you didn't finish it."

"Why would I finish it? Then I would've found out who the bad guys were. This way, I can always wonder."

I blinked. Had he just said what I thought he'd just said? But he kept grinning at me and I knew my ears hadn't deceived me, so I told him (because, come on, I just had to):

"That may be the dumbest thing I've ever heard anyone say in my life."

Pedro took a bow in his chair, as if I'd given him a sweet compliment.

"So, you finish any books?" I asked him.

"I finish plenty of books. I just never finish a mystery. Then again, I don't read a lot of mysteries. Maybe you can recommend a few."

"So you can start them and never finish them."

"Well, you can't not finish something until you've started it."

He was playing with me. That much was obvious. He was *always* playing with me. And part of me felt relieved by that revelation. His kind of playfulness was, in a way, like the other side of the coin to Alik's kind of playfulness. Pedro might just be the help I needed. Now I only had to ask him.

"Want to know my favorite book? It's called *Miracle Mongers and Their Methods: A Complete Exposé of the Modus Operandi of Fire Eaters, Heat Resisters, Poison Eaters, Venomous Reptile Defiers, Sword Swallowers, Human Ostriches, Strong Men, etc.* by Harry Houdini. That one, I finished. Have you ever heard of Harry Houdini?"

"Yes, I've heard of Harry Houdini."

"Hey, you asked me if I'd heard of Carissa Miller."

"Why is that your favorite book? Is it because its title is a thousand words long?"

"No, but that doesn't hurt. And the cover's fun too. It's a picture of Houdini flourishing all these playing cards, except each card is a different picture. Like one is this guy eating fire and one is this guy walking across hot coals, and one is this guy swallowing poison—"

"Are they all men?" I asked.

"The human ostrich might be a woman. It's not clear. So was that it? The something serious you needed to talk about. Was that it?"

"Was what it? We haven't talked about anything yet."

"Kat, we've talked about possibly stolen pianos and broken oboes and mystery writers and jewel thieves, not to mention fire eaters, heat resisters, poison eaters, venomous reptile defiers, sword swallowers, human ostriches, strong men, etc. What else is left?"

What else, eh?

I told him what else.

31

I shut the door before I did. I sat in one of the room's scattered plastic chairs. I told my story. All the while, the flesh of the apple atop the piano cycled through every shade between white and brown till the whole of it looked like caramel mush. Halfway through the story, I had to get up and move around just to keep my butt from getting sore.

Pedro didn't move at all, except to tug on his long, dark hair every now and then.

When I finished my story, finally, I sat back down and asked him the inevitable:

"What do you think?"

"What do I think? I think it's a lot. I think it's unbelievable."

My heart sank to my shoes. "Does that mean you don't believe it?"

"Aw, Kat, now here I thought we'd gotten to know each other the past few weeks."

"I do think that," I replied. "That's why I came here. But I still have to ask. You know I have to ask. Do you believe me?"

"I do."

"Even though it's unbelievable."

"Especially because it's unbelievable!"

I sighed. "That's not as reassuring as you think it is."

"You want reassuring? OK, how's this? You want me to help you outsmart him, right? Beat him at his own game? Before he kills again?"

"Why? Do you have a plan already?"

"No, but I know you have a bad plan. You can't beat a man at his own game. It's *his* game! You'd just as soon try to play 'Little Sunflower' better than the González brothers. You can't. You never will. But try to get them to play one of your tunes by your rules. That's how you stand out."

"Yeah, fine, that's nice and all, but if you could be less metaphoric and more specific, it would be better. What can I do specifically to stop him?"

"How should I know? I've only been sitting with this for five minutes."

Pedro was right. I had no reason to be upset with him. I should have been grateful that he didn't pull a Dev and suggest I get a shrink. I gave him the CD with all the digital pictures on it, hoping his more experienced eye with photography might see something I hadn't. It couldn't hurt, right?

I gathered my stuff and headed out. The sun had already begun its evening nap, and the snow on the ground had frozen to a smooth plaster. Jesus, how long had I been in the band room with Pedro? I checked my wristwatch. 4:06 p.m. Well, Jesus squared. I ambled down the school steps to the sidewalk when . . . oh, come on . . . out of the corner of my eye, I saw, parked in the visitors' lot . . .

Per Alik's promise, Hermann had chauffeured me this morning to school. Since he had no idea when school actually began, I had told him to show up at our temporary apartment, ready to go, at 6:00 a.m. . . . which he'd done without a complaint. And I'd be lying if it didn't feel a little cool to not have to take a city bus at the crack of dawn. You don't want to know the type of people one meets at the crack of dawn on a city bus. But please tell me, Jesus, please tell me that Hermann hadn't sat here *all day long* just waiting for me to come out.

Why should I have cared if I'd inconvenienced the accomplice of the man who'd murdered my mother, condemned my father to death, and ruined my life (not to mention the lives of countless others)? Well, for one, hello, I'm a human being. Empathy much? And two . . . I don't know . . . ever since I'd found out what had happened to Hermann as a child, I felt for him. We were both Alik's victims.

Hermann must have noticed me coming, because he got out and hurried to the passenger side to open the door for me . . . only to slip along a patch of ice and snow and (as my aunt might say) go "ass over teakettle." I rushed toward him, treading with a bit more caution than he had, and tried to help him to his feet, but that just emphasized how large he was and how tiny I was (and how silly we must have looked).

"Are you OK?" I asked.

His sunglasses had fallen off. The resemblance to his brother was much clearer now—uncanny, even. The small, dark eyes. The broad forehead. Not every feature was identical. Alik colored his hair and Hermann didn't. Alik's cheeks were sunken and Hermann had (again, as my aunt might say) "more meat on his bones." But they were unmistakably kin.

Hermann reset the sunglasses to their proper place, leaned on the front hood to stand, and then continued past me to the passenger side. Still courteous, despite the fall. I thanked him and took my seat, and soon we were threading past the factories of Fort Point on our way through the lit-up heart of Boston and then to Cambridge.

It didn't take us long to hit traffic. It never does in Boston.

I lowered the volume on the stereo. "Can I ask you a question?"

"A question?" He frowned at the stereo. Its low volume was making him fidget. "OK."

"Your brother, Alik . . . the things he does . . ."

"Everybody likes Alik."

"Right, but you and me . . . we know otherwise. We know about the bad things he does."

What was I doing? Good question. I wasn't entirely sure, myself. Maybe I was trying to figure Hermann out. That moment from my last morning in England, when Hermann had caught me snooping in the basement, still clung to my brain like a leech. The fact that he was aware of his brother's misdeeds . . . well, on our fun jaunt out to the prison, Alik wasn't exactly cagey in talking about what he had done and planned to do. Even with the Weill at medium volume, Hermann must have heard it all. Maybe I needed to know just how complicit he was.

Maybe it was the only answer I had any hope of getting, and I needed *something*. It was now or never. I posed the question: "You know what he does . . . what he is still doing . . . is *murder* . . . right? You know it's bad . . . don't you?"

Hermann paused for a moment. His large hands were tight on the steering wheel. Then he replied:

"He's the smart one. And everyone likes him. Everyone likes Alik."

And that was that. He turned the volume up on the music. What was learned? Damned if I know. I mean, I was glad I'd asked, but at the same time . . .

If I knew my brother (or sister) was a criminal, would I have turned him in, or would I, out of love, have helped him get away with it? I guess I'll never know how I'd react if my brother or sister broke the law. Alik had made sure of that.

I think I would have been a good big sister. In another world. I would have been forced to become a role model, and I would have too. I would have excelled, but I wouldn't have bragged about it. I would have become a math whiz so I could help my brother or sister with their times tables, and they would look up to me and everything would be as it was supposed to be.

We crawled forward with the traffic. Up ahead, the giant Citgo sign glowed with electric fakery in the orange-blue sunset. To our left, a dude on a motorcycle fiddled with the chinstrap of his helmet. To our right was the curb and the sidewalk and a thousand men and women in coats and scarves and earmuffs and hats, hustling their way home. Not far ahead of us, although still a good twenty minutes in this traffic, my aunt was preparing dinner. Meat loaf? Baked ziti? My uncle had loved her baked ziti. He'd eat it greedily by the pound (not that he ever said thank you). I had a feeling she wouldn't be making baked ziti for a long, long time.

Eventually, we arrived back at the apartment. I would say "home," but we both know that'd be a lie. It was a nice little complex near Harvard University, so tree lined and brick and not at all the gray, neglected ruins of Southie. No, this was not "home," though would I have felt more at home back in a mini mansion in Los Angeles? Doubtful.

Hermann and I climbed the steps of the gated (!) parking garage (!!) to our floor in the building. I entered the apartment first and immediately knew from the smell of fresh-cut herbs and the sound of sizzling oil that my aunt was definitely not cooking baked ziti. As I turned the corner and stepped into the kitchen, I saw that my aunt wasn't cooking anything at all. Alik stood by the stove, my aunt's *Kiss Me, I'm Irish* apron over his pleated outfit, as he used a fork to manipulate several pieces of breaded chicken along the bottom of a large pan.

"There she is," he said, raising his voice over the sizzling. "And how was school?"

"Where's my aunt?"

"I'm right here," she replied, a joyful lilt to her voice, as she sashayed past me and joined Alik at the stove. Her station apparently was the pot, whose lid she lifted and whose contents she observed with a squint. "Why are you home so late?"

"Mock trial."

Alik cocked his head in interest. "Oh, really? Are you an attorney or a witness?"

"I'm a witness," I said to him. "Or have you forgotten?"

At that, I shuffled to my bedroom, let my book bag sink to the floor, and then let my body crash against my bed. It was a better bed than the one in South Boston. Softer. I shut my eyes. My stress must have melted to exhaustion, because the next thing I knew, my aunt was shaking me awake for dinner.

The fried chicken turned out to be chicken schnitzel, an Austrian dish Alik had boasted his father used to make. Mention of his father reminded me of Hermann, who, like always, was absent. Probably forced to eat alone. More of a servant than family.

Reason #816 to loathe Alik Lisser.

I was serving myself some of the green beans my aunt had boiled when Alik nonchalantly raised a glass of wine and said, "To new friends."

My aunt raised her glass of wine. After a gentle glare from her, I raised my glass of Sprite.

"It's strange," he continued. "Even though I'm going to be in New York for a few days, I'm going to be thinking about you. You've become an important part of my life."

My aunt blushed.

But he wasn't talking about her. Just like he wasn't simply casually mentioning this trip to New York. No, Alik was putting me on notice: his alibi was set, the murder would be soon, and there was nothing I could do to prevent it.

And he was right.

32

That night, I had a nightmare.

Dev was dressed as Santa Claus (?) and was wrestling on the T with Pedro, who was dressed as John Lennon, complete with granny glasses (??). Dev elbowed Pedro in the face and knocked his granny glasses off, and when the glasses hit the floor of the train, they shattered into a million little glass shards and the glass shards were all, like, screaming in pain (???) and Pedro also fell to the floor and Santa Dev was standing over him and then Alik was standing over Santa Dev and Alik was ten feet tall and all the glass shards came together and formed a knife in Alik's hand and he started to cut into Santa Dev's head like it was a cake and it *sounded* like he was cutting into a piece of wood and—

I woke up, drenched in cold sweat, and utterly at a loss for words, thoughts, actions, breath, anything. I mean, Jesus H. Christ, what the heck was *that*?

I reached for Dev's pager. Then I checked the time. 3:18 a.m.

I sighed and lay back in my cold and sweaty sheets.

Alik was set to be in New York City over the weekend. He was to attend a conference on Saturday afternoon, and on Sunday, he was set to see a Broadway show. I had no doubt he'd already made sure there would be evidence of him at both. All the better to solidify his alibi while he was actually ending someone's life.

But how could he be in both places at once?

I thought back to my mother's murder. According to the novel *Double Frame*, Adrian Lescher was in his (nonexistent) London cottage when the mayor of Los Angeles, an old friend, begged for his assistance on the high-profile case. If any of this were true (which, I now knew, was a big *if*), then at the very least, after Alik killed my mother in Los Angeles, he flew from Los Angeles to London in enough time to answer his phone. Since the novel depicted Alik walking the scene of the crime less than twenty-four hours after the murder occurred, and since a flight across the pond (and across most of the United States) had to be, what, twelve to fifteen hours long, it seemed mathematically impossible for him to have made the two flights (unless Dame Carissa had fudged the timeline).

What seemed more likely, especially now that I had seen Hermann without his glasses, what seemed *obvious*, in fact, was that, whatever the timeline, whatever the case, Alik used his brother, probably often, to allow him to be in two places at once. How hard would it be to dress Hermann up in nice clothes, give him a hat and cane, and have someone at a distance recognize that figure as Alik Lisser?

Theory: Alik would indeed go off to New York City and do whatever schmoozing was required, make sure he was spotted by as many people as possible, and then on Sunday, Hermann would attend the Broadway show while Alik scurried back to Boston and played devil.

Thoughts? Suggestions? Criticisms?

Even if I was right, it did absolutely squat in helping me figure out 1) who Alik was targeting or 2) how Alik was going to target them or 3) when or 4) where exactly the targeting would take place. I'd guesstimated the frame of the painting, but the actual canvas was still blank and would remain so for three more days, until, suddenly, permanently, it would be splashed bloodred.

No pressure.

I paged Dev the moment I woke up, waited for him to call me back, page me back, anything, waited as long as I could until I had to go.

I did get some good news on that bright, crisp Friday morning: a piece of composition paper, the kind with music staffs inked across it like heartbeat monitors without the heartbeat, was folded in two and stuffed inside my locker. As before, Pedro's handwriting took me a moment to decipher. His letters ran all over the page, as if he'd been riding a roller coaster when he put pen to paper. But how he wrote it didn't matter. What he wrote mattered a great deal.

I THINK I'VE FOUND SOMETHING IN THE PHOTOS.

MEET ME IN THE DARKROOM AT 3PM.

Slog through six hours of classes till 3:00 p.m. and the potential undoing of Alik Lisser? No, thank you. I walked very, very briskly down a flight of stairs and down two corridors until I reached the front office and Miss Taggart, who was on the phone (as she often was). In a few minutes, the first bell would ring, and the kids who weren't late to school would hustle their butts to homeroom and the kids who *were* late to school would trickle in through the front doors and check in with Miss Taggart so as to avoid being marked absent and having the vice principal give their mother or father a call around 9:00 a.m.

I'd had my share of tardies. Often the result of staying on the city bus when it arrived at the stop in front of the school, the staying on the bus being a result of the stomach acid rising into my esophagus, the stomach acid being the result of terror at the prospect of leaving the bus and therefore stepping into the swarm of noise and hormones, not to mention the grueling (and mandatory) handing in of homework and answering of questions. How did everyone without anxiety problems deal with it all? Maybe that explained the flasks and bottles and thermoses of ill-gotten booze that many kids stashed in their lockers. Well, I didn't have any booze, I didn't want any booze, and the seats on the bus weren't *that* uncomfortable, and I'm rambling, sorry, but yes, I'd had my share of tardies.

In other words, I was familiar with Miss Taggart's morning routine. So I hid out in the restroom by the front office, waited for the first bell and morning announcements, and then skedaddled to her desk. Morning announcements were when Miss Taggart stepped outside and fed her nicotine habit. It was understood that if you arrived at school during morning announcements, you signed yourself in on her computer. That's just the way it was.

I waited until some freshie I didn't know finished his minute at the computer, and then I took a seat. The software she used required a user to type in their name to bring up their profile. Then all a user had to do was check a box indicating they were tardy. Did everyone exploit this highly exploitable system? What do you think?

I typed in Pedro's name and viewed his profile. I could have screwed with him and marked him as tardy or absent. Instead, I just memorized his Friday schedule. I got up to leave, remembered what I'd forgotten, and typed in my name to check the tardy box. No need for the vice principal to call my aunt and wonder where I was.

I waited outside Room 1440, where Pedro had his Period One class, and when I saw him strolling down the corridor, headphones on, tapping out a beat with his fingers on his thighs, I jumped out and ambushed the fool.

He didn't seem startled. That disappointed me. He took off his headphones.

"What's up, Kat?"

"What's up is I'm not waiting till three p.m. What did you find?"

"I'll be late for class."

"Yeah, I have a feeling this won't be your first time."

At that, he smirked. Ran his hands through his long hair. Then he led me down to the basement. I thought I knew all the high school's hidden nooks (excellent places to eat lunch without fear of being bothered), but he brought me into a maintenance closet I didn't even know existed. With all the pipes and wiring, there wasn't much room for us to stand, so as a result, my lips were inches from his Adam's apple.

Hey, *he* chose this narrow closet.

He tugged on the light (one of those bare plug-string bulbs) and took out a thin packet of paper from his backpack. The paper was all bent and wrinkled, as if he'd slept on it, but the images on the paper were unmistakable. These were printouts from the CD.

"So," he said, "you know what negative space is?"

"You mean, like high school?"

"Sort of, but no. In all art, there are the parts in the thing the artist chooses to decorate and there are the parts in the thing the artist chooses not to decorate. Like the rests in a song or, like, a silhouette in a drawing. Hold out your hand. I'll show you what I mean."

I held out my hand. He placed a piece of paper flat against it and then placed his hand flat against the paper. I felt the bumps along the top of his palm where his hand became fingers. Even though his hand was nearly twice the size of mine, our lifelines ran parallel.

"If I were to trace our hands," he said, speaking softer now, "the parts of the paper that I didn't trace would be the negative space. Make sense?"

"Yes," I replied, even softer still.

"When you learn to become an artist, you learn to look out for negative space. It can be just as important. So you're trained to see what isn't there as much as what is."

I gazed into his gaze. "And what did you see?"

He slowly slid the piece of paper out from between our hands, so that now our palms were bare to each other, and showed it to me. It was the photo of Alik's corner in the basement, with the TV atop the VCR atop the desk and the file cabinets all along the side.

"What do *you* see?" Pedro asked.

"I just see what's there."

"And what's that?"

"A TV atop a VCR atop a desk," I replied, "and file cabinets all along the side."

"Do you notice anything unusual about the TV or the VCR? See anything that should be there but isn't?"

My imagination went instantly to the video Alik had shown me, the footage he'd manipulated to frame my dad. I tucked both hands into my pockets and shook my head.

Pedro swapped the photo for another one, this time of the corner with Alik's science equipment and array of weapons. His lab. Where he perfected his kills.

"Anything missing here?" Pedro asked me.

I shook my head.

He swapped that photo for another one. Alik's large desk by the large window in the large book room.

"All I know about this Alex Blister guy is what you told me. Wealthy, genius, manipulative psychopath. If he's all that, and I'm sure he is, what's not in this photo but should be?"

"I just see what's there," I replied, and wiped at my wet eyes. "Just tell me, for Christ's sake."

"I'm sorry. I didn't mean to . . . I just . . . See, this is why it's bad to explain how the trick works, because it never . . . What's missing is the past fifteen years. Where's his computer? Why is he still using a VCR and TV from, like, the age of disco? Even his science equipment is outdated. I checked with Mr. Handy to be sure."

"Maybe he just likes antiques."

"But that's the thing," said Pedro. "He *relies* on this stuff. He uses it to help him function in the world. Except the world's moved on and he hasn't."

I was suddenly reminded of Alik's lecture back in October. A lifetime ago now. How he'd railed against DNA evidence. He had made it sound so reasonable at the time . . . but what if *time* was the point? Had Pedro figured out Alik Lisser's Achilles' heel?

And if so, how could I use it to take that inventive psychopath down?

33

I still wasn't any closer to figuring out who the next victim was going to be, but I wasn't about to sit around doing nothing, so after I got home that afternoon (and paged Dev yet again—it was just that he was busy, right?) and dropped off my stuff, I took the T back to my old neighborhood. The rest of the trip I made on foot, and some late-day sleet made it difficult to see, but I could have found my way to my chosen destination with my eyes closed.

Even when I was smaller and places like post offices seemed like palaces, I could tell that our neighborhood library wasn't anything special. The carpet was a sort of dull brown, like mud that's gone dry, and the overhead lights made everyone, no matter their race, look like they had jaundice. In all the many, many hours I'd spent at the library, I'd never *not* seen an OUT OF SERVICE sign on the restroom door. Fortunately, the librarians had their own restroom in the back that they let most people use (if they asked nicely).

There was half a dozen homeless people in the Dorchester Public Library that afternoon, below the usual amount. I walked among the mildew of the stacks (God, I love the smell of a used book!) to a part of the library I'd actually never used before. There were two microfilm readers in cubicles by the reference section. I looked around for the actual microfilm, couldn't find any, wasn't even sure what it looked like, and then did what any sensible person would do.

I went to talk to a librarian.

I've made the library sound like a slum, and I guess it was, but it was also magical, and a lot of that magic was due to the librarians, true wizards one and all, and when they shared their magic with you, well . . . you were set. When Miss Sharon had introduced a troubled girl to the world of Carissa Miller, she'd performed nothing short of a healing spell. Sure, not all librarians were good-natured (the doofus at my school library came to mind), but neither were all wizards.

For example, the librarian at the reference desk, old Mrs. Addams, usually operated somewhere between cooperative and constipated, always helpful but always complaining. We didn't chat much, but we knew each other, and she greeted me with a not-quite-warm stare as I came close.

"Saw you over by the machines," she said. "Useless without film, don't you know."

"Yeah . . . uh . . . do you have the *Los Angeles Times* for 1985?"

"I might just. Stay here."

She tottered off to who-knows-where, toting a full, fat ring of keys that jangled with each step of her orthopedic loafers. In the meantime, I glanced over the brim of her desk to see what she had been reading. I'm always curious what people choose to read—aren't you? You can learn a lot about a person by what books they—

Sex after Menopause. Well, OK then.

After spending the next few minutes looking everywhere *but* the reference desk, I spotted Mrs. Addams by the machines, already feeding the microfilm into its . . . what? Mouth? Opening? Orifice? Ugh, seemed like that stupid book had infected my brain. I quickly joined her, sat down, and let her show me how it all worked.

Then I began to research.

My mother was murdered on Saturday, September 28, 1985, so I started there . . . then realized my mistake and skipped ahead a day so I could read about what had *happened* on September 28, 1985. The controls on the machine were easy to operate: roll the dial to the right to go forward, to the left to go back. The microfilm had the entire newspaper on it, so I had to roll forward through every section, every ad page, *everything* in order to advance from one issue to the next. It was tedious, but it was better than nothing.

And here it was. Front page of the *Los Angeles Times*, September 29, 1985.

BARBARA ACKROYD, AGE 26, PAINTER AND WIFE, MURDERED

Headline as big as the top row of an eye chart. And below it, a photograph of my mother I'd seen before. Hopeful eyes, freckled button nose, and a smile like a slice of sunshine. Even in black and white, even on the grimy screen of an old microfilm viewer. Looking at me from another world (where she was, what, only ten years older than I was now?) where not even the sky was the limit.

My dad was the one who'd taken that photograph. It was how they'd met.

She had been so young. Just out of high school. She became his muse, and he became hers, and then I came along and became theirs. And then Alik came along and drowned my family in blood.

So yes. I had seen that photograph before. The original, also black and white, had hung in our house, where my mom and my dad each had a workroom. Sometimes it hung in his. Sometimes it hung in hers. Moving it back and forth must have been a private joke between them. It wasn't much larger than a sheet of paper. It was framed in thin green wood. And like everything else of material worth from back then, it had gone the way of lawyers.

But here it was again. Here she was again. Hopeful, freckled, sunny. Mom.

One of my aunt's friends in the neighborhood, Carla Capullo (age fifties, piano teacher and widow, alive), once asked to see my scrapbook. This was about a year after I'd been relocated to Boston, and even though I didn't keep a scrapbook, even though I'd never kept a scrapbook or even a diary, I must have known what Carla Capullo meant, because I remember my answer as vividly as if I'd given it that morning:

"I don't need to keep one. I have my memories."

I also remember how confused Carla Capullo had seemed by my answer, as if I were some weirdo, and she always kept her distance from then on (which was fine by me, because the woman absolutely *reeked* of cigar smoke, like she sweated it out of her pores). But look how adorable eight-year-old me was! So sure of herself!

Oh, Little Katie, stay ignorant. It's saner.

I sat in front of the microfilm machine, perusing issue after issue of the *Los Angeles Times*, until Mrs. Addams herself tottered over from the reference desk and flicked its switch, telling me that it was time for me to go home. I'd only gotten through the end of October. The story had stayed on the front page almost every day, although never in as striking a headline as on September 29 and rarely as the lead story.

I had a feeling that trend would change on Saturday, November 2, 1985, and when I returned to the library the next morning and reacquainted myself with my grimy little time machine, my suspicions proved accurate.

Top story, giant headline:

FILMMAKER BILL MCCANN ARRESTED IN CONNECTION WITH WIFE'S MURDER

Accompanying it was not a sweet photograph of my dad in happier times but instead his mug shot, in color, five-o'clock shadow along his jaw and a look of confusion in his green eyes, same as mine, as if he had no idea how he'd ended up on page one alongside this news report.

Far as I can remember, that look of confusion never left his green eyes. The last time I saw him in person was at his sentencing. By then, arrangements had already been made to send me off to Boston (not that I had been asked). The judge thanked the jury and banged his gavel, and my dad stared back at me with green confusion as the guards walked him out through the side door.

Was Alik Lisser in the courtroom that day? I bet if I flipped forward nine months, I could read about it in the newspaper. He definitely had testified in the trial. I bet he'd wowed the jury.

I read more. 1985 became 1986. My father's trial didn't actually begin until January 1986, but the *Los Angeles Times* still had readers to entertain, and so every few days, there would be a new article about my dad or my mom or anyone even remotely associated with the case (such as Alik Lisser). Every so often, my name came up, but I quickly skipped past whatever exploitative nonsense the writer had to say there. Speaking of exploitation, should they have even been publishing my name at all since I was a minor at the time? Talk about exploitation.

By noon, my eyes were itching from the soreness of staring at a grimy screen for hours on end, so I decided to take a breather. I hopped on the T and rode it back to Cambridge. Without a book to escape into, I instead occupied my time by going over what my stroll down microfilmic lane had taught me . . . which was what, exactly?

I already knew that Dame Carissa had stretched the truth in *Double Frame*, but what struck me now (and, I suppose, makes me seem like an idiot in retrospect) was how *compressed* she had made everything. Like, the novel took place over the course of a *week*. Most of her stories did. Most mystery stories did. I guess it made the sleuth that much more impressive for having solved the case so quickly, but real life was never quick. In fact, if someone did solve a crazy, complicated murder in real life in, like, three days, wouldn't that have been suspicious?

No, in real life, Alik Lisser had to be slower than Adrian Lescher. Alik Lisser took weeks.

How could I use that?

And what about the fact that Alik apparently was in London at the time of the murder (or at least shortly thereafter)? He had to have been to have received the phone call from the chief of police, who had invited him to fly across the pond and help with the investigation. According to an interview with Alik, that phone call had been made on October 1. The LAPD had caved in to the pressure to seek outside assistance on *day three*, for Pete's sake. Day three!

Though this begged the question:

How did Alik know the police chief was going to contact him at all?

Because as far as I knew, he only committed murders that he then was guaranteed to "solve" (not counting the ones he framed as suicides or accidents, like his old pal on New Year's Eve and my uncle). How had Alik known ahead of time that the chief of police of Los Angeles, California, would be pressured by the powers that be to call for help, much less to call *him*?

Unless the newspapers had it wrong. Who was their source again who'd told them that the LAPD had reached out after a mere three days to seek help from master sleuth Alik Lisser? Alik Lisser.

I mean, nobody denied it—at least, not that I found—but that lack of a denial didn't prove a thing. Could be their official public quote in ongoing investigations was "no comment," and that quote didn't change even when some gloryhound from across the pond gave an interview.

34

Maybe Pedro could make heads or tails of it. And wouldn't that be something—if *Pedro* solved my mother's murder. Not that he was, you know, completely useless. His brain definitely did its own thing. Maybe the result of all those photography-chemical fumes.

I got off at my stop, and as I climbed the steps to Harvard Square, I was greeted by sheets of frozen rain. Thank you very much, God, you son of a bitch. I pulled the collar of my coat close to my neck and plunged into the bombardment of icicles. My wool hat and mittens quickly soaked through. I quickened my pace, though not so quick as to slip on the sidewalk. This wasn't my first ice storm. But because I kept my gaze low, it was as a reflection in a half-frozen puddle that I first saw the red and blue lights flashing near my temporary home . . .

Oh no.

No, no, no.

What if I had been wrong all along?

What if my aunt wasn't safe at all and I had left her there, alone, to be . . .

I rushed toward the yellow tape. Under the yellow tape. On to the front door. A beat cop tried to stop me, but I was too small, too quick.

Damn it, how hard would it have been to tell my aunt what I knew? How hard would it have been to warn her about Alik Lisser? Sure, she wouldn't have believed me, but at least I would have made her think twice about being alone with him, at least I would have done *something*.

Another cop grabbed me by my bicep, stopped me in my tracks. There were many cops. I saw that now. Nearly a dozen. Strangers. And—

"Here she is," said that familiar voice. He emerged out of a wet shadow, black umbrella in hand, black eyes upon me. "Here's my girl."

35

"I arrived moments before you," Alik said, holding the front door open. He loomed over me like a leafless elm. "It's like fate."

"Is she dead?" I had to concentrate just to speak. Each word took effort. The world tipped. I shut my eyes to keep from throwing up. "Did you kill her?"

"She? No, no, the victim is male. Hermann called me up. I was at my conference in Manhattan."

The victim was male?

Dev. Oh God.

I should have paged him more. I should have gone to the MIT campus and tracked him down.

"Let me show you."

I didn't move.

"You'll want to see this, I am sure of it," he said.

I could barely speak. "Is it Dev?"

"There is a simple way for you to learn."

"No," I said. "No. You tell me. You tell me right now."

Alik frowned. Crossed his arms. Sighed.

Then, finally, finally:

"Well, if you *must* know, as far as I'm aware, the victim was well into his twilight years. Now, does that satisfy your curiosity? May we proceed?"

A rush of warmth flushed into my veins. I wasn't aware I'd gone so cold. My shoulders relaxed. My lungs exhaled. My mouth refilled with saliva and breath. I was going to be OK.

But then I remembered that, even if the victim wasn't Dev, it was still *someone*, and all that relief caught in my throat like a chicken bone.

Damn you, Alik. I followed him past the security desk, where the guard recognized us and waved us through, and down one of the red-carpeted corridors on the first floor. The final door on the left, #112, was barricaded with more police tape and by another stern beat cop. I didn't recognize him or any of the cops outside. Cambridge had its own police force, and they did not socialize with my uncle.

"You can't be here," the cop said.

"*Ja*, we can," replied Alik with the calmness of a cutting blade, "and I'd be happy to tell you why. See, my name is Alik Lisser."

"Who?"

Got to love *that* answer. I wanted to give the cop a high five.

Undeterred, Alik continued, "I understand your situation. I was you once . . . many, many years ago. But knowledge is power, and nobody likes to share power. You have my sympathies. Perhaps if you could get the attention of the lead detective, all will be revealed."

The cop clearly wasn't sure what to make of this old man and teenage girl. Who could blame him? Then he picked up his walkie and had a chat with, well, somebody.

"'Who?'" I muttered to Alik. "That's got to hurt. 'I'm Alik Lisser.' 'Who?'"

"He's young," Alik replied. "He doesn't know any better. Much like you. For example, you're probably feeling emboldened by his ignorance. If I'm not protected by my reputation, that must make me vulnerable, so what's to stop you from informing this young officer of the law everything you know about me, *ja*? Surely the thought has crossed your mind, and if it hasn't, it should have. And you can. You can tell him all my little secrets. And let's say he believes you, child that you are. You do know what his next question will be, right? 'Where is your proof?' Well, where is it?"

I didn't even bother matching Alik's glare. Yes, it had occurred to me (briefly) that his anonymity here made him more vulnerable, but more vulnerable isn't the same as an easy target, and I *didn't* have proof. Of course I didn't have proof. Alik clearly hadn't waited until Sunday afternoon to slink back to Boston and do his dirty business. He had popped away last night or early this morning. He said Hermann had called him, and maybe he had, at least to create a phone record—though if he hadn't, if there was no phone record, was *that* the proof . . . ?

No. I was trying to outsmart Alik, and Pedro was right. Outsmarting Alik meant playing his game. If I was going to defeat him, I had to force him to play my game.

I just had to figure out what my game was, and meanwhile, on the other side of the door, lay a dead body, a dead male, somebody innocent who could have still been alive had I acted faster, another name to add to the long, long list of Alik's victims, another name to join my mother (and, indirectly, my father), and, God, so many others.

After a few minutes, a Black woman in a white trench coat stepped out of the apartment. She nodded to the cop, who gave us some privacy.

"Glad to see you," the woman said. "I'm Detective Anita Riegert. Which of you is Alik Lisser? No, I'm kidding."

She shook Alik's hand, then looked to me. "Let me guess. You're his biographer."

"She's actually my protégé," said Alik. "Thank you for speaking with us, Detective. I take it you've heard of me?"

"I have, I have. Does your protégé have a name?"

"Kat," I whispered, then wondered why I was whispering, then wondered what it was about Detective Riegert that made me feel a bit in awe. I'd met female cops before. Maybe it was her self-confidence? "Kat McCann."

"Well, Alik, Kat. How can I help the two of you?"

"Actually, we're here to help you, Detective. If you've heard of me, you know of my particular expertise, *ja*?"

"The thing is, though," she replied, "we're not really in the habit of turning to outside help. You ask me, I say who says no to assistance, especially assistance with your pedigree, but my boss has this strict policy when it comes to psychics, private eyes, and, what do you call it, foreign intervention."

"Let me tell you something, and maybe you already know it—there's a wall between the kitchen and the dining room for a reason and the reason is—"

"—that most people don't want to see how the sausage is made. You're right, sir. I could not agree more. But my boss isn't most people. If I solve a case, he needs all the details."

"Then give him all the details, and if he gets mad, give him my phone number. Better yet, give him Ted Kennedy's phone number. Ted is still one of your senators, isn't he? He and I go way back."

"I'm sure you do," said Detective Riegert.

Alik held out his hands in supplication. "Use me, don't use me. But I had to offer my services. For my own peace of mind, *ja*? I knew the man in there. Law professor, right? Jules Rothstein?"

"How did you know Mr. Rothstein?"

"I've had an informal relationship with Harvard for a number of years now. They reached out to me—well, many universities reach out to me, but not many universities are Harvard. I'm actually teaching a lecture there this semester on criminology. I always liked Jules. Quiet fellow, but some excellent theories on mens rea as it relates to transferred malice published in the—"

"OK, OK. Five minutes," Detective Riegert said. "That's the best I can do. Five minutes under constant supervision."

She opened the door wide for us to enter. So Alik entered.

I did not.

Hell no.

"Kat," he said, "come now."

"I'd actually feel more comfortable if she waited outside," Detective Riegert replied.

With some effort, Alik leaned on his cane and bent down until we were eye to eye. "Don't you want to see me at work? Who knows what you might learn about how I've done what I've done for so very, very long?"

He didn't wink at me, but he might as well have, because we both knew he was right, so, yeah, I followed that bastard, that monster, the devil, into his crime scene.

36

It was a nice apartment. A studio, from the looks of it, so much smaller than the one me and my aunt had. But cozy. Lots of light blues and whites. The walls displayed clusters of photographs. Family and friends, probably. A goldfish tank sat by a window. The bed was made. Powder-blue blanket over white sheets.

No signs of struggle out here.

Someone was kneeling in the bathroom, not far from the tub and the checkered tiles around it. I inched in that direction to get a better look and saw a man in a jumpsuit scratching at the bathroom radiator with a Q-tip.

"Let's leave Lem alone," Detective Riegert said. "He's collecting samples."

"Evidence?" I asked.

"Potentially."

"So that's where the body was discovered, then?" asked Alik. "In the bathroom?"

"Can't you tell?"

"I can assure you, Detective, that I have deduced a great deal in the short time we've been allowed entry. On a basic level, it is obvious the victim knew his attacker. There is no sign of struggle. It is peculiar to attack someone in the bathroom, but not impractical if you know what you're doing. Bathrooms are corners in which one's victim can be trapped, *ja*. This implies premeditation. I wish you had preserved an outline of the body with chalk or some such so that I could—"

"A chalk outline? This isn't Victorian England. We use photography."

Alik pursed his lips in disapproval (though who knows what he disapproved of more: what she'd said or the dismissive tone in which she'd said it). Her mention of photography reminded me of Pedro, though, and I suddenly saw an opportunity . . .

"So, Lem's collecting DNA samples?" I asked Detective Riegert.

"That he is. Lem is a DNA pro. Aren't you, Lem?"

In response, Lem grunted. Alik grunted, too, though softer (and for different reasons).

"Then Lem will need to get our DNA too," I said. "Right? I mean, just by being here, we're leaving our DNA, right?"

"Aren't you clever," Detective Riegert replied, and then she picked up two baggies from the kitchen counter. "That's what these are for. Hope you two don't mind a cheek swab."

Alik grunted again. "And if I say no?"

"Why would you say no?"

"An argument could be made that it's a violation of privacy. To use the parlance of your Constitution, 'unlawful search and seizure.' An argument could be made that I'd decline out of principle."

"You're just afraid they'll store your DNA and then use it to clone you," I told Alik. "Somebody's seen *Jurassic Park* too many times."

I added a Tyrannosaurus roar for good effect. Detective Riegert chuckled.

Alik did not chuckle. And that made me feel *great*.

"Even though I haven't seen *Jurassic Park*," he replied, "I suspect I can still be of assistance."

He took a few long steps toward the bathroom and studied it for a minute.

"Cracked the case yet?" Detective Riegert asked.

"No, but I can share some preliminary observations. The victim was poisoned or strangled, correct?"

“What makes you say that?”

“There are no bloodstains. Not even a drop. Granted, the killer could have cleaned up after he was through, but then there’s the fact of the body, discovered as it was in the bathroom, and had the victim been bludgeoned or shot or stabbed or otherwise punctured, he would have presumably still bled out after the killer left. I want to add that these are preliminary observations and not definitive conclusions. No, it’s far too early for that. Was he poisoned or strangled?” Alik was already inching his way into the bathroom for a closer look. “The location of the body in the bathroom tilts the needle toward poison, but not determinately. Were there marks on his neck indicative of a rope or a pair of hands?”

“Yes to strangulation. No marks on his neck.”

How could someone be strangled without leaving marks on their neck?

In a Dame Carissa mystery, peculiar deaths were to be expected, but those were novels and those people weren’t real . . . except they had been real, each one a fictional name hiding a flesh-and-blood human who had fallen under the machinations of Alik Lisser. And I had spent years enjoying their tales. In the chat room, we’d once ranked the most deserving victims. I remember squirming during that bit, hoping nobody picked my mother . . . but I’d had little reason to worry. *Double Frame* was nobody’s favorite story. Nobody but me.

“What was . . .” The words caught in my throat. I had to force them out. “What was his name again?”

Detective Riegert replied, “His name was Jules Rothstein. How about we step out for a moment, let the expert do his thing?”

We exited through the fire door not far from Jules Rothstein’s apartment and stepped into the alleyway behind the building. The detective leaned against a brick wall and lit a cigarette and then said:

“Don’t smoke.”

“I don’t.”

She shrugged. "Then you're way ahead of me at your age. They're lung torpedoes. So, how did a kid from Southie end up apprentice to the—what do you call it—wizard of crime-solving?"

"What makes you think I'm from . . . I mean, who's to say I'm not from here?"

"Because you're not," Detective Riegert replied with a chuckle, "and it doesn't take a cop to recognize that accent."

I had an accent? I didn't think I had an accent. Nobody ever told me I had an accent. I guess everyone has an accent of some kind, but I just assumed I sounded like, I don't know, *me* and not like my classmates, some of whom have a Very Strong Accent, dropping their *r*'s like the letter was silent unless at the start of a word / *aw at the staht of a wuhd.*

Did I do that? Sure, maybe sometimes.

If my mother and father were alive, would they even have recognized my voice?

(Then again, if they were alive, I never would have relocated to the Land of the Invisible *R*.)

"You didn't answer my question," the detective said, exhaling smoke like a dragon.

"How did I end up with Alik Lisser?"

"That's the question."

"It's a long answer."

"I imagine it is."

"I got a question for you," I said, "if it's OK."

She shrugged again, which I took for a yes, and so I continued:

"It seemed like you were, I don't know, humoring him . . . us . . . and then you suddenly let us inside the crime scene. Why?"

Riegert eyed me for a second, flapped her white coat close to her body, and then nodded. "You *are* a bright one, aren't you?"

Now it was my turn to shrug.

"It's a couple of reasons. For one, this case . . . it's a weird one, and it can't hurt to have an ally with connections if things get ugly."

"What makes this case weird?"

"I'll get to that. Also, dude knew the deceased . . . Maybe he can help point us to who might have a grudge, aid us in building a suspect list. And third . . . dude knew the deceased and insists on viewing the crime scene? I don't care if he's Sherlock Holmes. That's not normal. See above, regarding suspect list, if you know what I'm saying."

Did I know what she was saying?

Yes, yes, a thousand times yes!

The insane roller coaster ride my emotions had been stuck on for months now (if not years) shot up to its highest point. I could see everything from up there. I could even see the end of the ride, with me stepping off while Alik remained bound to the coaster for the rest of his life.

But where to begin?

You're right about Alik Lisser. In fact, ten years ago, he murdered my mother.

Or how about . . .

You have no idea how right you are, Detective. Alik Lisser is a serial killer. He's Sherlock Holmes as a psychopath.

Or maybe . . .

You think Alik Lisser maybe killed Jules Rothstein? Maybe? You better sit down, because Jules Rothstein is just the latest in a long line of . . .

But then I saw Dev's face. Dev, who'd dodged this bullet and had probably never been Alik's target at all. Dev, once my ally, now who knows what, and all because I had told him the truth. This truth. I had gambled and lost. I had scared him away.

And back to the earliest point, what proof did I have, really? She was a police detective. Even if she believed me, she'd need evidence, and I had nothing but a sob story and a whole lot of conjecture. Alik had been careful. Alik was always careful.

I had to be careful too.

Detective Riegert was being careful. She was setting traps. She was gathering DNA evidence against him already. All I had to do was wait for that DNA evidence to tie Alik to this murder, and then, and then, everything else would be easier.

And if I could find a way to speed things along, maybe *help* her tie Alik to this murder . . .

"My mom was killed when I was six years old," I said. "Alik Lisser is the one who figured out who did it. He saw what no one else saw, and that evidence he found . . . it sent my dad to prison for life."

"Damn." She exhaled smoke. "That's a lot for anyone to carry. Wait. I know this story, don't I? It was big news. Your mom was Barbara Ackroyd and your dad was—wait, don't tell me—Bill McCann."

"All of which is to say I didn't always speak like I was a Southie, but I guess ten years is enough to change anyone. I've been living with my aunt and uncle. Well, until recently. My uncle died not too long ago. I think that made the news too. He was a cop. BPD. They say he fell and hit his head on the fireplace and then—"

"—fell face-first into the fire. Well. You poor thing."

"I know, right? I mean, what are the odds?"

Detective Riegert nodded in sympathy. "Kat, some people live their lives surrounded by death. I've seen it."

She wasn't biting. I had to be more explicit.

"No, you're right. Like, Alik, for example. He invited me to his real nice house over Christmas, and he told me that it used to be owned by a buddy of his, but that buddy died, which is how he got it. And then there's one of his closest pals, who was standing, like, right in front of him when *he* died. This was over New Year's. Then he comes over here for a job teaching, and he meets my aunt and uncle and then my uncle dies. But you know about the Carissa Miller books, right, all based on his real-life cases? Every other one is about him solving the murder of a friend or an acquaintance. It's like everyone he knows ends up dead. I better look both ways before I cross the street, am I right?"

The detective looked at me funny, and that was good enough for me. The seed had been planted.

"Well," she said, finally, snuffing out her cigarette on her heel, "we probably should get back."

"Yep, yep. Got to collect our fun DNA."

"Want to know a secret?" asked Riegert. "The crime tech in there . . . he was just finishing up before I let you in. The scene's already been swept for prints, DNA, all that forensic shit. It's really not that big an apartment. I just added the threat of DNA collection to see how Alik would react."

Then she laughed and laughed and held the door open for me while I laughed and laughed on the inside. Any false sense of security Alik Lisser might have had "contaminating" the crime scene with his DNA . . . all for nothing. And let me tell you: I'd never had a cotton swab scrape the inside of my cheek before, but as the crime technician did the same to Alik, my nerves came alive and sang out in beautiful harmony, all amplified by an emotion I never thought I'd feel again: hope.

37

Our next stop was the morgue. Apparently, no facility in Cambridge was equipped to deal with whatever was weird about Jules Rothstein's death, because we had to cross back over the river to massive Mass General. Alik had already obtained the go-ahead from Detective Riegert. If only he knew she was giving him just enough rope to hang himself . . .

On second thought, I hoped he *didn't* know. He probably didn't know.

He couldn't know, right?

As Hermann shuttled us into one of the cement labyrinths that functioned as the hospital's parking garages, Alik *seemed* not to be aware of the danger he was in. He seemed positively giddy, humming along with the discordant notes of *The Threepenny Opera.* He must have noticed my noticing, because he turned around in his seat and said:

"I love autopsies."

Of course he did. How very unsurprising and gross.

"*Ja*, human anatomy is endlessly fascinating," he continued. "We have mapped out galaxies we will never reach, but we are still mapping out the human brain. Do you know why the heart is on the left side of the body instead of the right? It's a trick question. The heart is not actually on the left side of the body. Imagine an asymmetrical triangle. Can an asymmetrical shape be perfectly centered? No. The left ventricle is larger by necessity. It's the engine that pushes blood through the aorta and, from there, everywhere. Not everyone's heart leans left, so to speak. There exists a condition present in one percent of the population where the heart favors the right side. But surely you recall the story of the priest I murdered in Brussels."

I did. It was one of Dame Carissa's best. It centered on a beloved Catholic priest who—

You know what? No.

Dame Carissa spent her career protecting this son of a bitch. She didn't deserve the courtesy. Alik certainly didn't. You want to read about how he "solved" the murder of an innocent man (by, keep in mind, pinning it on another innocent man)? Go ahead. Head toward your nearest bookstore or library, you ghoul.

Hermann idled the car in a handicapped spot while Alik and I followed the garage signs toward the hospital's cross-shaped White Building. As we did, we passed an elderly couple heading in the opposite direction. Like Alik, the man walked with a cane. Like me, his companion was short, female, and, from the scowl on her face, seemed like she'd rather be anywhere else.

Once inside the White Building, it was more signs and more walking. Not until we were alone on a descending elevator did Alik speak:

"Don't think I haven't noticed how much more confident you have become over the past few weeks. That remark about *Jurassic Park* was cute, though I imagine it was more for the detective's benefit than my own. What did the two of you discuss when you stepped out?"

"Cigarettes," I replied.

"*Ja*, I noticed an air of tobacco smoke on her. There was a time not too long ago I could have told you the brand she preferred, but age dulls the senses. To many, it dulls the mind. Senility—that's my only real fear."

"Not afraid of going to prison?"

The elevator doors opened to the basement level. "Why would I be afraid of what will never come to pass?"

There were fewer signs down here. Fewer rooms. The other floors displayed photographs of happy children. This floor displayed no photographs. The paint scheme was the same light green.

Alik seemed to know the way. Maybe all hospital basements were the same, and this was hardly his first morgue. Alik gave his name to a guard, who then activated a pair of double doors. After that, it was a left and a right, and then we were there.

The morgue had two rooms. I'd read enough to know the room with the equipment was the lab and the other room, which I was *not* going to visit, contained the bodies, presumably in a many-doored fridge. There were no bodies in the lab, and the coroner was spritzing down the metal examination table with, I swear to God, the same all-purpose blue cleaner my aunt used in our apartment in Boston.

"Hello," he said. His Swedish accent ebbed and crested like happy energy. "You're expected. Welcome. I'm Dr. Nilsson."

Alik nodded his greeting and introduced me as his squire. My soul vomited.

Dr. Nilsson smiled at us both, his wise old eyes twinkling behind his tiny spectacles. "You are here about Rothstein, Jules, yeah? Let me get the file."

He set the cleaner down and picked up a manila folder.

"Yeah, it's a weird one," he said. "Like out of a mystery story."

Dr. Nilsson splashed out a dozen photographs onto the examination table. I instantly recognized the checkered bathroom tiles and—

Oh God.

I mean, yes, I'd seen dead bodies before. More than any person my age should ever have seen. But this . . .

Jules Rothstein was sitting in his half-filled tub. He wore a tweed jacket, tweed slacks, socks, black shoes. The archetypal professor. However, I couldn't tell you whether he wore a tie or a belt or what his face looked like. I couldn't tell you any of those things because Jules Rothstein was *folded over* at the waist, face down in the water. A contortionist naturally could have pulled off that position or, I don't know, a flexible yoga mom, but not this elderly professor, not naturally.

And then the déjà vu hit me. Had I seen something like this before? How was that possible? Where could I possibly have . . . ?

Oh.

I looked at Alik, aghast.

Alik looked at the coroner.

"I would have to agree, Dr. Nilsson, *ja*. Exactly like out of a mystery story. 'Two in a Tub' by Carissa Miller, if I'm not mistaken. The killer renders the victim unconscious, drags them to their bathtub, half fills the tub with water, and then sits atop the victim's back until their weight pushes the victim's face underwater. Death by drowning. Also, unusual in the author's oeuvre, in that she wrote the tale from the point of view of the killer, rendering her series detective to the role of minor character."

If Dr. Nilsson picked up on the fact that Alik was referring more or less to himself, he appeared oblivious, simply nodding along politely . . . though I can only imagine the look of disgust on *my* face. Alik had murdered Jules Rothstein in the exact same fashion that somebody . . . no, that *he* had murdered somebody else thirty years ago.

Why?

"What are the specifics here, Doctor?" asked Alik. "I assume you've completed a full study of the body."

Dr. Nilsson tapped his index finger on one of the photographs. "Cause of death is 472 milliliters of water found in lungs. Multiple contusions to spine but only one break at the L3. And then there's an additional lateral contusion on the front of his throat here."

"I'd like to view that myself, if you wouldn't mind."

"He's back here," the coroner replied, and ambled into the other room. Alik was halfway there, too, when he realized I hadn't moved an inch from my spot beside the table.

"Come now, Kat," he said. "Half an education will only unlock half the doors."

"What if I don't want to see what's on the other side of those other doors?"

"And here I thought you'd grown a backbone."

"What good did a backbone do Jules Rothstein?"

"Have it your way, little mouse."

And he left me alone. Alone with the photographs. Alone with my thoughts. And maybe it was the chill of the morgue, but that hope Detective Riegert had ignited inside me . . . that hope of final, real justice for Alik Lisser . . . it flickered a bit.

38

When I got home from the morgue (jeez, what a phrase!), I crashed on my bed. I'd vowed not to get used to the fancies of this temporary flat, especially since they were Alik's gifts and were just a sinister excuse for him to have me close, but a soft bed was still a soft bed, and what were these pillows made out of? Actual clouds? I became instantly comfortable, which was the reason that I didn't respond at first to the fact that my closet was beeping. After all, it's not like it beeped every second. Maybe once a minute.

Did I know why my closet was beeping? I did not. And besides, the day had been so long already, what with the library research and the crime scene and everything, and the beeping didn't seem like it was going to stop, so I could just check on it later.

Oh, if only I was that type of person, the type who would have been content to let a mystery wait. Pedro could have waited. Pedro could have stayed in bed with the cloudpillows. Pedro could have stayed in bed with me and—

Ahem. Sorry. What was I saying? Right. The damn beeping. I groaned in the general direction of the closet to let it know how I felt and then shambled out of bed to smack whatever had decided to ruin my afternoon. Was it possible the closet had a smoke alarm running low on batteries? We had a smoke alarm in our old apartment that sometimes did that. It would really tick my uncle off (but then again, what didn't?), and he'd search every drawer for the right batteries, yanking them open and slamming them shut and—

And my closet did not have a smoke alarm. It did have Dev's pager, tucked into one of my Keds, the green ones with the flimsy soles that I couldn't wear in the winter. I vaguely recalled putting it there during the move from South Boston to Cambridge. Was the pager running low on batteries? Was that why it was beeping? No, stupid, wake up, the pager was beeping because that was what pagers did.

I checked its tiny screen. Dev had paged me at 10:02 a.m. And again at 12:49 p.m.

And again at 1:04 p.m.

Did he have questions about dead Jules Rothstein? Was he wondering if maybe I had been right and Alik Lisser had claimed a victim? Was he paging me to apologize and offer his help? As if. For one, there was no way he had learned the news (if he had learned the news) as early as 10:00 a.m. Maybe by 12:49 p.m. And for two, even if he had learned the news, what in that news would make him connect the death of an old professor to Alik?

So, with another mystery in need of solving, I called Dev back. He didn't pick up. Of course he didn't. When did Dev ever do anything on anyone else's schedule? I fell back into bed and wondered what had been so important that made him page me three times. He and I hadn't spoken a whole lot recently, not in the chat room and certainly not outside it. Maybe he missed me. Or maybe he was checking to see if I'd thrown away his Christmas gift. Maybe I should've thrown it away, or at least left it at the old apartment, but . . .

But that thought went unfinished as my mind sank deeper and deeper into the cloudpillow's cloudpillowness. I didn't dream. I must have been too comfortable to dream, or too tired. When my aunt woke me up for dinner, it took me a whole minute to crawl out of my sleep cocoon, and even then, reluctantly.

That daze lasted me through all of Sunday too. To be honest, it's a wonder my brain was functioning at all. Information overload. I lumbered from bed to kitchen to computer to bed to computer and may have sleep-lumbered for some of it. Was sleep-lumbering a thing? And speaking of the computer, you know who *didn't* show up at all in the chat room? Not once Saturday night, not once Sunday afternoon, not once Sunday evening. According to Marigoldeneyes, the last time WmbleyLnDet had made an appearance was Friday around 2:00 p.m., and only to brag to anyone and everyone that he had just finished the latest Peter Lovesey novel and (applause, please) had correctly predicted the ending.

Typical Dev.

But then poof: he vanished.

Atypical Dev.

I did try to call him on Sunday. I think I did. I must have. But he didn't pick up, and he sure didn't page me again. Still, I wasn't *that* worried. Alik had done his thing. Dev was safe.

Right?

And the last thing I wanted was to remind a freakin' serial killer about the existence of a friend of mine, though I had no doubt Alik needed reminding. He'd met Dev in October. Dev had practically fallen to his knees in worship. But the repeated pages followed by dead silence . . . it wasn't good.

So I took a chance. On Monday morning, after gobbling down a Pop-Tart, I knocked loudly on Alik's apartment door. Hermann was waiting for me in the car to take me to school. He could wait a few minutes more.

I knocked loudly again. I knew Alik was awake. He was always awake.

The door opened. He was awake and fully dressed. Dapper as a Copley Place mannequin.

"Good morning," he said. He sipped tea from a small porcelain cup. "To what do I owe the honor?"

"Did you do something to Dev?"

He sipped some more tea and then cocked his head to make it look like he needed to think for a moment, the bastard.

"Cut the crap," I said. "You know who he is. Is he OK?"

"Is he? Well, I'm not sure. I hear the lifestyle of college lads these days can be extravagant."

I gritted my teeth till my jaw ached. "Did you . . . do something to him?"

"Why? Did something happen to him?"

I shoved him. The tea spilled a dark stain across his dress shirt. Good.

"Did you hurt him?"

Alik reached for a side table to steady his balance. "As far as I know, Dev is perfectly fine. *Ja.* You have my word."

For all his many, many faults, Alik did believe in playing fair in this sick game between us. If he had injured Dev, or worse, he would have said so. I was (almost) sure of it.

At school, I zipped down the stairs to the music room. Pedro had told me that was where I'd be able to find him Monday morning, and sure enough, I heard his chaotic jazz music bebopping from down the hallway. If only the shadowy, submerged school basement didn't remind me of the shadowy, submerged hospital basement and the morgue and, ugh, hello again, anxiety-stomach.

I must have pinged his ESP, because a moment before I stepped into the band room, the music shifted abruptly from chaotic jazz to Carole King's "It's Too Late." I guess I should have been impressed, but I'd had it up to here with Men Trying to Impress Me.

"Kat!" said Pedro, spinning toward me on his piano stool. "Top of the morning and all that!"

He tucked a few strands of hair behind his right ear and grinned with, I assume, genuine happiness to see me (yeah, yeah, assume nothing, bite me). In spite of my foul mood, I found myself grinning back at him like a fool. Then I reached into my book bag and took out my wrinkled-spine paperback of *Adrian's Dozen.*

"A gift?" he asked.

"Research," I replied, and filled him in on the events of the past two days. I may have left out the bit about Dev. I mean, I had Alik's (relative) assurance that Dev was OK, so why complicate things?

Pedro listened with his whole body, leaning in, absorbing every syllable like I was relaying the secrets of the universe or something. Only when I was finished did he speak: "Well, gosh. And he based the murder on a story in that book?"

"'Two in a Tub.' It's the last story. I was thinking . . . maybe if you read it . . . you might be able to help me figure all this out? Because I'm clueless." I handed him the book and then added, "But you gotta promise to finish the whole story. None of that stupidness about reading everything but the end."

"I promise," he said, and added the paperback to his own pile of textbooks and notebooks.

The rest of the day was, well, the rest of the day. Nothing really happened (not that I was paying much attention). That is, nothing really happened until dinnertime, when Alik showed up with a large pizza.

I was on the computer at the time (still no sign of Dev). How ironic, if that's even the right word, to be in a Dame Carissa fandom shrine while Alik Lisser himself stood ten feet away. Not that they would have believed me. Not that I would have believed any of them had they claimed the inspiration for our favorite fictional character was standing ten feet away from them. And none of that was to even come within a mile of the horrible truth of it all. But the chat room didn't exist for truth. I saw that now. It existed to worship the entertaining lies that a cowardly woman told on behalf of a psychopathic man. When Dev met Alik back in October, hadn't he kept referring to him as Adrian? It made sense. I saw that now.

Over pizza, Alik told me and my aunt about his day, about how he had deepened his investigation into the death of his colleague, Jules Rothstein. He made it sound so heroic. My aunt certainly bought it, patting him on the back of his hand and telling him how incredible he was.

For me, it was all I could do not to barf. I sat dutifully silent, alternating sips of water with nibbles of cheese and sauce and crust. Then came the real reason he was there:

"I've learned that tomorrow is the funeral," he said. "Tomorrow morning, to be precise. You would be amazed how often a killer, compelled by guilt or ego, attends the funeral of his victim. It would be a real boon to have a second pair of eyes, someone who has proven herself to be clever and reliable, on the lookout for unusual behavior."

Of course my aunt said yes. She didn't even ask me if I *wanted* to skip school and attend the funeral of a murder victim. Neither did Alik. And I was tempted to speak up, tell them both how ridiculous an idea this was. But I was more tempted by curiosity. *Why* did Alik want me to attend the funeral of his murder victim? What was his game here?

39

The next morning I dressed in my blackest blacks and sat silently in the back seat. Mount Auburn Cemetery turned out to be a vast plain of frozen grass and frostbitten tombs. For whatever reason, Hermann didn't stay in the car but accompanied us on the walk, adjusting his sunglasses every now and then because, while it might be a whole lot warmer in the summertime, nothing's as bright as the wintertime sun. Every now and then we passed a genuine mausoleum, some history-book name like *Adams* or *Hancock* carved into its granite.

After a few minutes, the path inclined up a small hill, and it was near the top of this small hill where the mourners were gathered. There weren't many of them—maybe twenty, tops—and most of them were old men in dark suits. They stood about six feet away from the coffin, which sat on a sort of hammock above the freshly dug grave. The dirt from the grave formed a mound beside the hole, and a shovel was stuck into the dirt mound like Excalibur in its stone.

When we arrived, Alik activated his fake-empathy switch and began to chum it up with the mourners. Clearly he knew people no matter where he went (and they always knew him). Maybe these were other criminology professors, and that's how they knew each other. What was it he mentioned the other night about how often killers attend the funerals of their victims?

How many had Alik attended? Was this part of his victory lap?

Had *he* been at my mother's funeral?

The nearest train must have arrived recently, because soon another group of mourners joined us on the hill. Overall, they were younger than the first group, middle-aged instead of one-foot-in-the-grave (so to speak), and while they, too, were mostly men, I did notice three women in the bunch.

Jules Rothstein now had thirty people at his funeral (if I had to guess). Was that a good amount? Alik continued to make his way through the crowd, greeting everyone as if he were the host of the thing. Then again, he was, wasn't he? I overheard him say to more than one individual that he was dedicating his time and energy to "unearthing the monster who did this."

This was recess for him. This was his f'ed-up playground.

Eventually, one of the older men, a pocket-size Bible clutched in his hands, separated himself from the group and stood beside the coffin, facing us. The man (a rabbi?) adjusted the bobby pin that attached his yarmulke to his bushy, white hair and waited as everyone else quietly bunched up like a choir. Alik took his place at my side. Someone behind us muttered something about the lack of chairs.

The rabbi began:

"You believe funerals are about endings? Seems like the obvious conclusion. Here is the cause of our gathering, the end of a life. Death is an ending we're all guaranteed, but we don't like it, so we wrap the dead body in a shroud and then wrap the shrouded dead body in a coffin and then wrap the coffin containing the shrouded dead body in dirt. Out of sight, out of mind, and let us continue in our delusional fog, please, that *our* lives will not also end like this. In Judaism, there is no promise of an Afterlife. There is only the question, and the question is the answer."

The question is the answer? Well, that was right up Pedro's alley. He would have loved this eulogy, though I had a feeling he wasn't Jewish.

"Jules Rothstein made the study of uncomfortable endings his life's work. He and I would debate about science versus faith. He believed that science could answer all questions and I would remind him that his favorite book was *Frankenstein*, a novel critical of scientific zealotry, and he would shrug as if to acknowledge that to be a man is to be contradictory, and what a sense of humor the Almighty must have. But the Almighty is not laughing this morning. This I know with all the faith in my heart."

And look, there was Detective Riegert, leaning against an oak about fifty yards away and smoking one of her lung torpedoes. I assumed she was here for the reasons Alik had said, about the killer attending the funeral of their victim, and hey, here he was, Detective. Slap on the cuffs and drag him in.

"Jules and I grew up in the same village just outside Kiev. It's true. Though the Kiev of his youth was not the Kiev of mine. The Kiev of his youth, the Kiev of the 1930s, was gripped by famine, and then worse. The Kiev of the late 1940s, my Kiev, was a living organism of bulldozers and rebirth. So Jules became a scientist and I became a rabbi. He survived a horror show of a childhood, became an expert in criminal forensics, and was murdered in his bathtub. This sense of humor the Almighty has, it's not subtle."

Was this why Alik had brought me here? So I, too, could bathe in the glow of his own friggin' "divine humor," his own God complex? It made as much sense as anything. Whenever we were out, which wasn't often, and we passed someone who was dressed nice, my uncle used to mutter to my aunt, "There goes another peacock." Even on a Sunday. It fit, didn't it? He was a peacock, a showboat, a . . . whatever the word is. Was that the extent of it, bringing me here? Just to witness him strut? Because if so—

Hold up.

Was that . . . walking up the hill toward us . . . Was that Dev?

What in the name of Christ was *he* doing here?

OK, maybe there was a reasonable explanation. Maybe Dev had Jules Rothstein as a professor, maybe he was his favorite professor ever, and he saw that his favorite professor had died and was just here to pay his respects.

Yeah. Because that was Dev. Respectful.

He was sad about something. His mouth and jaw were twisted into this taut line of grief and . . . bruises decorating the right side of his face? Yellowing bruises, by the looks of it. A few days ago. And a fat lip still several sizes above normal.

He had reached out to me for help and I hadn't been there.

If Alik was surprised by Dev's appearance, he didn't show it. He just stood beside me the whole time like a gargoyle, like the rabbi's eulogy had enthralled him. Had he not seen Dev yet? Oh, who was I kidding . . . Alik Lisser saw everything, and whatever reason Dev had for being here now, it had to do with him.

I know, I know, assume nothing and all that, but come on.

Because Dev was late (as always), he was left standing in the back of the group. I turned to go to him, and Alik suddenly gripped my forearm with a steely claw.

"Mind your manners," he muttered.

I struggled to break free, but he wouldn't let me budge. Meanwhile, the rabbi had begun to recite a series of prayers. A few of the other mourners, those who knew Hebrew, spoke along with him, but most of us just remained respectfully silent while, down by the oaks, Detective Riegert was flicking ashes into the grass.

"Tradition dictates," the rabbi said, switching back to English, "that we conclude our service with the Mourner's Kaddish. Let us take a moment to dwell on the unusual language in the Mourner's Kaddish, and I don't mean that it is in Aramaic, though it is. What is unusual, I say to you, is that nowhere in the Mourner's Kaddish is mentioned the word 'death' or 'grief' or 'loss.' Were you to hear the Mourner's Kaddish without its title, you would assume it to be about praising God, nothing more, and you would not be wrong. Because in this moment of death and grief and loss, our relationship with the Almighty must not pause. Even as we suffer, even as our faith is tested—especially when our faith is tested—we exalt the Holy One, praised be He."

He then intoned the Mourner's Kaddish, which may not have been about death but sure sounded solemn. As he spoke, a gravedigger used a crank to lower Jules Rothstein, coffin and all, into his grave. The rabbi then motioned for us to pay our last respects. This involved the mourners, one by one, picking up the shovel from the dirt mound and tossing a few ounces of dirt onto the coffin.

I went to join the line, but once again, Alik's steel claw gripped my forearm. So instead I had to watch as everyone else said their goodbyes. At least they knew the man.

Before long, it was Dev's turn with the shovel. The look in his eyes, like this was the very last place on Earth he wanted to be. I wanted to shout out to him, say something—anything—but where to begin? Then he saw something behind us that made him freeze mid-shovel. I glanced to see what had him so terrified. All I saw were two uniformed cops. Sure, they were slowly approaching, but what did Dev have to fear from the police . . . ?

Ah, but you've already put it all together, haven't you? You've figured out why Dev was at the funeral, or why he had reached out to me repeatedly over the weekend, or at least why the sight of the police had turned him into a deer in headlights.

Congratulations. Pat yourself on the back for having the emotional distance to see the obvious. Because I didn't understand it at all, not until Dev dropped the shovel and began to run.

40

Who would have guessed I'd one day be sitting in a metal chair in a blank, beige room inside a jail, waiting to speak with an incarcerated friend, though my anxiety probably was a tiny spark compared to the lightning storm Dev must have been feeling. It had been more than six hours since his arrest at the cemetery. Would he be in an orange jumpsuit? Would he be shackled?

Why I was at the jail was obvious. I needed answers. I know, I know—I *always* needed answers, but this time was different. This time was personal. Nearly as personal as what Alik had perpetrated back in 1985. More so, in a way. This time, he had targeted someone specifically to get at me.

How I was at the jail was less obvious but weirdly similar. Alik had made it happen. On our way back from the cemetery, as I sat in shock in the back seat, Alik had simply turned around in his front seat and asked me if I wanted to see my pal.

"It will be a couple hours before you can," he had added, "but given that I helped the police nab their suspect, I've little doubt they will allow me this one small favor."

What he really meant was to remind me this was a favor I would now owe him, the evil son of a bitch. But what other choice did I have? When your only path forward required you to make a deal with the devil, you made the deal. And you ended up in a conference room in the Cambridge jail.

The far door opened with a loud clunk, and a guard led Dev in. No to the orange jumpsuit (he was still in his funeral clothes), but yes to the shackles. Dev sat down across from me. The guard remained on our side of the door. I'm thinking privacy is the first of many rights you lose when you've been arrested.

My dad would have known.

"How are you?" I asked him, then felt stupid for asking it. What was he going to say? That he was peachy? "Tell me everything. Maybe I can help."

He shrugged his broad shoulders. "What's there to say? You were right. About everything. And I didn't listen. I didn't listen and here I am."

"You're not here because you didn't listen. You're here because Alik Lisser is a monster. But if you tell me what happened, maybe we can figure out a way to—"

"—to what? Stop him? Professor Rothstein is dead. There's no stopping that. And we've both read enough mystery books to know that if the cops have enough evidence to get a warrant for arrest, it's pretty f'ing serious."

"Do you know what their evidence is?"

"I know all of it," Dev replied. "You want to know how? They showed me. They've even got my tooth in a little baggie."

"Wait, what?"

"Friday night, I'm on my way to a Kappa Sigma kegger, and the next thing I know, I'm waking up in a homeless shelter in Brookline, my mouth full of bloody gauze, and the left side of my face feels like it's been hit by a Mack Truck. Check this out."

He leaned down so his shackled left hand could pull back his left cheek and show me the gap where one of his lower back teeth was missing.

"And you have no idea how that—"

"No! Someone must have roofied me at the party. Or before the party. I don't know. Whatever they gave me knocked me out hard enough for someone to take out my tooth."

"For Alik Lisser to take out your tooth."

"Yeah. Except I didn't know that part till yesterday. Sunday. I spent all Saturday trying to retrace my steps, asking everyone I knew if they had any idea why I was missing one of my f'ing teeth, and the answer had been right there all along. For months. I was a real dick. I'm sorry."

"Sure. Thanks. Maybe when we figure this thing out, you can buy me an Orange Julius. But back to Sunday. What happened on Sunday?"

"Oh, well, Sunday was the day I met the bogeyman." His chains rattled in his lap. "Except I met him once before. Back in October. Remember that? I was tripping over myself trying to get him to sign my books. But he was wearing his mask then. He showed his true face on Sunday."

"Dev, what happened on—"

"I'm telling you what happened. I'm telling you, but I'm taking my time because telling you makes it real. Saying the words makes it real. Like every time I rattle these chains, it makes it real, and I don't want it to be real, Kat. I want it to just be a story in a book. Those words. Flat words. Two-dimensional."

"Dev." I felt for him. I did. But I had a feeling we didn't have an eternity to chat, that another one of those things you immediately lose when you've been arrested is time. "Please."

"OK, sorry, yeah, Sunday. I went to meet up with my comp-sci study group. We like to meet in the Hayden Library because Jonesie can always get us one of the rooms with more than one dedicated wired LAN port. Plus, Hayden has the best vending machines. I'll admit I was a little lightheaded. I had gotten a prescription for Percocet from the infirmary and may have taken a few before I set up for the study group. You would have done the same if your back tooth had been forcibly removed from your jaw and you had no memory of it! It was on my way to Hayden that I ran into Alik Lisser. By which I mean, I'm walking across the quad, trying not to slip on the ice, and I hear Alik Lisser calling out my name! Can you imagine? I was confused because of the meds, I was confused because Alik f'ing Lisser was right there at

MIT, standing about as close to me as Frank is right now. That's Frank, by the way. Say hi, Frank."

Frank, the jail guard, said nothing.

"Frank's quiet now," said Dev, "but wait till you don't get up fast enough, and then it's all 'You better stand up now, or you won't be able to stand up for a week.' Isn't that right, Frank?"

"Dev."

"I'm getting to it. Alik calls me over, so of course I go to see him. He's got his cane. He's sitting on a bench. He tells me he remembers me from his lecture. He asks how I'm doing. I tell him I've had better weekends. Then he asks me if I'd heard yet about Professor Rothstein. Did I know that he was found dead in his apartment? I did not. Didn't I have Professor Rothstein last semester for Intro to Criminal Forensics? Yes, I did. Did I do well in his class? 'No, Mr. Lisser, actually, I didn't do well in his class. No one did. No one ever did well in his class, but I thought I was smarter than them. I thought I could buck the curve. Why are you asking?'"

"When you didn't do well," I asked, "did you confront him?"

"Confront him? No. No, I didn't confront him. I may have stopped by his office hours and questioned his definition of fairness. I certainly didn't send him an f'ing letter."

"What letter?"

"This letter. I don't know. Lisser said the police found a typed letter in his apartment. Anonymous. Some threatening letter. From a former student."

"Oh Christ, Dev."

"I didn't write it! But he said he was doing his due diligence and speaking with former students who may have had a reason to hold a grudge. It's not like Rothstein ate my firstborn child! He gave me a C. And for that, I'm going to kill the man? No. But then there's my tooth."

I knew it before he said it. It was obvious. Alik had planted Dev's tooth at the crime scene. It must have come out in a struggle, the conclusion would be. And then I remembered how Rothstein had gone down. Someone had put their arm against his throat and squeezed. Wasn't that a wrestling move? Add to that Dev's obsession with Dame Carissa's novels, and they could draw a clear line from where he learned about this particular form of bathtub murder. And did Dev have an alibi? Nope. He had no recollection of his whereabouts for Friday night.

It was as perfect a frame as the one Alik had fixed for my father.

He'd won again. And this time, I'd let him do it. No, worse than that—I'd been an accomplice. I'd helped him find a perfect patsy. Dev wouldn't have even been on Alik's radar if it wasn't for me, and he certainly wouldn't have targeted him.

"My parents got me a lawyer," Dev replied. "My arraignment isn't until tomorrow morning, but I already spoke with her on the phone. She thinks if I plead out, I could get ten years."

"But you didn't do it."

"Remember what you said? You said Alik Lisser does this all the time. That means he succeeds *all the time.* And ten years, I'll still be in my twenties."

"Dev, please. Don't plead out. I'll fix this. I'm to blame and I should be the one who . . . I will find a way. I promise. Look at me. You plead guilty, and that's it. You plead not guilty, and that gives us months to figure this thing out. We'll work together. I'll tell you everything I know. We can beat him. He isn't God."

He looked at me with those little-boy eyes. "Isn't he?"

41

Dev made me promise that I wouldn't attend his arraignment, so the next day, while he was in court, I was in English class. I was learning about rhymed couplets. Dev was pleading for his freedom—or at least, I hoped he was. I'd promised not to attend his arraignment if he promised to plead not guilty, but the way he'd said it, with absolutely no hope in his voice . . .

"Kat, could you give us the rhyme scheme of a Shakespearean sonnet?"

Ms. Peorini waited with crossed arms for my answer. The class waited for my answer.

"Um," I replied, ever soft.

"'Um' is not quite what I was looking for, Kat. Try taking notes, if it's not too much trouble. That applies to all of you. This will be on the quiz. Let's review."

Some of my classmates glared at me. As if it was my fault they now had to take notes. I imagined my seat was a pool and I sank into it until I was underwater and invisible.

Underwater like Jules Rothstein.

I popped back up. No more hiding. No hiding until this was all over.

One way or another. Even if it was just me.

Because when I had arrived at school, Pedro wasn't in the band room or the darkroom, and at first I got worried that Alik had somehow targeted *him*, too, but then I spotted him by his locker right before homeroom. I spotted him by his locker laughing with Sadie Jackson, and there was only one reason any guy laughed at anything Sadie Jackson had to say—well, two reasons, featured that morning in a fuzzy pink sweater that Pedro just couldn't keep his eyes off.

Now I know, I *know*, Pedro had every right to laugh with Sadie Jackson or ogle Sadie Jackson or ogle whoever he wanted to ogle. Ogle away, Pedro. It wasn't like we were dating. We hadn't even kissed. We had almost kissed, maybe, once, but *almost* didn't matter, and what if only *I* assumed we were going to kiss, which was entirely possible. It's not like I had any experience in this area.

And yes, I *know*, with people *dying* and Dev in deep trouble, what right did I have to worry about Pedro and his ogling (hello, priorities, Kat), except I'd be lying if I said it didn't bother me. Turned out a person could worry about literal life and death *and* have their heart broken at the same time.

Now Sadie Jackson (yes, *that* Sadie Jackson), who sat to my left, passed me a folded-up handwritten note.

I unfolded it and read it:

YOU SHOULD KILL YOURSELF.

The writer signed the note with a smiley face.

I glanced over at Sadie, who pointed to her left to Barry Barkhurst, who sat to *her* left. Barry, who probably liked to spend his spare time kicking small animals, leered at me with a sadistic grin. All things considered, I wasn't bullied a whole lot, mostly because I spent so much time and effort hiding, but when I was, I just absorbed it, sucked in my tears, and went about my day. I mean, what was the point, anyway.

Except that day, I didn't just absorb it. Maybe it was all that was going on. Maybe it was the emotional pain I was already feeling. Or maybe—just maybe—all I had experienced these past few months had changed me. But instead of just ignoring the note or crumpling the note, I ripped out a page from my own notebook, wrote a reply, folded it up, and gave it to Sadie to pass to Barry, which she did.

And he read it.

And that sadistic grin of his shrank into confusion, and then fear.

What I'd written:

THANKS! I WILL BE SURE TO STAPLE THIS TO MY SUICIDE NOTE SO EVERYONE WILL SEE WHO INSPIRED ME!

And you better believe I signed my note with a smiley face.

Come lunchtime, I did my usual dodge of the cafeteria and secreted myself into a corner of the library. I'd originally tried my hidey-hole underneath the third-floor staircase, but a pack of potheads had already settled thereabouts with their bong. The library was always a good option, even this library. I took out my PB&J (and watermelon Capri-Sun) and my copy of *A Treasury of Great Mysteries, Volume 2* (so chosen because none of Dame Carissa's stories had made the cut) and fell into a semiconscious fugue of nibbling and reading. This was probably why I didn't notice Pedro sit across from me until he whistled a few bars of that ingratiating hit from a few years ago, "Don't Worry, Be Happy."

"Hi. Wow, Kat, when you read, you really read."

"Wow, Pedro, when you make an observation, you really make an observation."

He replied with that smirk-shrug of his, but I refused to be charmed. All I saw was him doing it to/with/for Sadie Jackson. Instead, I just asked, as coldly as I could:

"Can I help you with something?"

His smirk-shrug deflated. "Are you mad at me?"

"Like I said, when you make an observation . . ."

"I saw you, you know. This morning. By the lockers."

"I saw you too," I answered, trying to chew peanut butter and jelly as nonchalantly as one could (which, I got to tell you, is very difficult, what with the peanut butter turning to glue in your mouth and the jelly getting stuck to your lips).

"Nothing happened," he said. "We were just talking."

"And now *we're* just talking."

He sighed and tucked a loose tangle of hair behind an ear. He bit down on his lower lip, making his left cheek dimple.

Nice try, buddy. Still not charmed.

"Kat, you remember what I said about frying-pan kids and cookie-jar kids and how cookie-jar kids are obsessed with reaching the end, even if they have to jump to conclusions to get there?"

"I remember that it sounded stupid then and it sounds stupid now. Why do you ask?"

"Because you're jumping to conclusions! I was not flirting with Sadie!"

I shrugged and bit off another bite of sandwich. "So what if you were?"

"Because you want me to only flirt with you! Or was I not supposed to say that part out loud?"

I froze mid-chew.

"Kat, I like games as much as the next person who likes games, but some games . . . this game you're playing now . . . is not a fun game for me. And I'm guessing it's not fun for you either. I like you. And you know I like you. And I know you like me. And maybe Sadie was flirting with me a little. Maybe she didn't have any reason to believe she wasn't supposed to flirt with me."

I tried to reply. I did. But the gobs of food-glue in my mouth made that impossible. I held up a one-minute finger, sucked down most of my Capri-Sun, and then finally, *finally*, said what was on my mind:

"You could have given her a reason. You could have said something."

"Yeah. Well." Back into aw-shucks mode for Pedro. "I said something just now, didn't I?"

Why, yes. Yes, he did. And I, distracted doofus that I was, was only now registering the fact that He Said He Liked Me. I needed another

Capri-Sun for this. Too bad I only had the one. Poor planning, Kat. And don't keep the boy waiting. Say something!

"I like paper," I said.

Oof. I like paper?? What was *wrong* with me? Every atom in my body winced in shame. Even my organs winced.

But he just nodded. "Oh yeah?"

"Uh-huh. Paper smells nice. And it's smooth. And sometimes there are words on it."

"I've noticed that."

"And paper is really trees, so libraries are, like, indoor forests."

What, your brain has never been broken before because someone you like told you they liked you back? How nice for you. I, inexperienced in these things, was about to make an observation about the natural beauty of a paper cut, when Pedro saved me from continued embarrassment in the simplest, most chivalrous way possible.

He leaned across the table and kissed me.

He tasted like cool-mint Aquafresh.

Did we use the same toothpaste?

He kissed me and I kissed him and we kissed each other, and then the bell rang. Somewhere in that time, my heart skipped a beat and my toes curled up and *all* the clichés happened, but who cares, really. We kissed. What else mattered than that?

"So," he said, standing up, "I'll see you after school?"

"Sure. Wait. No! Shit. Sorry. I mean . . . I can't. I need to check on Dev."

"Who?"

Ohh, right, maybe I hadn't ever mentioned Dev to Pedro. Weird.

"He's just a friend," I said. "An older friend. A college friend. From online. We went to Alik Lisser's talk last October. Stop looking at me like that. He's just a friend. Who's in jail, actually, because of me . . . well, because of Alik, but only because Alik is fixated on me . . . Oh God, I'm a bad person, aren't I? My friend's in jail and I'm making out in the school library."

"I hear libraries are like indoor forests."

"I'm a bad, bad person."

"See, now that hurts. Because that implies I have bad, bad taste, and sure, I can't hit a fastball or fix a car like my older brother could or like my old man still can, but I've got great taste. And you're great, Kat. You're just overloaded with bad, bad problems. Deal with them one at a time and cut yourself some slack. And remember that you're not alone because you've got me. And your friend isn't alone because he's got you. So go check on him. And then, maybe, if you want, call me after."

"I don't have your phone number . . ."

He took a Bic pen from his pocket and wrote out his seven digits on my right palm.

"There," he said. "One bad problem solved."

42

Once my last class ended, I took the quickest route to the parking lot. I had to find out what went down at the arraignment. Knowing Dev, the answer could have been anything. I rushed to the familiar rented Cadillac, opened the door, and—

"There she is."

Alik. Sitting in the back seat. Waiting for me.

He was smoking one of those thin panatela cigars that Adrian smoked in the books, that *Alik* smoked back when I was six, the cedar smell of it clawing at me, trying to regress me . . .

Yeah, I opted for the passenger seat in the front.

Hermann, unreadable as always, shifted into Drive and off we went, *Threepenny* soundtracking us. I lowered my window to half-mast (despite the frigid temps) to suck out that cloying cigar smoke.

"How was your day?" Alik asked. "Did you learn anything of value?"

Oh, was I obligated to answer him? Heck no. I bided my time alternating thoughts of whether I'd left Detective Riegert's card on top of my nightstand or on top of my dresser with thoughts of Pedro's minty lips . . .

"I wanted to thank you in person, Kat. The past few weeks have been exhilarating."

Blah, blah, blah, screw you.

We met the traffic on the bridge in record time. The Charles sparkled underneath us, as it sometimes did when it was in the mood. My sixth-grade teacher told us that a person can never step in the same river twice, that the water's always flowing somewhere, but I don't know. It was still the same river, and we were still the same people.

Alik was definitely still the same person, still blathering on from the back seat. "I'm going to write a book about our recent events. It feels obligatory. I actually have a few of Carrie's old manuscripts, complete with editorial notations. Any suggestions for a title?"

Yeah, Alik, I had a few suggestions. I doubted any of them were fit for print. I had *no* doubt he knew how things went down during Dev's arraignments. He probably even attended, got some sort of voyeuristic thrill from it all. But there was no need to feed his massive, insatiable ego with my questions. I could wait a few minutes and find out on my own.

Then he said:

"Your aunt's already begun to pack. I don't imagine it will take long."

Pack? What did he mean?

"I covered the cost. It seemed only fair, since I covered the cost of the move *to* Cambridge."

Ah. Of course. He had accomplished what he came to do. He didn't need me under his thumb anymore. He was sending us back to Dorchester. What a coincidence his renovations of our old dump had finished up this very week. Oh well. No more bougie Harvard Square apartment. No more rides to and from school. No more Alik popping up unannounced.

Good.

"Gone quiet, *ja*?" Alik puffed at his thin cigar. "I respect a little quiet in a little mouse. Though I hope it isn't because you believe the words of a little mouse can have no big effect. Your words can change minds. Take, for example, your compatriot Dev. His lawyer's words—big words, I've no doubt—convinced Dev to confess to my crime, but then you spoke with Dev, and this morning, what did he plead before the magistrate? 'Not guilty.' You did that. I orchestrated it, of course, got you in to see him, pushed to make it happen—I *needed* him to plead not guilty—but the words were yours. Perhaps the one writing the book should be you. Even better, perhaps we could collaborate. *Ja*, that's a fine idea! We'll do it this summer."

Dev pleaded not guilty? To hear the news, even from Alik's lips, released a weight around my heart. There was still hope. There was still—

What was that other thing Alik was going on about? Collaborating this summer on a book project? If he thought that was even a *possibility*, the dude was crazier than . . . well, crazier than the crazy I already knew he was.

From the cleanness of the red brick on the buildings, we were nearing our temporary home in Cambridge. The sooner, the better. I hugged my book bag to my chest.

"To be honest, I don't like his chances. Your compatriot, I mean. If his lawyer couldn't convince him to take a plea, which was in his best interest, how effective do you think he will be at convincing twelve strangers of your friend's innocence when the evidence to the contrary is substantial. I should know. You will thank me, though. I put a good word in with the prosecutor. He did not seek remand without bail. Your friend Dev is home by now, I would suspect, though he cannot leave the Commonwealth of Massachusetts."

Go ahead. Keep trying to undercut my moment. But I've got hope now, nutjob.

Hermann sidled up to the curb and shifted into Park. I reached for the car door. Then Alik's long fingers cupped around my left shoulder and a cloud of cedar smoke floated in front of my vision.

"Listen to me closely. Dev will be found guilty, and he will die in prison like your father. He will die in prison unless you save him, and you can. Say the word, and the case against him will fall apart. I've already found someone else to blame. Say the word, and Dev will be freed of all suspicion."

I turned around and looked him straight in the eye. "Just like that, huh?"

"Well, like I said, you will need to come to England this summer. I really have missed the awe and wonder of a captive audience. And I was serious about the book. You can be my assistant. I'll give you top billing on the acknowledgments page."

"You think I'm going to live with you in England . . . ?" I couldn't help but laugh. Laugh right in his face. Laugh more freely than I had in months, maybe years, because really, have you heard anything as funny as *that*? "You think I'm going to be your assistant . . . ?"

"You had a good time this Christmas. For a while."

"Goodbye, Alik."

"You'll change your mind."

"And you're out of yours."

With that, I left the car and Kurt Weill and Hermann and Alik behind me.

In our (temporary) apartment, my aunt was sitting in front of my mother's painting. She was staring at it as if it were the Virgin Mary, as if she were praying, as if I were an intruder. Not that she glared at me or anything. She just gave me a simple smile and asked me how my day was. We talked for a minute about tomorrow's move. She'd already begun to box up "the unessentials." She then told me that the garage opener in my bedroom had been making noise all day.

Garage opener in my bedroom?

I went in to check . . . and saw what she meant because she'd left it on my pillow. Dev's pager. I guess it did look a bit like a garage opener. Not that I'd seen many, living in a tenement and all that. I picked it up and wondered why I hadn't even thought to bring it to school. It seemed like such an obvious omission, right?

His phone number scrolled across its little gray screen. I picked up the phone to call him. And I had every intention of calling him when I picked up the phone. But then I saw the other phone number, the one scrawled across my palm . . .

It wasn't as if I didn't know what had happened in court.

And I didn't expect to chat with Pedro for *that* long. Putting aside all my (considerable) drama, what did we really have to talk about, anyway? Well, as it turned out, a lot. Turned out we were two human beings who just liked each other. We talked about people we both knew, we talked about living in South Boston, we talked about the future. Pedro was in the back half of his senior year. Had he applied to any colleges? (Short answer: no.) Did he want to go to college someday? (Short answer: yes.)

And then we got to talking about other stuff that's none of your business.

By the time I hung up, I could smell minestrone wafting in from the kitchen. And I felt weirdly famished. So it wasn't until after dinner that I finally, finally called Dev.

"Hey," he said. He sounded depressed. Couldn't say I blamed him.

"Sorry I didn't get back to you till now," I replied. "I had school. And homework. Alik told me you plead not guilty. That couldn't have been easy."

"I don't think 'easy' is in my vocabulary anymore."

"Welcome to my world."

"Yeah? You got an f'ing murder charge pending against you?"

"I don't mean . . . Look, all I'm saying is, Alik has made both of our lives very complicated. And not for nothing, but if we're comparing war wounds, at least you've still got a mom and a dad."

He didn't say anything.

"Look," I continued after a sigh, "I'm sorry. I'm sorry I didn't get back to you till now, I'm sorry I got you in this mess, I'm sorry about what I just said. But we need to look forward. We need to strategize."

"Bring it on. You and me against the world."

I sat on my bed and stared at my palm. Pedro's digits had mostly sweated away, but I could still see their blue traces on my skin. "Well, that's the thing. It isn't you and me against the world. No offense, but you and me don't stand a chance. We need help. And we don't have to beat the world. Just Alik Lisser."

"Oh. Just Alik f'ing Lisser. I feel so much better."

I clenched my hand into a fist and smiled. "You should. Because I got a plan."

43

My plan was simple:

We needed help, right? We needed people who understood Alik Lisser so well they not only could predict him, they could also outwit him. We needed people who understood Alik Lisser so well that they could get *him* to play *their* game. Now if only I knew a group of people who had read and reread and discussed and rediscussed every Adrian Lescher novel every day for as long as AOL had had chat rooms . . .

Brilliant, right?

Sure, yeah, OK, Adrian Lescher was not Alik Lisser, but he was the next best (worst?) thing, and Alik had made the deliberate choice to re-create a murder Dame Carissa had immortalized years ago. All I had to do—all Dev and I had to do—was convince them to pitch in, and why wouldn't they? Dev's freedom was literally on the line. He may not have been anyone's favorite member of the group, but he *was* a member of the group. They would have his back.

"Though," I said to Dev, "maybe I should do the talking."

He promised to behave himself. And I believed him. If anyone knew the stakes, it was him.

We logged on that evening (me on my pawnshop Packard Bell, him on whatever gazillion-dollar computer he used at MIT) to catch the 8:00 p.m. crowd. All the regulars were there. Snooty Professor. Tweed. Maternal Marigoldeneyes. Even Kiwi_woolgatherer was there. The topic du jour was Dr. Fung (who *never* replied to me, by the way), who apparently had begun to gate some of his theories and evidence about Dame Carissa's disappearance to paid members only.

Professor.Tweed: This proves he is nothing but a mercenary unworthy of our attention.

Marigoldeneyes: Now now. Isn't everyone entitled to make a living?

Professor.Tweed: I'll wager Dr. Fung is here now, one of us. He wouldn't be the first interloper. Need I remind anyone of the AladdinZane debacle?

1975-Bob: whats that

Marigoldeneyes did a fine job summarizing the antics of my stalker from last year, and you'd think I'd be rattled by it all. She even reached out to me via IM to make sure I was OK. The funny thing: I *was* OK. With everything that had gone down after that, with all the death and misery that Alik Lisser had introduced (and reintroduced) into my life, a threat like an internet stalker seemed so, I don't know, small potatoes.

Or did it say something about me that I had attracted the attention of two loony tunes?

The switch in topic away from Francis Fung gave me the perfect opportunity to take the reins on Dev's behalf. It was time to rally the troops.

KMcCann14: On a more serious note, I got a favor to ask everyone. One of us is in trouble. A lot of trouble. As in Arrested. As in Charged with a Crime he didn't commit. Like I said: Big Trouble. But I know if we all work together, we can figure out a way to get him out of trouble. If anyone can do it, it's a room full of Adrian Lescher junkies. Are you with me?

I didn't have to wait long. The answers came quick and emphatic.

4Lollipop4: yes
AL4EVA: absolutely!!!

And so on. In less than a minute, everyone was on board. Even the newbies said yes (maybe just to fit in). Though it wasn't long after that minute that somebody realized the obvious:

Professor.Tweed: Why so uncharacteristically silent, WmbleyLnDet? the answer is one of two possibilities. Either you're *not* on board, which confirms you to be the cad we always suspected you to be, or you're already on board because you're the one of us who is in trouble.

AL4EVA: he could be afk :)

Professor.Tweed: The answer is one of *three* possibilities.

Well . . . it's not like we could get mad at them for solving a mystery.

KMCann14: You got it. I'm talking about WmbleyLnDet. And the reason he's quiet is because I asked him to be. Remember in the story "Bitter Death," when Leslie Lindon-Fry couldn't convince Adrian of her innocence because she got so emotional but her best friend was able to be more calm and rational about it and vouch for Leslie and that was what made Adrian take the case? This is like that.

4Lollipop4: plus Adrian had a crush on the best friend

Marigoldeneyes: I think he would have taken the case anyway. Adrian would never have let an innocent person suffer.

During all this, I got a few private messages from people asking for details. WmbleyLnDet was probably getting the same barrage. He was being a good boy and not writing in the main room, but he also wasn't messaging me. Maybe he really was Away from Keyboard.

Kiwi_woolgatherer: What are the police saying WmbleyLnDet did?

KMCann14: It's a murder case. A professor was drowned face-forward in his bathtub. Sound familiar?

Professor.Tweed: That's "Two in a Tub," first published in Ellery Queen in 1978. First-rate yarn, imho.

KMCann14: That's the other reason all of you are perfect for this case. The killer is using WmbleyLnDet's love of these stories to frame him.

AL4EVA: that could happen to any of us :/

Marigoldeneyes: It's exploitation!

Professor.Tweed: The way I see it, Occam's Razor may be applicable here. How can we be positive that WmbleyLnDet is innocent? No offense intended, of course.

And here came the hard part, the part I dreaded, the part I had to do perfectly. Because I really did know the room would band together and support one of their own. I was sure of it (even if Dev wasn't). But now it was time for the details. The Alik Lisser of it all.

OK, deep breath.

KMCann14: I know he is innocent because I know who really did it.

KMCann14: Let me explain.

KMCann14: My mother was murdered when I was 6 and Alik Lisser solved the case. Double Frame is that story. Her story. My story. My father's story. Because he was the one who was found guilty. You know that if you've read the book and you've all read the book. He died in prison. Fast-forward to last October and guess who's coming to my town? Alik Lisser. I had to talk to him about what had happened. He was there. Plus, it was ALIK LISSER. Like, imagine if you had the chance to meet Joseph Bell.

1975-Bob: whos joseph bell

Professor.Tweed: Joseph Bell was the inspiration for Sherlock Holmes. This is the Big Boys Table. If you're looking for the Little Girls Table, you might want to go elsewhere, imho.

1975-Bob: whats imho

KMCann14: And I met him. I met Alik Lisser. So did WmbleyLn-Det. And Alik was great. He listened patiently to all my questions about ten years ago and then he did something even greater. He invited me and my family to spend Christmas with him in ENGLAND.

AL4EVA: no way!!

KMCann14: It's true.

Kiwi_woolgatherer: It is true. I will vouch for her.

Thank you, oh, New Zealand shepherd. And sure, OK, so maybe I skipped over the part where I couldn't even open my mouth to say hello and Alik had to actually call me up before we could have a conversation, but I wasn't writing a memoir here. I was persuading my friends to do the right thing. And I was doing a pretty good job of it, in my humble opinion.

KMCann14: Trust me, I get it. It didn't even seem to be true at the time. And Christmas in England was amazing. In real life, Alik doesn't live on Wembley Lane in London. He lives in a cottage in the country with a basement lab full of old guns and poisons, etc, etc. Those days before January 1st were like a dream except I was wide awake and I had to keep pinching myself. Then on New Years Eve, I found out that it WAS all too good to be true and that the truth was actually a nightmare.

KMCann14: We went to London. We stayed at DAME CARISSA'S FLAT. Can you imagine?? I have pictures if you want to see. Anyway, on NYE, Alik hosted a party. That's when I met Korba the Greek. Real name: Cosmo Korban. Like I said, it was like I was in one of the novels. So surreal. But then things went from surreal to insane, because at midnight, DI Korban keeled over and DIED. Suicide by hemlock. HEMLOCK. And I KNEW for a FACT that Alik had HEMLOCK in his lab. So I gathered all my courage and I did the impossible. I confronted Alik Lisser.

KMCann14: And he CONFESSED to it. He confessed to ALL of it. He was PROUD of it. Korban had been getting close to the truth and so he had to die. What truth, you ask? Well, buckle in, because here's the SHOCKER to end all SHOCKERS: almost every murder Alik Lisser "solved," he was the one who DID IT. For years and years and years, he killed all these innocent people and he framed other innocent people and he did it because he COULD. He did it because IT WAS HIS HOBBY. He killed my mother and framed my father BECAUSE IT WAS FUN.

KMCann14: And when I threatened to expose him, he drowned that professor in a tub and framed WmbleyLnDet. He thinks he's smarter than everyone. He thinks he's better than everyone. But we've got a secret weapon he hasn't counted on: US. We've read all the books. We've all got, like, PhDs in mystery. If we work together, I know we can come up with a way to turn the tables on this psychopath. So: who's with me?

I didn't have to wait long. The replies came quick.

AL4EVA: lol you had us going there, KM!
Marigoldeneyes: Oh, it's all a prank? Thank goodness.
KMCann14: What? No. It's not a prank. It's REAL.
AL4EVA: whatever lol lol :)
Marigoldeneyes: So it's not a prank? I'm so confused.
Professor.Tweed: Fanfiction belongs on Usenet or one of those silly websites that "publish" this sort of thing. There are rules to this room, KMCann14. We thought you respected them.

Crap. I'd screwed up. I had to get them back. I needed them. We needed them.

KMCann14: It's NOT fanfiction! All of this HAPPENED!! All of this is HAPPENING!!! I can PROVE it!

I *could* prove it, couldn't I? I could point them toward the Boston newspapers. They could read about my uncle's death and then Jules Rothstein's death and . . . what did that prove, exactly?

I could point them toward the website for Harvard University. They could see that Alik was in town as a visiting professor . . . which meant what?

I had the digital pictures, but the best they showed, to quote Pedro, was what *wasn't* there.

Dev's name disappeared from the list. His fears had been confirmed. He had signed off. The mob had turned their back on him . . . and were charging on me. Even my ally, Kiwi_woolgatherer, picked up a torch.

Kiwi_woolgatherer: You expect us to believe that all this time, this man did all these terrible deeds and nobody suspected a thing? Carissa Miller, his friend, his confidante, never suspected a thing?

Well, I had dug myself deep enough. Might as well bury myself.

KMCann14: She knew. She knew and she let him do it because it gave her material for her BOOKS. She let him kill my mother and frame my father because it gave her MATERIAL. I know we all worship at her feet but the truth is, Dame Carissa is an ACCOMPLICE and a COWARD.

Professor.Tweed: Now that's a bridge too far, imho. Marigoldeneyes, you have a duty here as moderator.

Marigoldeneyes: He's right, KMCann14. I'm so sorry.

And with that, I was booted from the chat room.

44

I stared at the screen in disbelief.

Disbelief that my home had shut its doors to me.

Disbelief that my friends had not even given me a moment's consideration.

Most of all, disbelief at myself for thinking it would be otherwise.

I wasn't even aware I was crying until I felt a teardrop dangle from my chin. I let it dangle, let it drop. Let my eyes puff and my shoulders rock with every sob. And I'd been such a fool to—

The computer's speakers beeped. An IM appeared on the screen.

Kiwi_woolgatherer: Do you really believe Carissa Miller was an accomplice and a coward?

Sigh. Why not kick a person when they were down? I considered not replying. What would be the point? But Kiwi_woolgatherer had always been patient with me and, oddball though he was, I had trusted him once.

KMCann14: Yes.

About twenty seconds passed. Then:

Kiwi_woolgatherer: It makes one wonder about the timing of her disappearance. If she were an accomplice and a coward, as you say, imagine all the guilt and shame weighing her down every day.

KMCann14: She could have said something. She could have stopped him.

Kiwi_woolgatherer: Could she, though? Can a leopard change her spots? Can a coward be a hero? Imagine she tries to be a hero. Imagine that, for the paperback edition of her autobiography, she adds in all the details about Alik Lisser's misdeeds.

KMCann14: Without incriminating herself?

Kiwi_woolgatherer: She does incriminate herself. It's her first go at being a hero and she's pulling out all the stops.

Where was he going with this? I wiped away some snot and read on.

Kiwi_woolgatherer: She throws caution to the wind. She burns the candle at both ends. She piles on all the cliches. Imagine she is so incautious, though, that an old, devious friend of hers realizes what she's up to. He confronts her, threatens her. Not for the first time. But it's enough to batten down her heroism, and in the night, her cowardice reemerges and she does what all cowards do best. She runs.

Oh. My. God.

Kiwi_woolgatherer: She runs as far as she can. She runs all the way to the other side of the world.

KMCann14: She runs to New Zealand.

Kiwi_woolgatherer: Yes.

OH. MY. GOD.

The world spun around me. Down was up. The cursor on the screen slyly blinked at me, as if to tease me. *What are you going to say to that, Kat? What are you going to say now?*

It was possible Kiwi_woolgatherer was lying. Maybe they were giving me an outrageous story in exchange for the outrageous story they thought I'd given in the chat room. It certainly was easier to believe than Dame Carissa Miller pretending to be a shepherd from Christchurch, New Zealand, and hanging out in an AOL chat room dedicated to her fandom.

KMCann14: If you're saying what I think you're saying, why should I believe you?

Kiwi_woolgatherer: Good question. Assume nothing. I could tell you that my flat in London has a western exposure to the Thames. Oh, I miss that view.

KMCann14: I bet there are pictures of her home you can find in old magazines. That doesn't prove anything.

Kiwi_woolgatherer: Pictures of my home, yes. No pictures of Alik's home, though. No pictures of those creepy beds he keeps in the guest rooms or that ludicrous battlement of red herring he keeps in the cellar. Need I go on?

No. I was convinced. My mouth was dry and my hands were trembling and I was chatting with Dame Carissa Miller.

My favorite author.

Kiwi_woolgatherer: I am truly, truly sorry, Katie. That is your name, isn't it? Katie McCann?

KMCann14: Kat.

Kiwi_woolgatherer: Kat, for what it's worth, I tried to imbue your mother's novel with the pathos and empathy I felt she deserved.

KMCann14: It's an honor to meet you. It really is. I loved your books. They gave me a place to get away when things got rough. And things got rough a lot.

Kiwi_woolgatherer: That's why I wrote them. That's why any writer puts pen to paper. We write them so we can escape our rough lives and we read them for the very same reason. It's a symbiotic relationship. I've always believed that. It all fills the same need to escape.

KMCann14: And when you can't escape?

Kiwi_woolgatherer: We can always escape, Kat. As long as we have our books. As long as we have our imaginations. We are escape artists, you and I.

KMCann14: Sure, no, I get that, but Alik is not some ogre you invented. He's real. He's real and the violence is real and the blood is real and my mother is dead and my father is dead and no book is going to save me from that.

I wiped the back of my hand across my wet face, then continued to write. I had to be honest.

KMCann14: And you let it happen. You could have stopped him. You had so many opportunities to stop him. Why didn't you stop him??

Kiwi_woolgatherer: Because there's another word for someone who spends their life escaping from their life. 'Coward.' I don't know what else to tell you. If I could do it all again . . .

Kiwi_woolgatherer: But there I go escaping into whimsy. If I could do it all again, I'd make the same mistakes. To believe otherwise is delusional, and I've come to accept my limitations. Some days, I ask myself if I could go back to the day I met Alik, knowing what I know now, would I still have exploited his crimes to benefit my career? Would I have gone to the police? Does all that spilt blood counterbalance the wealth and privilege which paid for a western exposure of the Thames? We both know what my answer is, don't we? I know I'm damned. The ghosts appear every night in my dreams to remind me. So many ghosts.

KMCann14: That's because you owe them.

Kiwi_woolgatherer: I'm well aware of my debts.

KMCann14: Except I don't think you are. You say you're a coward. Be a coward. I can't force you to stick out your neck. But if I come up with a way to get Alik and I can promise it won't put you at risk, you're going to help me.

Kiwi_woolgatherer: That's a promise you can't keep. Trust me. I know him.

KMCann14: Yeah. You do. But you don't know me.

Silence.

But she didn't sign off.

I hated her. I hated her almost as much as I hated Alik. And why not? She'd helped make him rich and famous, and had he not become rich and famous, he would not have been able to slither into all those cases. That wasn't ink on her hands from all those nights of writing—that was blood.

Kiwi_woolgatherer: If you can devise a brilliant solution that insulates me from harm, I will help you. For whatever good it will do. You are not alone in this.

KMcCann14: Thank you.

Kiwi_woolgatherer: Also, for whatever it's worth, should you copy/paste this conversation and share it with anyone, I will disavow every word of it and then you will be alone.

She signed off.

Well. Whoever said don't meet your heroes wasn't kidding. Jeeeeesus.

Now all I needed was a brilliant solution that insulated her from harm. This had to be something Alik would never consider, not in a million years, something he couldn't ever be prepared for.

How do you outsmart a genius?

But first things first. I called Dev. He didn't pick up. Can't say I blamed him. Poor guy. He had turned down a plea deal, counted on another one of my "brilliant plans," and now he was facing prison time. I don't think I'd answer the phone either.

But I knew someone who (probably) would answer.

"Hey," said Pedro. "What's up?"

I could barely hear him over the jazz trumpeting in the background, so I asked him to lower the volume on his stereo. Then I told him everything. Everything. Dame Carissa may have warned me not to copy/paste our conversation and share it with anyone . . . but screw her. I *did* copy/paste the conversation, and now I was reading it to Pedro.

"Many amazing people are also awful people," he said once I was through. "Chuck Berry peeped on women while they used the bathroom. John Lennon straight up hit women. Alik Lisser is a psycho killer, and Carissa Miller was, like, his accomplice after the fact. That's a thing, right? Plus, there's the job she pretended to have when she came into the chat room. A shepherd. As in someone who watches over the sheep. Doesn't sound like she thinks highly of her fans."

"Ugh. I didn't even think of that."

"That's why I'm here."

We talked about other stuff (mostly none of your business) and that was that. What else was there to do? What would *you* have done? What *I* did was go to bed. The rules of the chat room dictated that all bans could be appealed after twenty-four hours. Tomorrow, I would email Marigoldeneyes and restate my case to her, and then I would restate my case to everyone else. Or not.

I lay back on my bed and stared at the insides of my eyelids. Even though stating my case for the chat room hadn't fixed anything, it had felt at least a little, I don't know, cathartic? Writing something down has a way of putting something into perspective.

Names and faces orbited my imagination. Alik flashes his bright false teeth in a smarmy grin. My mother and father take turns with a bedtime story. Pedro slides a finger through his long hair. Dame Carissa touch-types new pages for her revised autobiography. My aunt clutches the arms of her airplane seat. My uncle looms over us both as we lie on the kitchen floor. Hermann stands guard by his large car, eyes behind sunglasses. Detective Riegert's lips purse around a cigarette.

Francis Fung, PhD, updates his conspiracy website with fresh meat for his readers. Pedro cups my chin and presses his soft lips to my soft lips. Alik stares up at me from my mother's blood-wet body. Alik smears that blood on the bathroom windowsill beside the editing booths at 2240 East Magnolia.

Well . . . that was one solution I hadn't considered, eh? So bold, so perfect, that no one—not even Alik—would *ever* see it coming. I could do to him what he had done to my father and countless others over the years. I could frame him for a crime. I could frame him for murder. All I would have to do was find a victim. I could think of a dozen people off the top of my head. Classmates, mostly. It was empowering to think about (in a twisted way). Not that I'd ever do it.

Unless . . .

45

Dev's trial wasn't scheduled to begin until July. That gave me a hard deadline to put everything into motion, and I'd need every moment I could get. I'd also need all the assistance I could get.

And the first person I went to for assistance was Alik Lisser.

I waited a few weeks. My aunt and I had been relocated back to our old apartment in Dorchester, and I wanted to make sure everything was OK with her first. The neighborhood was the same armpit it had been when we'd left, but Alik had paid for our apartment to be fixed up. Gone was the redbrick fireplace (with my uncle's bloodstains on it), replaced now with a lovely white-brick fireplace that matched the new cream-colored walls. It was like living in a box of milk.

Apparently, Alik had shown my aunt a catalog, and she'd picked everything out, so you would think she'd be ecstatic over the changes. However, she seemed to spend most of her time sitting in my uncle's bear of a recliner, one of the few carryovers from before. One evening in early March, I woke up from a nap to find her in the recliner, burying her face into the plaid cushion as if to smell it (and by *it*, I mean *him*). I propped myself on the arm of the recliner and wrapped my arms around her in the warmest, clingiest hug I could muster. Mom watched on from her painting, which hung above the TV set.

That was the evening I called Alik. I shut the door for privacy, dialed the number he'd given me, and waited. And waited. For a second,

I thought his machine was going to pick up, but then the ringing stopped and he spoke:

"There she is."

I blinked. "How'd you know it was me?"

"Oh, my phone came with this little machine. It shows who's calling and it takes messages for me when I'm away, and it's even cordless. *Ja*, you Americans love your toys. How can I help you, my dear—or are you simply calling because you missed me?"

So gross.

"Does your offer still stand?" I asked.

"Which offer would that be?"

"I fly to England for the summer and in exchange . . ."

"In exchange what?"

"In exchange, you get the charges dropped against Dev."

"That is quite an offer," he replied, "but I don't see how I could possibly get the charges dropped. The evidence is, as you know, fairly overwhelming."

I didn't panic. Not yet. This was another one of his games, right?

"I do sympathize, Katie. It can't be easy standing by, helpless, while a good friend of yours is put before the magistrate. How about I take you out tomorrow for ice cream? I was a child once. I remember. Nothing calms a child's troubles like a nice scoop of vanilla ice cream. It's my treat. I will come by and pick you up after school and buy you a sundae. And we can talk about whatever you want."

Take me out for ice cream? What kind of off-the-wall, presumptuous, creepy, insane—

No, wait. Hold on. So we could "talk about whatever I wanted"? Why couldn't we talk about it now? Because the bastard was paranoid that I was taping our conversation! Ha, if only I was that clever.

The next day, I met Pedro in the music room. He was scrubbing a spray-painted swastika off the side of the piano. I went to the closest bathroom, soaked some paper towels, and sat down beside him to help remove the graffiti. While we did that, occasionally bumping hands in a bit of intentional clumsiness, I updated him on the latest, including the fact that Alik the Devil would be stopping by that afternoon.

"I want to photograph him," said Pedro.

"No. Why? No."

"I've never photographed a monster before."

"It's not like he has horns and a tail."

"I know that." Pedro lightly elbowed me. "I'll keep my distance. I know he's dangerous. But I want to, I don't know, capture him with my camera. Does that sound flaky?"

"Yes. And besides, I took plenty of pictures of him last Christmas."

"Those are digital pictures. Digital is so lifeless. Please? I'll be your best friend."

"You already are my best friend," I replied, lightly elbowing him back.

"See? I kept my word."

Sigh.

Which meant that while I waited after school for the dreaded Cadillac, Pedro positioned himself by a window in Room 480. I realized that since all the windows in the school were interlaced with wires to keep them from shattering, whatever photograph he hoped to get would make Alik look like he was behind bars. Maybe there was something to his flakiness after all.

Or maybe Alik wasn't even going to show up, because the buses came and went and I was left alone on the front step. I glanced up at Room 480. Pedro waved back to me. Then he abruptly stopped waving.

The Cadillac sidled up to the curb. Hermann did his chauffeur best, quickly strolling around the car to open the door to the back seat.

"Come on inside!" said Alik. "What a beautiful day for a scoop of vanilla ice cream!"

It was a beautiful day. The March thaw had begun. No snow-clogged sidewalks. No black ice. I could even wear my winter coat unzipped. But even if it had been ninety-two degrees and sunnier than hell, I was not going to have this man buy me a scoop of vanilla ice cream.

But I had to play nice. And I had to at least *try* to get Pedro his photograph.

So:

"If it's such a beautiful day," I said, "why don't you step outside?"

He frowned. He wasn't expecting that. Good. That meant he'd be curious. "I'm fine where I am. I've actually been here before, remember? I picked you up after your uncle had his accident."

"Yeah, I remember my uncle's 'accident.' But you don't have to be so cautious with your words. I'm not taping you now, and I wasn't taping you last night."

He studied me. In the dark of the car, his dyed hair seemed to disappear, making him look like a bald crone. Then he flashed a veneer-perfect grin and got out of the car, cane-first. Unlike his brother, he took his time strolling around the Cadillac to get to me. But he didn't stop there. He leaned over until his lips were an inch from my ear.

"Do you like your flat's refurbishment? I may have included some personal touches, and I know for a fact your aunt hasn't found them all."

And there it was. The new threat. If I was taping our conversation, if I tried to do anything to hurt him, he'd hurt her. At this point, I'd almost been expecting it. Almost.

My hands tingled. My mouth went dry. I persisted. I had to.

"Is there, like, a contract we should sign or something? In blood? To ensure that you'll do what you promised for Dev and then . . . only then . . . I do what I promised for you?"

He took a step back. Studied me. Assessed my worthiness.

"We understand each other," he replied. "'Signed in blood.' You are endlessly amusing. Are you ready for that sundae now?"

"I'll pass. Got homework. But as soon as Dev is free of all charges, we can eat all the ice cream in England. They do have ice cream in England, don't they?"

Later, at home, I called Pedro to ask if he got his special photograph. He seemed disappointed that Alik had no evil aura . . . which led to a discussion as to what color an evil aura might be, which led to him suggesting crimson, which led to me accusing him of hating on redheads, blah blah blah, you get the gist.

After I got off the phone, I sent out two emails to two people I'd never emailed before. Then I waited some more. A lot more. Because Alik wasn't going to do his thing for Dev until the very last minute.

Which meant late June. Also (not coincidentally) right before Dev's trial began.

And that left April and May for (in no particular order):

1. **School.** Not much to report there. I maintained my solid C average in most of my classes. No applause, please. Could I do better if I tried harder or cared more? Maybe. But what was the point? It's not like I could afford to go to college, and they don't ask to see your report card when you apply for a job at Dunkin'.
2. **Pedro.** See above. More of the same. I got to say, for my first real relationship, I was *killing* it. I just had to be myself and let him be . . . perfect. Not perfect as in, like, a Greek god or whatever, but perfect because he was him. Does that make sense? Does it make sense that, as the weeks turned into months and we learned more about each other and he even wrote me a frickin' *song*, my imagination went into high gear wondering when the other shoe was going to drop?
3. **Dev.** I tried to reach out to him at least once a week. But he never answered his phone. Never responded to emails. That at least made sense. If I were him, I wouldn't want anything to do with me either. But I was going to fix things. Or die trying.
4. **My aunt.** She's had a rough life, but this year was *especially* rough. She still had some friends in the neighborhood, but they kept their distance, as if my aunt's rough luck could be contagious. So she leaned on me. When she needed to pick up groceries, she'd ask me to come with her. When I

was home, she'd ask me if I wanted to watch TV with her. She told me stories about all the trouble my mother got into when they were younger. I told her about Pedro.

I never told my maunt about Alik or my plan to bring him down for good. If I had, she never would have agreed to let me go to England. It was too risky. And she was right. It was crazy risky. And so, on the first Saturday in June, I took the train to Cambridge to get some insurance.

Detective Riegert's desk was one of about a dozen in Robbery/Homicide. She pulled up a rickety chair beside it and popped in a stick of gum, and then she cut to the chase and asked what I wanted.

"In the next few weeks," I said, "something's going to happen. Maybe some new evidence will come to light or some old evidence will vanish. I don't know. But the case against Dev will suddenly fall apart. My guess is that you'll then be pointed toward another suspect who probably *also* is not guilty."

Detective Riegert crossed her arms. "And you know this how?"

"Because Alik Lisser is going to make it happen."

"Hey, I may not like the guy, but—"

"He murdered Jules Rothstein. And before you ask, no, I can't prove it. But maybe when the case against Dev suddenly falls apart, you'll remember I came here and said all this. You'll ignore his fame and all that, and you'll dig deeper. I guess I came here because . . . I need you to tell me you'll dig deeper. Please."

"You came all the way here just to say all that?"

What could I say? That I would have called, but I was worried Alik, in refurbishing my apartment, had tapped my phone? Not a chance. My paranoia would just make the detective believe me less. So I just nodded.

She sighed, spat her gum into her wastebasket, and finally said, "Be honest with me, kid. Are you in danger?"

"No," I answered.

That was the only lie I ever told her.

46

Because Harvard's spring semester ended way before my school year did, Alik had already been home for a while before it came time for me to head to Logan Airport and board my British Airways flight to Heathrow. Otherwise, I'm sure he would have insisted we fly together. Instead, I had my super-spacious row in first class all to myself. I could have stretched out and taken a nap if I'd wanted (and if I could have shaken off my nerves long enough). I wasn't as visibly a nervous wreck as my aunt had been on her trip across the pond. My anxiety remained on the inside: palpitating pulse, spitless mouth, wringing stomach. A steady stream of ginger ales from the flight attendant helped a little but couldn't quiet the voices in my mind and the dark possibility that this would be a one-way trip.

It probably would be. I'd been waiting for the other shoe to drop, hadn't I? Dying overseas at the hands of the monster who'd destroyed my family would be a heck of a dropped shoe. One of my email correspondents had sent me the package I'd requested, and its contents were currently hidden in my luggage between my two pairs of green chinos, but the real success of my plan depended on the reliability of my other email correspondent, and in our brief back-and-forth, he had already proven to be (unsurprisingly) erratic, asking way too many questions and committing to *probably* holding up his end (no promises).

Just like in December, Hermann showed up at the airport. Even though we recognized each other on sight, he was still holding a placard with my name written on it in pristine calligraphy. Unlike in December, the countryside we passed on our trip west was thriving, with fields white and yellow with sheep and barley while the sky was a cosmos of blue.

After an hour on the road, Hermann asked if I wanted to stop again at Stonehenge. It was clear from his excitement that he did, so I said yes, and we spent a good while wandering among the ancient monoliths. Despite the beautiful weather, it was still a bit chilly, especially with the occasional breeze, and I was glad I was wearing my (slightly oversize) army-surplus jacket.

"Carissa always loved this place," he said.

Oh yeah. He had mentioned that during our first visit to Stonehenge way back when. That was when he'd told me that I reminded him of her. Back then, it had felt like such a compliment . . .

We arrived at Alik's cottage around sunset. The man himself was waiting outside, leaning on his cane.

"There she is," he said, because of course he did. Because he *was* predictable.

On this, I was betting my life.

After a dinner of roasted chicken and herbed potatoes (which, I've got to admit, was absolutely delicious), Alik showed me our calendar for the next two months. Almost every weekday was blocked out to the same schedule: breakfast at 7:00 a.m., writing from 8:00 a.m. to 12:00 p.m., then lunch, rewriting from 1:00 p.m. to 5:00 p.m., then dinner.

"What do I do while you're writing and rewriting?" I asked, imagining long hours alone in the backyard with one of his old books.

"My process is collaborative. That's why you're here. I will regale you with my adventures, and you will write them down. Then you will type them up. You know how to use a typewriter, *ja*? It is not hard."

"You flew me all the way to England to be your personal secretary?"

"*Nein, nein, nein*—you are here to be my appreciative audience!"

That made more sense.

Then I pointed out one of the dates on the calendar that was circled: July 7. Lescher Day. Might as well call it Lisser Day. We weren't in Oz anymore. Unfortunately, we never were.

"Are we taking the day off . . . ?"

"We are, actually. As it turns out, I have special plans this year. A chap I knew at the Yard reached out. He is making a documentary about forensic science and wants to interview me first. How could I say no?"

"The Yard?"

"Hmm? Oh. Sorry. *Ja.* Scotland Yard. He is going to film my process for posterity. Isn't that nice?"

Oh yes. It was.

Writing in the morning meant sitting in chairs in the backyard (if the weather was cooperative) and him going on and on and on about this case or that case while I took notes with a gold fountain pen that was "one of many gifts from Her Royal Highness." He seemed to be picking and choosing the cases at random, bopping around the timeline, until I figured out (by week two) what all the cases had in common.

There were no frame jobs possible in any of them. These were the crimes he'd actually solved.

Writing in the afternoon meant him looking over my shoulder while I sat at his typewriter and turned the morning's notes into workable prose. Oftentimes, this meant typing everything he said, grueling sentence by grueling sentence. Sometimes, though, I didn't type what he said. Sometimes I improved on it in my own words. And when he reread the afternoon's typed pages after dinner, this time with the fountain pen in his hand for more notes, he could have crossed out my additions . . . but he rarely did. I checked the manuscript pages to be sure, and he always left the manuscript pages in the same place on his desk, just to the left of the typewriter.

By the end of July 6, our teamwork had resulted in fifty-four finished pages.

July 7, 1996, began with rain. More rain than I had ever seen come down in Boston. A real downpour.

The kind of storm that canceled plans.

Alik's guest was scheduled to arrive at 10:00 a.m. This gave me and Alik time to have a more-relaxed-than-usual breakfast. He had replaced the arty black-and-white photograph of Paris (which had replaced my mother's painting) with another piece of abstract art, this one featuring gold rectangles.

"Another gift from Her Majesty?" I asked him.

"Because of the gold?" He smiled. "*Nein, nein*, this is a work by Gustav Klimt. You have not heard of Klimt, have you? Of course not. American education remains an oxymoron. This was my father's favorite painting. Why he liked such gaudy nonsense, I'll never know."

"Didn't you say this friend of yours was bringing a camera? Aren't you worried people will see that and think *you* like 'gaudy nonsense'?"

"Did I forget to mention the painting is worth three million pounds? And it's not like this is the first time I've allowed the press access to my domicile. It would be rude of me, public servant that I am, to turn them away."

He sipped his tea and returned to the paper. I sipped my tea and thought about my parents.

After breakfast, Alik slipped into a suit and touched up his hair. Whatever black dye he'd used smelled like turpentine. Maybe it was turpentine. When the doorbell rang, Alik remained in his seat at the desk, jotting notes on my pad, and let Hermann answer the door. I sat curled up on the couch with a truly massive edition of Audubon's illustrated *Birds of America*.

"Dr. Fung!" greeted Alik. "Always a delight."

Yes, *that* Dr. Fung.

(All will be revealed soon. Relax.)

"I really appreciate your doing this," Fung replied.

Francis Fung, PhD, looked exactly like he'd appeared on his website, receding blond hair bound into a ponytail and quite slim. Surfer-dude vibe with a posh I-have-a-country-house accent. "The tiny mouse on the divan is my assistant, Kat McCann. She's interning from America to help me with my memoirs. Say hello, Kat."

"Hello," I mumbled.

"From the looks of her choice of reading material, it appears my assistant is feeling a bit homesick today. Could I interest either of you in a spot of tea?"

"Actually," said Dr. Fung, "do you mind if we get started?"

Dr. Fung immediately turned on his camera (a small, fancy model very, very similar to the one I'd "borrowed" during Christmas break) and mounted it on his shoulder.

"From Scotland Yard to Spielberg." Alik chuckled. "I'll bet there's a story to be found there."

Dr. Fung shrugged. "Not an especially new story. Injured in the line. Accident in the lab. Not my fault. Add to that a dash of office politics, and the choice wasn't really a choice. Similar story to yours, now that I say it out loud."

"Well. All the luck."

"Can we get started, please?" Fung said again, and so they did. Alik commenced with a general tour of the cottage. I could have acted then. It wouldn't have taken me long to get what I needed from my suitcase in the guest room. But Alik's tour was on the move, and even though they walked at the pace of a man with a cane, I couldn't risk even the possibility of being caught. Plus, if Dr. Fung kept to the plan, I would have a better opportunity very soon—

"Did Carissa Miller spend much time here?"

—and bringing up Dame Carissa was officially *not* part of the plan. Damn it, Dr. Fung.

"Some," replied Alik. "She preferred the city, but every so often, the hills and dells of rural England called, and she answered."

"Do you miss her?"

"*Ja*, every day. When you know someone for as long as we knew each other—and then to no longer have that person in your life—it's as if a limb has been severed."

"Severed? That sounds like you assume foul play."

DAMN IT, DR. FUNG.

"I assume nothing," Alik answered, unfazed. "It was merely a figure of speech."

Then Dr. Fung, thank God, shifted gears:

"Of course. I didn't mean to imply otherwise. Oh no, looks like the rain's going to stop soon. I so wanted to capture some B-roll of you strolling in the gloom. For ambience."

And so the two of them headed outside.

I waited until I heard the front door shut with a clunk, and then I set down the Audubon tome, rushed to the guest room, and scooped up the package from my suitcase.

By now you've figured out what it was, right? What I was going to use to frame Alik? He had chased Dame Carissa into hiding because she had updated her memoir to include all the horrific details of their partnership.

How perfect then to use that revised manuscript to frame him for her murder.

And once Dame Carissa understood my plan (and that it really didn't require any sort of risk on her part, coward that she was), she had been more than eager to participate. Some drops of her blood on the title page to further implicate him, and then into the post the revised manuscript went (to be delivered to Pedro's address juuuust in case a certain someone was keeping an eye on me). When Dr. Fung and Alik came back inside, the camera would pan in real time to the file cabinets, and guess what revised manuscript Ms. Kat McCann had hidden in one of its drawers, and, wait, was that dried blood on its cover?

Flawless.

Honestly, the trickiest bit had been convincing Francis Fung, PhD, to participate. He never did reply to that first brief email I sent. It took months to get him on board, once with a more detailed email, and then by sending him a few of the digital pictures I'd taken to prove I was legit.

Then, in late March, he finally replied.

He asked for more pictures, more details.

I was happy to provide them.

By late May, he was still on the fence. Part of it, according to him, was the fact that I was "nothing but a child." As if children didn't have anything worthwhile to offer. As if children, because they were children, were unreliable in all things. But part of it was that I didn't share the *entirety* of my plan with him.

"He keeps trophies," I'd written. "He keeps them in a file cabinet in the basement of his cottage. I GUARANTEE that he has something about Carissa in there. Come on July 7. Pretend you're making a movie about him. He'll love that."

And he did.

And now I needed to live up to my guarantee. I rushed down to the basement to put the pre-bloodied manuscript into the very same file cabinet drawer in which Alik kept all the evidence/trophies from my mother's murder. I picked the file cabinet's lock (a feat I'd been practicing every night since I'd arrived) and slipped the manuscript into the drawer, and I shut the drawer and scampered back up the stairs and shut the basement door behind me just as the front door opened with a clunk and the two men trundled back inside.

47

Dr. Fung dried off his lens with the hem of his pink raincoat. He muttered to Alik (with Oscar-worthy nonchalance): "Now, let's move on to the main event. Lead me to your laboratory."

"Do you know why I've agreed to so few profiles? It's not from lack of interest, I assure you. Can you guess the reason? *Nein?* It's because most people prefer their windows to the world a tad bit opaque. It adds mystique to existence. But most people don't realize this about themselves, and so they invent shortcuts to knowledge like the World Wide Web. Have you been on it? I deeply hope it's just a fad. The acquisition of information should require hard work—as I'm sure you would concur—and even then, again, let's not forget the value of mystery. It's our curiosity that has allowed us to become the species that we are. Satiate that curiosity too quickly and we will lose our way."

"So, is that a no to the laboratory . . . ?" asked Dr. Fung.

Alik replied with a noncommittal shrug. Acquaintance or not, he clearly wanted to make Francis Fung, PhD, who'd driven all the way here for this very purpose, work for this golden opportunity of documenting the great man's great sanctum. And Fung clearly was not used to begging anyone for anything.

Which left it up to me to save the day.

"It's a good point," I piped up.

They both glanced at me, Alik with genuine interest and Fung with a look that could best be described as Have You Gone Mad, Little Girl.

"You show the world your lab, and you might as well show them the secret ingredient to your recipe for chicken potpie. You show the world your lab, and everyone will know the quick and easy way to become the next Alik Lisser. I'd keep that door locked if I were you."

"And I," replied Alik, "would keep facile manipulation by reverse psychology to a minimum. But it's a kind gesture you're making for Dr. Fung, and it reminds me of the importance of kindness. I apologize for forgetting it."

Alik leaned on his cane and reached into his pocket for his key. He then reached for the basement doorknob with the key and—

—discovered he didn't need the key at all when the knob turned without any resistance in his grip.

Crap, crap, crap. Crap on a cracker. Crapasaurus Rex.

"Hmm," he mused.

"Everything OK?" Dr. Fung asked.

"*Ja, ja.* Another lesson in kindness. My manservant forgot to lock up. Come, come. Let's descend into my lair and learn my secret recipe for chicken potpie. You may join us, little mouse. What better way for an apprentice to learn her craft."

Thank you, Occam's razor, for having my back.

Alik flicked on the light switch, and we climbed down the stairs. Dr. Fung kept a hand on the railing to steady his balance while he filmed everything: The corner with the desk and wall art and file cabinets. The corner with the poison samples and the lab table of weapons. The flamboyant red curtain aglow with gray daylight.

"Why don't you walk me through your typical process?" Dr. Fung asked.

"Ah, but there is no typical process. Each case presented its own unique set of problems and therefore its own path toward a solution. You can have all the best equipment in the world, but without the insight in knowing just how to proceed in this specific example, you might as well put a robot in charge and yourself out to pasture. Oh, no offense intended, Francis."

"None taken, Alik. And how about the file cabinets? What are those for?"

My stomach knotted with anticipation. I reminded myself to swallow to keep my mouth from drying up.

Here we go.

"My notes, mostly. Esoterica."

"Oh, I'm sure the public would be fascinated to see some of that."

"*Ja*, I'm sure you're correct, but here I must draw my line. Would you ask your wife to show you her diary?"

"No," said Dr. Fung, "but I would ask Louis Pasteur for his lab notes. As would you. We all stand on the shoulders of giants. Let the next generation perch on yours. Otherwise, what am I doing here?"

I bit my lip. It was a good pitch. A good lure.

Would Alik take the bait?

"How about only one drawer?" I piped up again. "That way, it's not like you're handing over your entire diary. Just a page."

Alik smirked at me. Then at Dr. Fung.

"One page," Alik said. Then, straight to the camera, he added, "Pick wisely."

Yes.

Dr. Fung made a show of trying to choose. He peered at the cabinets like he was only allowed to take a single item from the world's prettiest, freshest breakfast buffet. He took his time and then some. He really sold it. Then he pointed to the cabinet drawer I'd told him about in our email exchange—middle of the pack, bottom. The one he'd come all this way to see. The end of his long and lonely search for justice.

He pointed to the cabinet drawer. And Alik glared at me. And I knew the jig was up.

"Nein," said Alik.

"Excuse me?" asked Dr. Fung. He angled his camera from the drawer to Alik's face. "I don't understand."

"*Nein?* I understand. My little mouse understands."

Alik's gaze pinned me to the spot. I couldn't speak. I couldn't move. I now understood why deer froze in headlights . . . right before getting smashed to gory death.

"Hermann didn't forget to lock the basement door, did he, Katie? But somebody did forget. What, I wonder, will we find inside the drawer?"

Dr. Fung had his camera angled on us. "I still don't understand."

"I told my apprentice you were coming today, and she decided to play a little trick. Open that drawer and you'll find it for yourself, I am certain. But be warned, Francis. It is just a trick, just as how it was she tricked you to select that drawer. In card magic, it's called a force. I have a book all about it upstairs in my library."

Dr. Fung angled the camera away from us now. "Inside this drawer?"

"It will appear incriminating, whatever it is, but it will be nonsense, because there is no evidence that incriminates me in any crime, is there, Katie? Just the wishful thinking of a teenage girl with fantasies of—"

"Oh my God."

The drawer was open. Dr. Fung had his camera recording its contents. He shifted the camera to focus on Alik.

"It is true. God. Why?"

"What is it?" Alik chuckled. "A doctored photograph of me shooting JFK?"

Dr. Fung stepped aside. Alik stepped toward the open drawer. He peered inside.

He gasped. He actually gasped.

Oh, what a wonderful sound that was. Just a quick intake of breath, yeah, OK, but it snapped me out of my deerlike paralysis.

"Are you telling me that manuscript is not real?" asked Dr. Fung. "Are you telling me that blood is not real? If I tested that blood, Alik, whose will it match?"

"*Nein, nein* . . . She . . . she did this . . ."

"Carissa Miller disappeared over five years ago. That girl couldn't have been more than eleven. And from the sound of it, American. What did you do?"

"Turn that camera off," muttered Alik.

But that just made Dr. Fung zoom the camera in for a close shot of Alik's face. So Alik raised his cane and smacked Dr. Fung in the wrist, forcing him to drop the camera. It clattered to the floor.

Dr. Fung clutched his bruised wrist but did not cower. "Did you kill her?"

"Nein!"

Then: the creak of the steps. Hermann must have heard the commotion. He stopped midway down the stairs and asked:

"What is going on?"

"What's going on is your employer just became the prime suspect in the possible murder of Carissa Miller."

"It's a trick! I'll prove it!"

Alik snatched the manuscript from the drawer and fanned through the pages. So certain he'd see gibberish or the same words repeated over and over again instead of what he *knew* was real, what he knew were the contents of Dame Carissa's revised autobiography, in which she exposed him. This manuscript, with her real blood on it, which had no provable way of getting there other than he put it there with all his other "esoterica."

"Alik," said Hermann slowly, "you hurt Carrie?"

"Nein." He waved off his brother like a mosquito. "It's a setup. Circumstantial."

"When she went away, you promised me you didn't hurt her! You promised me!"

"And I didn't."

"It looks a lot like you did," Dr. Fung said. He picked up the camera. "Got any comment?"

But Alik didn't have a chance to comment or quip or anything, because Hermann launched himself at him with furious speed, past me, tackling his brother against the cabinets.

"You promised me!" he cried out, and he punched Alik square in the nose, bending it almost ninety degrees. He punched him in the mouth, shattering the veneers with a loud crack. He had brought his fist back to punch him a third time when Dr. Fung, of all people, stepped in and grabbed Hermann and pulled him away.

"He'll get his," Dr. Fung said, "but not like this."

That moment gave Alik all the opportunity he needed, and he limped past them and toward me. No, not toward me—toward the poisons and knives and guns behind me.

But I had a weapon of my own. Tucked in my back pocket. Just in case everything went wrong. And as Alik, eyes huge with fury, blood spilling down his chin, came within arm's reach, I slipped the letter opener from my back pocket and held its tip to his throat.

As he, at one time, must have done to my mother.

"No," I said. "No more."

Behind him, Dr. Fung drew back the hammer on his own weapon, a revolver.

Alik Lisser, the famed detective, sighed and coughed as his nose and mouth bled all over the basement's polished white tile.

48

Alik had been right. As always. The manuscript with Dame Carissa's blood *was* only circumstantial evidence. But circumstantial evidence was still evidence, and it was enough to get authorities around the world to reopen Alik Lisser's many cases.

Especially once the damning revelations in Dame Carissa's revised manuscript became public.

Especially once Hermann started telling them everything he knew.

Frankly, it was *a lot*. Between the public outrage and the many, many, many investigations, it didn't look like *any* justice would be happening for a while. Fortunately, in America, we're famously impatient. Also in America, we had Detective Riegert reopening the Rothstein case once Alik had magically orchestrated the charges against Dev to be dropped. Her forensics wizards located and identified several strands of dyed hair they had gathered in their initial sweep of the crime scene, hair that proved a perfect match to one infamous Austro-British detective.

There must have been a hundred photographers on hand from around the world when Alik Lisser, extradited and handcuffed, was escorted off a British Airways plane by a small army of Massachusetts's finest.

The picture made the front page of the *Herald*.

It reminded me of the coverage of my mother's murder.

At first, my aunt couldn't believe it. Then she didn't want to believe it. Then she scolded me for putting myself in danger. That's when I knew we would all be OK.

We didn't talk about my uncle. The details of his murder had not yet been disclosed by the press. Since Dame Carissa (whose secret existence in New Zealand I never shared with the press or the authorities) hadn't written about it, and since the police had no reason to question anyone about it, the only people who knew the truth were me, Pedro, and Alik. If my aunt ever asked me about my uncle's "accident," I would have told her the truth . . . but she never did.

But she must have wondered every now and then, right?

Because he was a flight risk, Alik Lisser was held without bail. Because he was a celebrity, he was remanded not to the local jail with everyone else but instead, in a deal with the feds, to a more secure and private cell at Fort Devens. Yep, the very prison I'd taken him to months earlier.

That was where he was when I went to visit him the Sunday before Labor Day (by then, I'd turned seventeen and didn't need adult supervision inside the facility). Pedro borrowed his father's Oldsmobile station wagon to drive me out. For the journey, I'd decided to bring along *The Empty Coffin* by, yes, Carissa Miller. I'd learned as Alik's stenographer that its central murder was one of the ones he *hadn't* committed, so I guess it felt safe. I read it out loud to Pedro as he piloted us west. Every so often, he pointed out lines he especially liked.

She was a talented writer. Just a reprehensible person.

Once we reached the prison, I let Pedro keep reading while I followed through with the necessities indoors: walk through a metal detector, sign the ledger (like I'm checking into a bed-and-breakfast), raise my arms while a female guard pats me down. Then I followed a male guard to the visiting room.

It was not much different from the room where I'd met up with Dev. There were only so many different ways to set up a thing like that, I guess? I took my seat and waited. I didn't have to wait long.

Alik was led in by his chains. Like cattle at auction. Without his cane, he walked with a heavy limp. So three-legged cattle at auction. Since he wasn't allowed any of his special creams and balms, he finally looked his age: white hair, taut cheeks, yellow teeth. The guards secured his chains to hooks under the table.

"There he is," I said.

He nodded. "Came all this way to gloat?"

"Well, I mean, you taught me how important it is."

"Is that it, then, little mouse? Going to follow in my footsteps?"

"No," I replied. "I don't think anyone's going to be doing that."

"There's the real tragedy. You see that, don't you? Do you know how many men and women I have inspired to become officers of the law? Now all they have is cynicism. That's on your hands."

"They're still a lot cleaner than yours."

"Is that why you're really here, then? For an apology?"

I shook my head. "What would be the point?"

"Agreed. Then what? You must have come all this way to ask me something."

"Oh, I don't know." I sat back in my chair. "It's not enough that I get to see you like this?"

"How's my brother?"

I frowned. I had no idea. Once Alik was arrested in the United States, I'd kinda lost track of things in the UK (and elsewhere). Was that bad? Most of his crimes *had* been committed overseas. All those victims—both the people he'd murdered and the people he'd framed.

"The warden doesn't let me read any of the newspapers," he continued, "and my legal representation in America has had difficulties establishing a rapport with my legal representation abroad."

"You still expect to get out, don't you?"

"What I expect is, most municipalities will recognize the futility, not to mention the expense, in litigating dead cases—so to speak. As to local matters, well, we're looking at a case where the police can't seem to make up their mind as to whom the culprit is. First they pin it on a college student. Then they pin it on me, and let's be honest, right now, I'm a very convenient target."

"I'll be testifying against you."

"*Ja, ja*, but you are a child. And it's not as if you *saw* me do anything. But I digress. You came all this way. How can I help you?"

"You suggested you made 'personal adjustments' to our apartment. The police did a sweep of the whole place and found nothing. No recording equipment. No hidden blowpipes filled with poison darts."

"And your question is?"

"There never were any personal adjustments, were there?"

"What you're really asking me," he said, "is whether or not you're safe. There are no assurances in this life. Do you know how often meteorites crash into our planet? Do you know how many cerebral hemorrhages go undetected? Are any of us safe?"

And that, I knew, was as close to a confirmation as I was going to get. As close to peace of mind for me and my aunt as Alik was ever going to share. And that was fine. Maybe not definitive, but enough.

I got up to leave.

"Wait, please." Alik leaned forward. "I have a question for you."

I hesitated, nervous.

"When did Carrie find you? Her plan—framing me for her murder—your participation was essential. More to the point, how did she know to find you? Did she hire someone to follow me?"

"Those are all great questions."

"I know they are."

"And I can answer every single one of them."

"Then do so."

His gaze was so insistent, so brimming with curiosity, so hungry for closure.

"Nah," I said. "I'm good."

And I left.

ACKNOWLEDGMENTS

The author would like to single out his family for their patience, his friends for their kindness, his writing group for their wisdom, his agent and editor for their tenacity and faith, and his team at Thomas & Mercer for midwifing this story into the world.

ABOUT THE AUTHOR

Joshua Corin is the author of the Xanadu Marx series, the Esme Stuart series, and a cornucopia of comic books for Marvel, among many others. His work has been translated into over a dozen languages.

Joshua wrote this novel alongside his cat, Princess Tater Tot, in Atlanta, Georgia.

For more information visit www.joshuacorin.com.